HUNTING A KILLER

"In the short term, I'm going to work on getting some cameras installed at the Dane house, so we can see what's going on. Tamara, let us all know when your next open house is," Lilly said.

"It's tomorrow, but maybe I should cancel it," Tamara said.

"No, don't cancel it," Lilly said. "We can take shifts babysitting the house the morning of and make sure nothing happens to it during the day."

"Will that help us figure out who killed Gladys?" Ernie asked.

Lilly took a deep breath, reached over and grabbed her friend's hand. She did not let go and looked around the table. "Let's leave that to Bash. For now."

"Are you sure?" Delia said.

"Here's what I'm thinking. Tamara may end up on the suspect list for killing Gladys. If someone's going after Tamara's business, they may be going after her as well and trying to frame her. Let's look out for our friend and collect all the facts whether you think they're relevant or not. Then maybe we can put this puzzle together . . ."

Books by Julia Henry

PRUNING THE DEAD

TILLING THE TRUTH

Published by Kensington Publishing Corporation

TILLING THE TRUTH

Julia Henry

KW 2022

Kensington Books
www.kensingtonbooks.com

KENSINGTON BOOKS are published by

Kensington Publishing Corp.
119 West 40th Street
New York, NY 10018

All Kensington titles, imprints, and distributed lines are available at special quantity discounts for bulk purchases for sales promotion, premiums, fund-raising, educational, or institutional use.

Special book excerpts or customized printings can also be created to fit specific needs. For details, write or phone the office of the Kensington Sales Manager: Attn.: Sales Department. Kensington Publishing Corp., 119 West 40th Street, New York, NY 10018. Phone: 1-800-221-2647.

Kensington and the K logo Reg. U.S. Pat. & TM Off.

First Printing: September 2019
ISBN-13: 978-1-4967-1483-1
ISBN-10: 1-4967-1483-0

ISBN-13: 978-1-4967-1484-8 (ebook)
ISBN-10: 1-4967-1484-9 (ebook)

10 9 8 7 6 5 4 3 2 1

Printed in the United States of America

To Bryan Spence and Glenn Lentz,
the best brothers-in-law I could have asked for

CHAPTER ONE

Lilly Jayne had considered saying no to the invitation for tea, but her curiosity got the better of her. That, plus her good manners. Her mother, Viola, rest her soul, would have haunted her forever if she had said no to Braden and Miranda's invite. Especially now that she had been named the executor of such a large part of Harmon Dane's estate.

They'd called after they met with Harmon's lawyer, as Lilly had predicted they would. After a terse conversation, the three of them agreed to meet at the Star Café to talk in person. Lilly was a big believer in face-to-face conversations, especially when they were difficult. She could have as easily invited them to her house, but then she couldn't escape. She found both Braden and Miranda tiresome at best, and this conversation wasn't going to represent them at their best. Frankly, she also thought that they were less concerned by her late friend's recent death than they were by what he left them in his will. Harmon deserved better, not that she was one for public wailing. No, Lilly Jayne was far too much of a cranky Yankee for that. Nonetheless, she grieved the loss of Harmon, was honored that he had asked her to help honor his final wishes, and felt determined to make his relatives step up to do their part.

Lilly walked down the front stairs and put her purse on the side table in the front hall. She looked at her reflection in the mirror and smiled faintly. Little curls of her white hair were flying about, not surprising in the August humidity. Her black cotton dress with white cabbage roses skimmed over her solid shape, nipping in at the waist thanks to a thin red belt, and then scooting out to a full circle skirt. Her white canvas sneakers were fairly hip these days, but that wasn't why she chose them. She'd been wearing them for years. Lately, though, she'd had to add inserts to help alleviate the pain of her aching knees. She took a tube of lipstick out of her purse and rolled the red balm over her lips. Today's earrings were white roses, which complemented her black-and-white rose necklace.

Lilly was tempted to jump on her Vespa to drive into town but changed her mind. The helmet wreaked havoc with her hair, and summer traffic made navigating downtown more challenging. Driving made no sense, since parking was sure to be a challenge. Besides, since she had plenty of time the walk would do her good.

She almost called out to Delia, her housemate, to let her know she was leaving, but then remembered Delia was down at the town hall today. She'd been filling in as an interim town clerk and spent many hours there going through records, trying to get the town back on track. Lilly sighed. Since her husband, Alan, had died two years ago, she'd gotten so used to having Delia around; Lilly was going to miss her when she moved in to the room she'd rented in Burlington later this month to start teaching in Boston. Granted, Delia would be teaching two freshmen sections of research techniques, not her dream topic, but academic careers took a while to build. Lilly sighed once more, and then gave herself a shake. No time for a pity party. She couldn't, wouldn't, ask Delia to put her life on hold any longer.

Lilly closed the front door behind her and double-checked that it was locked. She hated that she had to worry about that, but she did. Curiosity had led more than a few tourists up her front path and into her front hall this past summer without an invitation. She found it disconcerting, to say the least. She'd taken to locking her front door to make sure that her privacy was just that, her privacy. She suspected most of the folks had wanted to get to the back of the house to see her famous gardens, but they never got that far. Thankfully, because her house was so old that no building codes were adhered to, there was no way to get to the back of the house from the side yards. From the street, to the left there was a large greenhouse butted right up against her neighbor Roddy Lyden's fence. To the right her driveway ran all the way to the back of the house, dipping down to a large stone wall at the end. There were no stairs up the stone wall and into the backyard. You had to get to the backyard through the garage, which Lilly and Delia kept closed.

Lilly enjoyed her privacy almost as much as she enjoyed working in her gardens. Almost. She had invited folks over in May for a garden party, and that had turned out to be quite the event for a number of reasons, not the least of which was when her friend Tamara got pushed into the koi pond, and the late Merilee Frank pilfered a family treasure. What a chain of events that party had started. Still, she was considering inviting people over for a fall open house, but with Delia leaving, Lilly wasn't sure she was up to planning the party on her own. Not that she would have to. Her friends Tamara O'Connor and Ernie Johnson would be more than happy to help. But she wasn't going to mention it to them until she committed to the idea herself. Once they had the possibility of a party in their heads, it would be hard to dissuade them.

As Lilly turned to the right to head towards the center of town she paused for a moment outside Roddy Lyden's house. She halfway hoped he would be outside working on his front garden, not that it needed the work. But he wasn't. She hadn't seen Roddy for a couple of days, which was a long time for them. Since he'd moved in, especially since all that happened in May, they talked or texted practically every day. She made a mental note to give him a call later, when she got home.

Lilly walked down Washington Street towards the center of town, a rotary around which most of Goosebush drove at least once a week, if not daily.

The rotary was sometimes referred to as the Wheel since it was the retail center of town. The businesses directly on the Wheel had all been there for years, though not in their present states. Most, except for the post office, were now serving a different purpose. Lilly's destination, the Star Café, was a prime example of a repurposed storefront. While she was growing up, the Star had been a Woolworth. The original store was four stories tall, with a brick façade, tall tin ceilings, worn wooden floors, and complete with an ice cream bar in the front and a cafeteria in the back. Stan Freeland had taken over the building after it had been underused for many years. He turned it into a bookstore and café in the front, and a restaurant and bar in the back. On the second floor there was a theater space. The top two floors were used for storage and some artists' work spaces. Stan was young but had a vision for the building he was determined to see realized. As far as Lilly could tell, he was successful. The Star was always packed.

Lilly walked in and looked to her right. She gave Stella Haywood a small wave and a smile and looked to her left. Stella was the youngest sister of Bash Haywood, the chief of police for Goosebush. Lilly had known Stella forever, and was pleased that the younger woman had found a good job at the Star. After a few fits and starts, Stella was finally on a solid path.

Miranda and Braden were both there already, and Stan had brought them a pot of tea. She took a deep breath before she walked over to them.

"Have fun," Stan whispered to her as he walked back towards the coffee bar. Stan was thin and had a shaved head, a small goatee, and large black-framed glasses. He looked like a humorless hipster, but his loving restoration of the old Woolworth displayed an old soul with a great imagination he coupled with a solid business acumen.

"Good afternoon, Stan," Lilly said. "Could you bring me a cup of tea?" Lilly plastered on a smile, and walked over to the table. Braden started to stand up, but Lilly waved him back into his seat.

"Braden, Miranda, I hope I'm not late," Lilly said. She knew she wasn't. Lilly Jayne was never late.

"No, we just got here ourselves," Braden said. "We ordered a pot of Earl Grey. You're welcome to share if you'd like."

"That's fine with me," Lilly said.

"It's a little pedestrian for my taste, but it will have to do," Miranda said.

"Miranda is a bit of a tea snob," Braden said. "She has started to grow her own tea and make her own blends."

"Oh really? My friend Delia Greenway, you know Delia, is doing research on plants that can be made into tea as well as serve other uses. She mentioned that she tasted a delicious blend lately. Maybe it was one of yours?"

"Not likely," Miranda said. "I only make blends for an exclusive group of customers. Delia isn't one of them."

"My mistake," Lilly said. She narrowed her eyes and looked right at Miranda. A thoroughly unpleasant woman, a few years younger than Lilly herself, Miranda wore her steel gray hair in a top knot held in place with a silver clasp. She now wore her normal uniform: layers of scarves and a flowy jacket worn over black jeans and a black T-shirt.

Miranda Dane had never worked a day in her life, at least as far as Lilly could tell. She'd relied on her cousin Harmon's goodwill, living in what used to be a gardener's cottage for a long-gone estate. Harmon had bought the cottage for his mother-in-law, and when she passed, Miranda moved in. Miranda had always implied that she helped take care of Harmon in his later years after his wife died. But every time Lilly had gone over to see him he'd been waiting on Miranda hand and foot.

"Thanks for coming to meet with us, Lilly," Braden said. He flashed his overly white smile at Lilly. "We met with the lawyers this morning and wanted to check in with you. I'm not sure if they've been in contact—"

"They have," Lilly said.

There was a pause in the conversation. Lilly wasn't going to fill it in for them. This was their meeting, though she had a pretty good idea what they wanted to meet about.

"Of course they have. You're the executor of his estate. We're here to talk to you about Uncle Harmon's endowment. The one for the birds," Braden said.

"For the birds is right," Miranda said.

Lilly took a deep breath before she spoke. "Do you mean money he left for the nesting grounds by his house, to ensure that it be taken care of and expanded if possible? The Dane Sanctuary?"

"Dane Sanctuary? I didn't realize it already had a name," Braden said. Stan brought a cup over for Lilly, and Branden poured her some tea.

"It does," Lilly said, taking the cup. "Your uncle had been talking about it for years. It was actually in memory of your aunt. He was planning on establishing it this fall, so it would be ready for the nesting next spring. We'd been talking about the launch party plans a few days before he passed."

"So, you were in on it with him?" Miranda asked.

"In on it? In on what?"

"This cash drain on his estate," Miranda said.

Lilly put her teacup down and stared at the other woman. Braden quickly jumped in to smooth things over, his normal role in these tedious conversations.

"Uncle Harmon thought he had more time," Braden said. "We all did. I can't help but think when he wrote the will and left such a huge amount of cash for this effort that he expected to have the house in Florida sold, so there would've been more cash overall. He *was* planning on selling the Florida house, you know. Buying a smaller condo," Braden said.

"He had mentioned that possibility, but I don't know that he was planning on it—"

"Well, he was. He never would leave that whole Florida house to Mimi. A condo, maybe. But the whole house? I don't think so," Miranda said.

"Mimi is, was, his sister. I have no doubt he intended to take care of her," Lilly said.

"Of course he did," Braden said. "Lilly, the problem is that the family is house rich and cash poor. Uncle Harmon was very generous. Sure, he left Miranda her cottage, but she has to add the value of it to the pool. Once we sell his house it will be in the mix, but that's taking a long time. Meanwhile he didn't leave us any money to pay inheritance taxes with—"

"Or to live on," Miranda said. "We need some of the bird money."

"Just for a little while until we sell his house— then I can pay it back from my inheritance," Braden said.

"We discussed that this wasn't the best time of year to put the house on the market," Lilly said. "The house is wonderful, but it will need a very specific buyer." She thought it was in very poor taste that Miranda pushed to put the house on the market so soon after Harmon died. Harmon left it to Braden, but the younger man didn't want to live on Shipyard Lane. The will made it clear that the value of the Goosebush houses were to be factored into Braden and Miranda's inheritance, and that Mimi's house was hers alone. Harmon may have intended to clarify these issues over time to stop the sniping, but time was not on her old friend's side. She wished, not for the first time, that she'd talked to Harmon more about the best way to deal with Braden and Miranda, who had been challenging the will from the outset. But who was she to judge them? Lilly did not have money issues, nor did she have relatives who lived off her goodwill.

"It's a great house, I'm sure it will sell. But it may take some time," Lilly said.

Harmon's house *was* a great house, Lilly thought.

Always one of her favorites. But not without its issues. First was the nesting sanctuary that Harmon
had created. That could preclude access to the
beach depending on what Dawn Simmons, the scientist Harmon had been working with, found in
her research and recommended long term for the
sanctuary.

Then there were the restrictions on the land itself, which had been established when the spit of
land was sold to the original owners, who called it
Shipyard Lane. Three houses sat on the edge of a
small cliff, overlooking a rocky beach and the
water. The view was spectacular, and the elevation
made the houses fairly immune to storm damage.
All three houses were identical, built by the same
builder at the same time. They had a walking path
along the front, which led to Harmon Dane's
house and a staircase down to the beach. They also
had a gravel road on the back of the houses, where
the occupants parked. But the agreement when
the houses were built was that nothing could be
done to any one of the houses that wasn't done to
all three. And that they would all stay the same
size. It was a gentlemen's agreement that had
worked for many years but had hosts of issues once
the middle house was sold to Alex Marston and he
started to explore the possibility of adding a floor
with expansive outdoor decks. He'd been shut down
quickly enough by both Harmon and his neighbor
on the other side, Gladys Preston. The three neighbors had been sparring ever since.

Lilly took a sip of tea, put her cup back down on
the saucer, and looked up at Miranda and Braden.
"I'm sorry. I can't help you with this. The money is

still in escrow, and even though it is a generous endowment, it will be spent on the sanctuary as Harmon wanted it to be used. As a matter of fact, it is likely we will need to raise more funds in order to fulfill Harmon's wishes. He and I discussed that, which is why we were making plans to launch the idea of the sanctuary publicly this fall, to get folks interested in supporting the idea. I am more than willing to do that for Harmon and look forward to seeing his wish fulfilled. It is the least I could do for him. I won't be able to help you with your cash flow problems."

"I wonder if this would all stand up in court?" Miranda said. "It could be argued that he was not of sound mind—"

"Harmon Dane was of very sound mind, up till the end. I still can't believe . . . he was always so healthy." Lilly cleared her throat. She looked down at her teacup and blinked back the tears that burned the back of her eyelids.

"Uncle Harmon benefited from modern medicine. He took a handful of pills every day to keep everything in check and balanced. But you're right, he always seemed so healthy. I still can't believe he's gone," Braden said. Lilly looked over at Braden, and noted that he had the good manners to look as sincere as he sounded. "I know he thought the world of you, Lilly, and that you'll do right by him. Miranda and I thought it was worth the conversation. It will all be fine, we'll figure something out. Thanks for coming by and being willing to listen."

Lilly stood up and looked at both of them. Harmon's cousin and ne'er-do-well nephew. Surely, her old friend deserved a better legacy than the two of them. "I'll keep you both posted on the plans for the sanctuary. Let's hope his house sells soon. Miranda, have you made plans to have your house appraised yet? If not, I can do that. It will help move things along. I'd imagine the value has increased substantially since the last time. We'll need to figure that out; it was a very generous gift from Harmon." Miranda choked on her tea, and Braden patted her gently on the back.

With that, Lilly Jayne picked up her purse and headed out of the Star Café. She was tempted to go home, but she felt the need to discuss what had just happened with someone who understood. She'd walk over and see if Tamara was in her office.

CHAPTER TWO

When Lilly walked out of the Star Café a wall of heat hit her and knocked her back. The Star wasn't even that cold inside. It was just that August heat was August heat. She wished she'd worn a lighter colored dress, but felt that in Harmon's memory, and given her role as executor of his estate, she should wear black. At least it was cotton, but the white cabbage roses didn't offer much respite from the sun. Her full skirt was also airy, as indicated by the gust of wind that pushed it up. No worries on that front. Lilly wore bicycle shorts under her dress. The better attire to ride her Vespa, as she often did, and not shock half the residents of Goosebush. Not that many folks would be shocked by Lilly Jayne. They'd long ago grown used to Lilly behaving as she wanted to.

Tamara's office was almost exactly across the street from the Star, but that's not how rotaries worked, even for pedestrians. Lilly took a moment to decide whether to go left or right. Right had fewer crosswalks, but Lilly noticed Gladys Preston getting out of her car, and since avoiding Gladys was in the best interest of Lilly's stress levels, she turned left. Gladys owned the house near Harmon's and had shown a great interest in the sale of his home. Understandable for most people, considering a neighbor had passed and new folks would be moving in, but Gladys didn't show that sort of concern. Gladys Preston was easily one of the most miserable people in Goosebush and looked at life through a prism of gloom. Her misery was contagious, and Lilly worried that a meeting with Miranda and Braden made her more susceptible to malaise.

"Oh Harmon, my friend, I'm not sure I have the patience to do the work you wanted me to do, but I promise I'll try," Lilly said quietly. If anyone heard her they didn't make any indication they had. Instead they smiled at her, nodded, and in some cases waved or said hello. Lilly had been hiding out at Windward, her home, the past few years while she was taking care of her husband and then deeply mourning his passing. People were glad to see her out and about.

Lilly headed left, walking slowly in the heat. She smiled, waved back, and said hello to a half-dozen folks before she got to the second crosswalk. She was pausing at the next crosswalk—the only crosswalk with an actual light since by Goosebush standards it was a busy entryway onto the rotary. As if drawn by a magnet, Lilly looked left at Bits, Bolts & Bulbs. The Triple B was owned by Ernie Johnson, Lilly's friend and her co-conspirator in all things gardening.

"I wonder if Ernie has more impatiens?" she wondered aloud. It was very late in the season, but Lilly still used the plants to fill in where things had died, and to gussy up window boxes—her own and the ones she gave as gifts to other people.

Lilly walked the block to the store and broke into a smile when she walked in the door. She'd traveled the world and had been to more markets than she could remember, but she knew one thing for sure. The Triple B was her favorite shop, ever. Ernie stocked it with home repair items, gardening supplies, a few small appliances, a healthy computer supply area, and a cookware section. The greenhouse off of the back of the shop had seasonal plants and herbs.

But the magic of the shop lay in the decor. Every month Ernie had a different theme for the store in addition to the seasonal offerings. This month's theme was adventure. He preferred it over the "back to school" trope that everyone else followed. He carried school supplies and a wide array of backpacks, of course. But he also carried maps, travelers' notebooks and inserts, compasses, birding books, and binoculars. Every month he created a different treasure map of Goosebush, with clues he'd arranged to be left at other stores, or in public spaces. Anyone who went to all the sites on the map got a prize. Other stores loved the increased traffic, and volunteers made sure the clues left in different sites were kept in stock. Kids and parents alike had taken to stopping by to pick up a map and go out on an adventure in town.

Lilly walked into the store and took a deep breath of the cooler air. She waved to the cashier, who in turn pointed to the greenhouse area. Lilly went over to the cooler and got a bottle of iced tea. She held it up to her forehead and went to stand in line to pay for it.

"Pay for it on your way out, Ms. Jayne. We both know you'll end up buying a plant or two before you leave." Lilly smiled at the cashier. For the life of her, Lilly couldn't remember his name. He'd only been there for a couple of weeks, and Lilly wouldn't worry about his name until he'd been there a month. Ernie tended to go through staff in the summer. Students went back to school. And a few folks thought it would be an easy job, not understanding the demands of a small, bustling business, so they didn't last long.

"I have no idea what you mean," Lilly said, smiling at him. She opened the top and took a deep swig of the tea concoction. The most important requirements for the heat of the day—that it was cold and wet—were met. Not much beyond that but, nevertheless, Lilly kept sipping it as she walked through the store towards the greenhouse.

"Lilly, what brings you here?" Ernie said. He was misting beds of flowers and moving things around. Ernie was the same height as Lilly, and always wore a white long-sleeved dress shirt with rolled-up sleeves and khakis when he was at work. His apron didn't identify him as the owner, just as another member of the staff. His receding hairline glistened slightly, and Ernie stopped misting, took out a handkerchief, and dabbed his brow.

"I had tea with Miranda and Braden," Lilly said.

"And you needed a plant fix to get right with the world again," Ernie said, replacing the handkerchief and turning the mister back on. He gestured to a stool by one of the tables. "Boy howdy, do I understand that. Braden isn't that bad, though he is a bit dim. But Miranda sits on my last nerve."

"She'd kick at a football game," Lilly said. She walked over and leaned on the stool, taking another swig of tea.

"She'd what?" Ernie asked. He stopped misting and turned to look at her.

"She'd kick at a football game," Lilly said. "My grandfather used to say that about people who complained a lot. I have no idea what it means and am fairly certain that he misquoted a quote and it stuck. That said, I've always loved the phrase. I'm surprised you haven't heard me use it before."

"I know you don't suffer fools gladly, but I don't think I've heard you say it aloud before," Ernie said. He turned the mister back on and moved to the next rack of plants.

"It must be the heat," Lilly said. She watched the plants perk up after their shower. Most folks would have missed that, but Lilly understood plants. "People are getting to me these days. Maybe I'm still a bit raw after Harmon's death."

Ernie looked over his shoulder and gave her a kind smile. "I understand that, all too well." Both of them were silent for a moment remembering the loss of their husbands.

"Losing someone who's been sick is one thing. But Harmon was healthy. We had lunched the day before he . . ."

"I know. He'd placed a huge plant order a couple of days before that," Ernie said.

"Did you deliver the plants?" Lilly asked.

"Some of them, per Tamara's request. She wanted to spruce up the place for open houses. But most of the plants are still here. See over there, those are the order." He gestured to two shelves of plants off to the side. They were blocked from being purchased by others by a barrier of blue painter's tape with a sign attached. "I keep meaning to talk to you about that. We should put Harmon's house on our project list, since he paid for the plants." The project list was for the Garden Squad, which included Lilly, Ernie, Tamara, Tamara's husband, Warwick, Delia, and Roddy Lyden. The list was an internal document of neglected gardening projects around town. The squad did their work under dark of night, when they wouldn't be noticed. They chose to be clandestine gardeners for two reasons. First, they didn't want folks to think they were for hire or starting a new business. Second, they didn't ask permission before they tackled a project. It was Lilly's philosophy that a badly tended garden was corrosive to Goosebush's soul. The rest of the squad agreed, and so they were guerilla gardeners.

"Agreed. I'd love you to come out and look at the sanctuary with me," Lilly said. "We'll need to hire someone to get the new habitats built. I hope you can help me with that, and give me some design advice."

"Happy to help," Ernie said. "Maybe we can discuss it at the meeting this afternoon."

"Meeting?" Lilly said. For someone retired, Lilly had a lot of meetings these days. Far too many in her opinion. She was losing track of her schedule.

"The Beautification Committee? We're meeting here in an hour. I thought you were early."

"No, but I'll try to be on time. I was heading over to talk to Tamara, but the call of the plants was too hard to ignore. I don't know how I missed this meeting . . ."

"I do," Ernie said. "We've changed the meeting four times this month alone. I half expect this one to be called off too. Hopefully folks will show up this afternoon."

"If nothing else we'll have a chance to talk. I'll make sure Tamara comes too. See you in a bit."

"Tamara, are you here?" Lilly called out. The annoying buzzer had let folks know that someone had entered the office, but no one was there to respond. "Pete? Anyone?"

"Be right there," said a disembodied voice that Lilly recognized as belonging to her best friend. Tamara came around the corner, a coffee cup in hand. She looked cool and chic with her ivory-colored linen sheath dress and impossibly high heels.

"Figures. It's been quiet as a tomb in here all day. Not a call, not a visitor. I take five minutes to make some coffee and someone comes in. Thankfully, it's just you."

"Just me? Should I be offended?" Lilly said. She sat down on one of the guest chairs in the waiting area and stretched her long legs out in front of her.

"Oh Lilly, you know what I mean. I'm in a bad mood because business is off." Tamara sat down at her desk and crossed her legs in one smooth move, not dropping any coffee. "Sorry, I should have checked. Would you like some coffee?"

"No, thanks, I'm still working on my iced tea. Isn't it normal for business to be a little slow in August? Didn't you tell me that once? Families relocate before school, people are on vacation."

"Usually. But I do have houses to sell."

"Including the Dane house," Lilly said, taking another swig of her iced tea.

"Especially the Dane house. Speaking of which, how did your meeting with Miranda and Braden go?" Tamara sat down on the chair next to the sofa and stretched her long legs out in front of her. Tamara and Lilly were the same age, though Tamara looked fifteen years younger. She was in great shape, always dressed to the nines with a simple elegance that Lilly didn't try to emulate.

"As you expected. They need money, wanted me to tap into the sanctuary fund."

"You can't do that, can you?" Tamara asked.

"No, I can't, even if I wanted to, which I don't. The money is still tied up in probate and will be for a few more weeks. At least. There's a lot to untangle with this will."

"Well, you're good at untangling, but I know this must be hard. Poor Harmon. He was such a good man. Hard to believe he's gone," Tamara said.

"I know. It's hitting me hard. This is going to sound unkind, but I don't think it is hitting Braden or Miranda as hard as it should. Do you know what I mean?"

"Harmon deserved to have better relatives,"

Tamara said. "He was smart to leave you in charge of things. I had no idea he was so serious about the bird sanctuary, though, did you? He left a lot of money for that."

"I'd imagine he expected his estate to have more cash when he passed. He should have left percentages of his estate to different folks, but he left that lump sum. I know he wanted to create a fund to support the sanctuary. His late wife loved those birds, and I think he was interested in helping them to preserve her memory. We'd talked about it, and I was going to help him with the garden part. Fortunately, the conversations were far enough along that I have a good idea as to what he wanted in that regard. That said, I had no idea he was going to put so much of his estate into the project. He had to have known that wouldn't make his relatives happy."

"Maybe he was past caring?" Tamara said. "He's been supporting that sorry lot for years. I'm all for seeing his wishes through, but I've got to admit it adds another layer of stress to selling the house. There are so many restrictions on the lot, not to mention the charming neighbors. That scientist, Deb?" Tamara stirred her coffee and blew on it.

"Dawn. Dawn Simmons."

"Dawn, right. She's coming in to figure out the work schedule for the sanctuary next week, right? That's going to be helpful, so we can let potential buyers know what to expect."

"Week after next, though Gladys Preston and Alex Marston are giving me a hard time about that," Lilly said.

"What kind of a hard time?" Tamara asked.

"Nothing I can't handle. Listening to them, you'd think we were about to build the Eiffel Tower instead of a nesting habitat. I'm not too worried about them. Gladys threatened to deny me access to Harmon's house via the shared driveway for additional vehicles. I did an end run and I'm going to have scaffolding set up using the beach at Swallow Point, so the scientists can use that to set up. There are also the stairs to the beach, so folks could park over there and come up to the house that way. I'm not about to let Gladys derail this project with her pettiness."

"We all need to not let Gladys get to us, but that's a tough one these days. Anyway, have you decided if Dawn's going to stay at the house or not?" Tamara asked.

"I haven't spoken to her, but that's one possibility. I'll let you know. She'll clear out for open houses and tours."

"No worries about that. You're footing the bill for her coming in, aren't you? Instead of waiting for the estate to pony up?" Tamara asked.

"The work needs to be done, and better sooner than later. I was going to donate to the sanctuary fund anyway, and this will help seed the work."

"What's the work they're going to be doing?" Tamara took a sip of her coffee, which had cooled enough for her to drink. Tamara was a hot beverage person, even in August. Lilly never understood how she did it.

"It's more of an assessment, really. Checking the old wooden stairs, figuring out what it will take to shore them up without compromising the nesting area, making sure the vegetation is going to hold, looking at the stone wall, that sort of thing. We need to assess the fence built along the side of the house as well. It runs right along the cliffside. Harmon liked it for privacy, but I suspect it will need to be taken down, or at the very least moved inside the property line to create more of a formal sanctuary space before the new owners move in. We're going to catalog the plants as well. This visit will last a few days, and then we'll make plans going forward. There will be some temporary scaffolding set up for the work this fall, nothing too invasive. Dawn and I are working on getting scientists, builders, environmentalists, and other folks all lined up. The schedule took some coordination, but between Delia and me, we got it done."

"The beach has its own set of issues for scaffolding, doesn't it?" Tamara asked.

"It does, but folks seem confident we can make it work. Thank heaven Harmon bought the beach from the town and leased it back for public use as a public space. He did that to prevent any other buildings going up, but it made this much easier."

"It was smart of him, and generous. Now that there's that small parking lot and the benches, a lot of folks use it."

"It's also dog friendly, as long as people clean up and keep them under control. That makes it a popular walking destination. The dogs don't mind walking over the stones to go swimming."

"Goosebush has other, better public beaches for folks to swim and sunbathe, but there aren't many dog options," Tamara said.

"We are blessed with lots of options, that's for sure. Anyway, I officially asked for the permits at the last town hall meeting, the one they held when you were on vacation. I'm surprised you didn't hear about that."

"Ray Mancini and I have been trying to meet all week, but one or the other of us has had to cancel. We're having a drink tonight to catch up." Tamara turned over a pad of paper and put her coffee mug down on the cardboard.

"After our Beautification Committee meeting?"

"What Beautification Committee meeting?" Tamara said, furrowing her brow and turning to the calendar that was open on her desktop computer.

"I'm glad it wasn't only me. Phew. I was at the Triple B and Ernie mentioned a meeting. I couldn't believe that I'd missed it on my calendar."

"I hate to sound paranoid, but it may not have made it to your calendar, or mine," Tamara said, turning back to Lilly. "You know who they added to the Beautification Committee, don't you?"

"We need to come up with a better name for this committee," Lilly said. "How about Team Beauty?"

"You know Regan got herself on the committee," Tamara said.

"Oh no," Lilly said, not trying to mask her distaste from Tamara. They'd been friends for over sixty years, and Lilly was grateful she never had to pretend she was anyone else in front of Tamara. "Who put her on?"

"Miranda Dane."

"Miranda Dane," Lilly said. She looked right at Tamara, who turned her gaze back to her coffee mug. "I'm not going to tell you I told you so, Tamara, but I told you so. I told you Miranda was going to be a nightmare to have on the committee. But no—you wanted to be nice to Miranda."

"Listen, Harmon's death was hard," Tamara said. "She had me feeling sorry for her. Besides, even you've got to admit, she's a good gardener."

"She is." Lilly was reluctant to admit it, but Miranda knew her plants. "But what a miserable person. And now she's ended up being the Benedict Arnold of Team Beauty and invited your business rival onto the committee."

"Yeah, well, there's that," Tamara sighed deeply. "Just think, two months ago none of us had heard of Regan Holland. Life was simple back then."

Indeed, none of them had heard of Regan Holland. But Regan Holland had heard of Goosebush. An ambitious real estate broker who had moved from community to community over the years, Regan Holland had apparently decided that Goosebush would be her latest conquest. She'd discovered that there was only one real estate agency in town. The agency run by Tamara O'Connor and her partners. Of course, if you asked most of Goosebush they'd agree that they didn't need more than one real estate agency. Folks who didn't want to go with Tamara went with a chain or sold their houses themselves online. But O'Connor Real Estate was all that Goosebush had ever needed. Until Regan started talking to folks, letting them know that they should be getting higher prices and commercial zoning should be spread out and one office was a monopoly. She hadn't convinced many people yet, but she was working on it by writing checks to sponsor events, taking folks out to dinner, and inserting herself into town business.

"I never asked you, how did the open house go yesterday?" Lilly asked. The segue wasn't out of thin air. Regan had been talking to Braden Dane, wanting him to give her the listing for Harmon's house. As executor of Harmon's will, Lilly agreed to keep Braden aware of bids and allow him to have the final say in the selling of his house. Tamara had the listing currently, but both women agreed they would make this a business transaction, with Braden in charge.

"The Dane house has a curse, I swear. Every time I have an open house something goes wrong. Last week it was the plumbing backing up, leaving me with black goo in the sinks and tubs. Yesterday there was a mouse infestation."

"Mice aren't unheard of in houses," Lilly said, making a face.

"Lil, when I say infestation, I mean infestation. There were dozens running all over the place, not even trying to hide. All of them, by the way, white mice, not field mice."

"White mice? Like lab mice?" Lilly shivered as she said the word *mice.* Lilly hated mice. Or, more accurately, Lilly was afraid of mice. One of the few things Lilly was truly afraid of.

"Exactly like. Someone had let them in and let them loose. Luckily, I got there early and figured it out. I canceled the open house. I've got somebody over there now doing their best to capture them all and to clean up."

"Any idea of who did it?"

"None that I can prove. Unfortunately for me, there are a few possible folks."

"Like Regan."

"Gladys Preston. Miranda. Maybe even Alex."

"Alex? Alex Marston? Why would he let mice loose in the house?"

"Alex puts a low bid in on the Dane house every few days. They're laughable. But I'm obligated to tell Braden about it since you've made him the point person on the house deal. He has held firm until recently, but he's starting to cave."

"He'd have to get that past me, and Miranda. And trust me, Miranda wants the house to sell for as much as possible. How much longer do you have the listing?"

"Till Labor Day. But Braden's losing faith, and that's not a good kind of client to have."

"I shouldn't have let Braden talk me out of being in charge of this sale once he decided to put the house on the market," Lilly said. "He's making a lot of terrible decisions about it, that's for sure. Who cares if we've been best friends forever? That wouldn't have compromised me on the business front."

"I know it wouldn't have, Lilly, but with Regan around, we need to tread carefully. This much I know, I've got to sell the Dane house."

"You will, you will. Meanwhile, let's head over to the Triple B for the meeting." Lilly finished her iced tea, stood up, and put the bottle in the recycling bin. Tamara would sell the house if the playing field was level. But it obviously wasn't. Lilly couldn't help but wonder who was sabotaging her friend and what she could do to catch them.

CHAPTER THREE

Tamara and Lilly arrived back at the Triple B together and went into the greenhouse for the meeting. When the committee was first formed, they could all fit in Ernie's office. But now, after seeing some of the work that the committee had done over the past couple of months there were more volunteers than they knew what to do with. The core committee, the voting committee, remained the Garden Squad itself, PJ Frank, and the board of selectmen of Goosebush. But other members, like Regan, Miranda, Gladys, the Goosebush Girl Scout troop, and half of Warwick O'Connor's lacrosse team, came to meetings regularly.

Everyone had an opinion on what needed to be beautified in Goosebush. Happily for all, a small fund had been established where people could apply for a grant, and then the committee would find volunteers to help do the work. Nobody knew about the clandestine work that the Garden Squad did to determine the viability of the projects. Everyone was surprised when one of the first projects was the reseeding of the lacrosse/field hockey/soccer/football fields at the high school. It wasn't a flashy garden or a reclaiming of land. The grass was always green. But folks on the committee knew that Warwick and his students spent hours, even days, trying to get the fields up to standard every spring, summer, and fall. Taking up the grass and adding new soil, an irrigation system, and sod were worthy investments. Tamara and Lilly worked hard on getting matching funds, and everyone agreed that the use it would get over the year was tremendous.

Alden Park was a perpetual project, but the discovery of some artifacts during excavation halted gardening progress in the name of academia. Delia was overseeing the project and was determined that no more work would be done until research was complete. Nothing in the town history showed Alden Park had been a dumping site, so the discovery of the artifacts was not anticipated. The hope was that the work would be done by next spring.

The list of projects that were seeking funding was short, which made it all the more contentious among the committee. Those under the age of thirty were all pushing for the public park near the beach to be finally finished, complete with an outdoor performance space for summer shows. The old beach house and concession stand were there already, offering the infrastructure of plumbing and electricity that could support the modest proposal.

"All that will do is cause commotion," Gladys Preston opined. "Commotion, beer drinking, and heaven knows what. Bad news when a bunch of teenagers are given a place to party."

"The empty parking lot offers the same opportunities," Ernie said. "And you know we all do everything we can to ensure that doesn't happen. If anything, this would make the parking lot busier at night, which would take away from it being a party spot. I, for one, love the idea of being able to have an outdoor theater close to the beach. It would be unique, and fun."

"As long as it doesn't ruin the dunes—" Miranda said.

"The whole idea is to create a place that will get folks off the dunes," Ernie said. He had to explain this at every meeting, but maintained his patience. Barely, at this point. "That part of the beach is in good shape, because it's the public part, where folks from other towns can come for the day. Their parking fees help maintain the beaches. We've built up the fencing, and there are clear access paths for folks. It's farther down, on the private town part of the beach, where we have to worry about the dunes and the plant life."

"How about the dunes for a project then?" one of the Girl Scouts asked. "The dunes we need to worry about?"

"On the docket for next spring," Lilly said, smiling. "The parking lot project needs to get started this fall if it's going to be ready for next spring. If we decide to go ahead with the performance area, we need to factor that into the work, and I'd like to get that done. But since the payoff won't be for months, I've been wondering if maybe we should do some sort of project that we can all enjoy this fall. What do you all think about planting a pumpkin patch and some other vegetables that we can harvest in September and October for the winter? We could use that lot we're planning to use for the new garden by the elementary school. Maybe we could hold some sort of festival this fall?"

"A craft fair, with local foods," Portia Asher offered up. Lilly hadn't seen the small, older woman sitting on a stool towards the back of the room. But once Portia spoke, the entire room came to attention. A public garden, where folks could have a patch of land where they could plant some vegetables, was surprisingly controversial in Goosebush. Nevertheless, Portia persisted, and Lilly's idea was one way to get folks used to the idea. The lot everyone was discussing was underused, overgrown, and owned by the town itself. Celebrating the use of the land with a festival was inspired, and was well worth the investment of time and money.

"PJ, maybe you could bring some of that cider you make to the fair," someone said. "That would guarantee a crowd."

"Watch out, folks, I've been brewing some new beers. I may have some to break out." Everyone laughed. PJ Frank didn't just brew some beer. He and his partner had started a small craft brewery that was producing local beers everyone was raving about.

"We've got two great projects," Ernie said. "Getting a spot ready for a fall festival, and getting the area near the public parking lot cleared and prepped for a performance space next spring. Since the beach project will take some planning, we won't be able to do a lot this fall, but we can talk it up, figure out a way to get folks excited about it, since it will take town support to pull it off. You think we can get enough volunteers to pull them both off? To get the beach ready to go, and get this garden planted?"

"You know, Coach O'Connor has been trying to get a 10K organized for this fall. A team building exercise," Harry Lentz said. Harry was one of the lacrosse players who came to every meeting. "Maybe we could measure the route, and get folks to start and end at the festival site, but loop by the parking lot area? Maybe there could be some sort of station for folks to get water or go to the bathroom there, with some entertainment?"

"Show folks what could be?" Ernie said. "That's a great idea, Harry. We could talk to—"

"Do we have time to get the plants ready to go for an autumn festival?" Regan interrupted the enthusiasm the students had started to show for the idea. "I don't know much about gardening, but isn't August pretty late to start?" Regan had a million-watt smile that was wasted on the people in the room, so she toned it down quickly.

Tamara turned to answer the other woman. "There are more than a few of us who could offer up some plants to transplant, I'd imagine. I know Warwick's got quite the pumpkin patch going, and there are some container plants we could offer up. That's how Goosebush works, you see, Regan. We all pitch in. We're in it together."

Nobody spoke for a couple of moments, knowing this was about more than plants.

"Well then, two projects ready to go. Anything else we should talk about—" Ernie finally said to fill the silence.

"There sure is," Gladys said, turning towards Lilly. "I want to know what this one has planned for this research project on the beach at Swallow Point."

"That project isn't the concern of this committee," Ernie said.

"Well, it sure as hell should be, and there's nowhere else to bring it up. I don't know anything about it, and I sure should. I live on Shipyard Lane. There's a covenant there; anything that impacts one house impacts us all—"

"This project doesn't impact Harmon's house," Lilly said, infusing her voice with patience she did not feel. She had gone over this a dozen times with Gladys both in private and in public. "As we discussed, years ago Harmon bought the land that included the beach to the side of his house and deeded the use back to the town. He even built the small parking lot for folks to use. It isn't a swimming beach, so the town was grateful that he was willing to maintain it. It also stopped a developer from buying the land and blocking the view for the folks up the street. Anyway, he also promised to protect the beach and the wildlife that was there as part of the deal with the town. Harmon always said he did this to make his house a bit more private, but he ended up falling in love with the birds and the plants that grew in that little spit of land. He left money in his will to protect that sanctuary and deeded the land back to the town in perpetuity provided the reserve was always protected and maintained.

"Now, the stairs down to the beach are precarious and may need to be rebuilt. Harmon was already planning that work when he passed. A work assessment is taking place in a couple of weeks. As part of rebuilding the stairs, a nesting area will be built. These new stairs aren't going to create public access to Shipyard Lane from the beach. If anything, I would imagine it will raise the property values for all three houses, since the reserve will ensure the land will be kept up, and the new stairs will be accessible to everyone on Shipyard."

"You would say that, wouldn't you, Ms. Holier-Than-Thou. I know what you're up to, don't think I don't," Gladys said. She got up quickly and knocked her stool over. She harrumphed as she stomped out of the greenhouse. After a moment Regan got up and followed her out, as did Miranda.

"Good riddance," Portia said loudly. Everyone laughed. "Now, let's get down to a schedule. These kids are going back to school soon and we're going to lose them. And if we want to pull off this road race, we need to get cracking. But let's get this straight—I'm not doing any running!"

The meeting broke up shortly after a schedule was created. Two groups set out right from the meeting to go on site visits and take some digital pictures. As they left, one of the Girl Scouts promised to help Portia gain access to the private Facebook group they were creating in order to keep track of the work.

Delia was amongst the last to leave the room. She continued to type for a few minutes while Ernie, Tamara, and Lilly chatted. When she finally looked up from her keyboard she blinked a couple of times as if assimilating back to the real world.

"I've shared the notes from the meeting on the Google drive we set up for the committee."

"Who has access to those documents?" Tamara asked.

"Everyone on the committee," Delia said. "I've got a private drive for the four of us plus Roddy and Warwick. I make copies of the notes and they go in there. I make copies of everything and put them in different places, so we don't lose them."

"Are you building in enough redundancies?" Ernie asked, gently teasing his young friend. Delia was, at heart, an academic. She'd spent years as a research assistant for Lilly's late husband, Alan Macmillan, and had moved into the house to help him finish his last projects. After he passed she had stayed on to help Lilly cope. Though forty years separated the two women, their friendship ran deep. Whereas Delia had the intellectual capacity to do a ton of work, Lilly helped her navigate emotional connections to other people. Delia didn't always pick up on social cues, but she was learning.

"If I've learned nothing these past two months, there are never enough redundancies," Delia said. "I also download them on my own computer and on an external hard drive. If they're really important, I print them out. I've also been embedding watermarks to prove authenticity. The town records are a real mess, mostly because they had been altered slightly over the years and I can't tell the difference between the original versions and the fake ones. Digital copies can be complicated for that reason, so I'm figuring out ways to encode version numbers."

"You're the perfect person for that job," Lilly said. "You've got that attention to detail that makes you such a great scholar."

"I've been thinking a lot about Alan lately," Delia said, looking at Lilly. "I hope that doesn't make you sad."

"I think of Alan every day. How could that make me sad?" Lilly gave the younger woman a kind smile, which seemed to fortify Delia. "Tell me, what's making you think about him?"

"Alan always told me to pay attention to the details. That the smallest piece of information could have the greatest impact. He also told me to fight for time to do the work right. That's one of the reasons I'm trying to make sure that the work we do on Alden Park moves at a pace that keeps up with the artifacts we're discovering. They don't make sense somehow, and the only way we'll figure out the mystery is by taking our time. I know Alden Park was supposed to be the next big project of the Beautification Committee. Thank you all for your patience with me on that—"

"Please, I for one am thrilled about the archaeological dig across the street," Ernie said. "For one thing, they're keeping me busy stocking shovels, brushes, buckets, and all sorts of other things they need." Ernie paused while everyone laughed. "Also, as one of the trustees of the library it thrills me that there's going to be an online and public exhibition of what's found in real time, rather than waiting for an academic paper to be published."

"Delia, what else is making you feel anxious?" Tamara asked.

"I'll admit it, entering the academic world this fall is making me feel pressed for time and nervous about a million other things. They've had me go over my syllabus for 'Historical Research in Real Time' three times and want me to make it more compelling so that the class fills. They also have me teaching two sections of the freshman research class online, which is new for me, though I'll admit it's less daunting than getting up and talking in front of sixty students at a time."

"Sixty? That's a lot," Tamara said.

"It's a core course for freshmen, starting this year. They've been finding that folks don't understand proper research and attribution techniques these days. Unintentional plagiarism is a problem, so they want to make sure students understand the proper techniques right away so they can't claim ignorance."

"You'll be great at it all," Lilly said.

Delia sighed. "This is the road that Alan and I talked about for my career, and now that I'm finally on it, I'm noticing a million other paths that interest me. Listen to me. It's probably nerves. I'm this close to living my dream."

"Dreams can change," Tamara said. Tamara looked over at her friend Lilly. No one understood better than Tamara how much Lilly would miss

Delia. And no one understood better than Tamara that Lilly would never say anything to Delia about that.

Lilly shot Tamara a look and got up. "You know, Delia, nerves are fine. I'm happy to look over anything you'd like me to, of course. In the meantime, I haven't been to Alden Park for a few days. Want to walk me over while there's still sunlight and give me a tour of the site?"

"Hold up, I'm coming with you," Ernie said. "I can't get enough of this adventure. Afterwards, dinner? Before the town meeting tonight?"

"Town meeting?" Lilly asked.

"Lilly, you didn't forget about the town meeting, did you?" Tamara said. "Lenny Andrus is trying to get a variance on his latest project."

"I didn't forget about it," Lilly said.

"Liar," Tamara said. Lilly smiled, and gave her a wink. Truth to tell, she had forgotten about it. Lilly took a deep breath. She was too busy these days, much too busy. If everything kept up at this pace she'd need to buy a planner, and she'd promised herself she wouldn't do that once she retired. What she needed was time off. She'd penciled out the two weeks after the scientists left as a vacation for herself. She'd rest then.

"What a dump!" Ernie said, helping himself to another serving of Lilly's potato salad. Lilly, Ernie, Delia, Tamara, Warwick, and Roddy were sitting in Lilly's kitchen, enjoying what Lilly's mother always referred to as a cold supper. Cold roasted turkey, ham, potato salad, coleslaw, green salad, rolls, chips, and a multitude of jellies, mustards, relishes, and other condiments folks could add at their whim.

"Why does he keep saying that?" Delia asked Roddy quietly.

"Ernie's playing into a stereotype doing his Bette Davis imitation," Roddy said. "But I think he means it as a compliment."

"Of course, I mean it as a compliment," Ernie said. "A dump from the 1800s. Who could have guessed it would be so fascinating?"

"I'm not sure I'd call it fascinating," Warwick said.

"You, my friend, need a tour from Delia. She explains what's going on like she's telling you a story, which she is. Layers and mounds of stuff covered over for all those years, waiting for us to find them. The rigor needed to make sure the layers are uncovered in due time so the story comes out as it should. Fascinating."

"I'm not exactly an expert, but I've been reading up. Dump sites are excellent for archaeologists," Delia said. "Think about what people throw away. Food scraps, broken dishes, clothes, all the stuff that reflects everyday life. Back then there was less waste than there is today, but it still gives you a good sense of what people ate, used for pottery, all that stuff. A time capsule of sorts for Goosebush. There may not be a ton of academic use for the findings, but it's still pretty interesting.

"The fascinating thing about this dump is that it was completely unexpected," Delia said. "And it seems to have been narrowly used."

"What do you mean 'narrowly used'?" Roddy asked.

"Alden Park has been common use ground for Goosebush ever since the town was founded. The artifacts are definitely from the mid-1800s, so they aren't from the time when the town had indigenous folks living here. From everything I've been able to find in the town records, it was never used as a public dumping site. So where did this stuff come from? That's why I wanted to bring some people trained to look at these pieces in to excavate. They will be able to place the findings on some sort of timeline. There doesn't seem to be a huge variety of things, so it may have been used for a narrow, specific purpose."

"Very interesting," Lilly agreed. "Of course, opening it up to academics does delay redoing the park indefinitely. But no matter, thanks to today's meeting there's plenty to keep us busy this fall."

"I take it the meeting went well?" Warwick said.

"Well?" Tamara said. "These days well is such a relative term. I guess it did go well. Once Gladys, Regan, and Miranda left, that is."

Warwick whistled through his teeth and turned the lazy Susan until the green salad was in front of him. He helped himself to a good portion of greens. "Those women do get around, spreading sunshine in their path, don't they?" he said, smiling at his wife.

She smiled back. "Indeed, they do."

"Speaking of which, what fun have we to look forward to tonight at the town meeting? I'm hoping we're done with the Shipyard Lane questions from Gladys," Ernie said. He helped himself to some more coleslaw.

"Nothing about that project is on the agenda," Delia said.

"Nor will it be," Lilly said. "We talked about the permitting at the last meeting. Gladys wasn't there, thankfully. The part of the project that is the town's business has been dealt with."

"It has indeed," Delia said. "It should be a quick meeting. Lenny has asked for a variance for a project he's working on. He asked that it be brought before the town meeting rather than being decided by the board of selectmen."

"Because the board would've turned him down flat," Tamara said.

"Can an individual really usurp the normal channels like that?" Roddy asked. "Seems like a dangerous way to run a town government."

"It could be, except that Goosebush is a small town. Folks weigh in on both sides of an argument and usually choose the side that is best for the town overall," Lilly said.

"Usually," Ernie said. "Of course, there is that tragic example of the old Girl Scout meeting house that was razed to build that god-awful sushi restaurant everyone thought would be a great hit here in Goosebush."

"A sushi restaurant? I love sushi." Delia said. "Where was that?"

"You wouldn't have loved this place. It was a couple of blocks away from the beach. It's an empty lot now. They used frozen fish and didn't buy local. Don't think that doesn't come up every few years at town hall meetings. Of course, the whole plan never would've happened if they hadn't called for a meeting when Warwick and I were on vacation and Lilly was taking care of Alan," Tamara said.

"Democracy really rests on the shoulders of so few people?" Roddy said.

"There have always been a few of us with, how shall I put this, a clearer vision than others," Lilly said. "We usually see to it that considerations are weighed carefully."

"Which is how Tamara got on the board of selectmen and why Lilly has to go to every meeting," Ernie said. "To make sure common sense prevails."

"Still, another town meeting? Does every town have these many meetings?" Roddy asked, adding a slice of ham to his plate and picking up a roll. "Not that I mind. It's a wonderful way for a newcomer to learn about the goings-on. But still, I feel as if I'm wearing out my seat on those bleachers in the school gymnasium."

"No, you're right, we've had more than our share of town meetings this summer. Lots to work through. The board of selectmen decided to do it out in the open. Transparency matters. We have to gain some trust back after what happened in May," Tamara said. "As for tonight's meeting, Lenny Andrus has decided to move from the renovation business into the construction business—"

"That I am aware of. I asked him for a bid on some work on my house, but he hasn't gotten back to me," Roddy said. "He let me know that he was more interested in new construction than renovating old. A shame, his work came highly recommended." Roddy finished making his ham sandwich and took a hesitant bite. He always enjoyed experimenting with Lilly and Delia's array of condiments, but he'd learned to move slowly. He'd had varying degrees of success combining flavors over the summer.

"There aren't a lot of empty lots in Goosebush," Delia said. "So now he's trying to get permission to tear down old houses and build new ones. That has enough permitting issues. But his latest scheme has him tearing down two houses and building four. The neighborhood he wants to build in is zoned for one-acre lots, but he says that isn't modern society. His Plan B is to build two two-family houses on the lots."

"And I assume the town of Goosebush is against more housing on these two lots of land? Even though in this part of town our lots are much smaller than one acre."

"This part of town is the historical district. Different rules," Tamara said.

"But to answer your question," Ernie said, "the town does want to stop Lenny. It's not that he wants to add housing stock. There are some questions about whether or not he can pull it off. Of course, no one will be so crass as to say that aloud. He runs a very small company, and from what I can tell, he does not have a huge cash reserve to invest in these projects."

"How do you know that?" Tamara asked.

"I'm telling tales out of school," Ernie said. "These are my business concerns, but not for the public."

"His application shows that he has enough money," Delia said dubiously.

"And I hope he does," Ernie said. "Anyway, I'll

be at the meeting, voting no. Is that the only thing we're voting on tonight?"

"There is a pro forma vote on Dump Day—"

"We prefer to call it Recycling Day," Warwick said.

"Which is?" Roddy asked.

"Which is one of the fundraisers we do for the high school sports teams," Warwick said. "Folks bring gently used furniture and home goods to the dump, students spend time cleaning, fixing, repainting, recovering, and repurposing them in some cases. They're shop projects for the semester. In December there is a huge rummage sale, and everything the kids worked on all fall is put up for sale. Helps raise money for the other sports teams, which don't get as much funding as the football team."

"That doesn't sound at all controversial—" Roddy said.

"The reason it comes up for open vote is the coverage it gets in the town paper and on the on-line blogs. It's as much to remind people to show up on Saturday and either help or bring their stuff," Lilly said.

"Small town," Roddy said.

"The longer you're here, the smaller it gets," Warwick said. "Sit near me tonight, I'll give you the inside scoop on some of the people who show up."

"Now Warwick, don't cause trouble—" Tamara said.

"Me? Cause trouble? Isn't that the mission of the Garden Squad? To cause trouble for the town?"

"Not cause trouble, just step in where needed," Ernie said. "Speaking of which, this project to create a performance space at the beach? It's going to need some extra effort on our part to make sure it gets pulled off well. We need to keep the scope small, but talk up the project positively. It would be a lot of fun for folks to use during the summer."

"Absolutely—"

"Of course—"

"I was thinking about that—"

"But that's for another day. Tonight, we vote on Lenny's project and remind the town that Dump Day is Saturday," Ernie said. "All the while Warwick and I will let Roddy in on some of the character foibles of our neighbors."

"Glad you'll be joining us. We always have fun," Warwick said

"It's the only thing that gets me through these meetings," Ernie said.

"You said it," Warwick said, catching the napkin Tamara threw at him with a laugh.

CHAPTER FOUR

"Are we ready for a vote?" Tamara said for the umpteenth time.

The school gym, where the town halls were usually held, was packed. On the one hand, that spoke well for democracy in action. On the other hand, it said a lot about the impending issue. More houses in Goosebush meant more property taxes. But it could also mean a decrease in property values if not carefully thought through. Goosebush was its own special bubble of a small town. Small enough for the individual to matter and folks to take a vested interest in each other's business. Issues that other towns were grappling with played out in Goosebush, just in a microcosm. Though the town had a reputation of being wealthy, like most places there were people on all parts of the economic spectrum. Affordable housing was an issue that the town was grappling with.

"Lenny Andrus doesn't have a bad idea," Ray

Mancini whispered to Lilly. Ray was on the town board of selectmen, but due to the nature of the meeting, the board was interspersed with the audience, and Lenny was being asked questions with Tamara moderating. "The problem is that Lenny Andrus had the idea. If something like this is going to happen, two lots essentially becoming four, I'd feel a lot better if it was somebody with a hell of a lot more business acumen than Lenny making it happen."

"I tried to hire Lenny a couple times, but he was always too busy, and I ended up hiring other contractors. When did he take up housebuilding instead of restoration work?" Lilly asked.

"This past winter. He flipped a house in the fall, and then flipped another one."

"Here in Goosebush?" Lilly asked.

"No, a couple towns over. He made some fast money. That can be addictive."

Both Ray and Lilly stopped talking and listened to some more of the questions and comments coming from the audience. After a few more minutes it was clear that both the questions and the answers were getting redundant. Ray stood up and stood beside Tamara. The other members of the board got up as well.

"Given the robust conversation, I don't think a voice vote will work," Tamara said. "We can do this one of two ways. Secret ballot or a show of hands."

"I say show of hands," Gladys Preston said. "Lenny may as well know where folks stand, so he can work the crowd better next time." Everyone laughed.

"Anyone have any objection to that?" Tamara asked. No one raised an objection, so Tamara conferred with her fellow board members. They agreed to each take rows of people and do the counts that way.

At the end, the concerns raised by Lilly must've been the concerns of most folks in the room since the vote went against Lenny by a healthy margin. While folks had their hands in the air, Lilly looked around. She noticed that Gladys had her hand up against Lenny's proposition. She glanced at Lenny and couldn't help but notice that he saw Gladys's hand as well. Lilly recused herself. If it had been close, she would've raised her hand against Lenny, but her vote wasn't necessary.

Next the pro forma vote was taken on Recycling Day, after Warwick gave his pitch to everyone present to please come on down and help pick over the findings in the dump or collect contributions. Folks clapped loudly for Warwick, grateful for the mood change in addition to being supportive for the idea itself. Warwick was very popular in town, and he got a huge round of applause once the vote was taken.

Folks left quickly at the end of the meeting. Lilly stayed back to help put things away and to show her friend support. Lilly knew better than anyone that Tamara did not cherish speaking in public. Most folks thought of her as an extrovert, but in fact, public speaking exhausted her.

"Nice job moderating that," Lilly said to Tamara. "Though the meeting didn't go quite the way I expected. I would've thought the idea of rethinking house lots in Goosebush would've had more support."

"I suspect the idea may have more support the next time it comes up," Tamara said.

"Preferably, if Lenny brings it up, he'll have a stronger business proposal that makes folks feel more secure in taking the leap. 'Trust me' isn't a great business slogan these days," Lilly said.

"Sad in a way. That was a good enough slogan for a lot of folks to build a business in the past. Including my parents when they moved here twenty-odd years ago," Warwick said. He and Ray Mancini were putting folding chairs on racks while Lilly walked through the bleachers with a trash bag.

"Your folks opened a small grocer, which grew into a liquor store as well over time," Ray said. "No one ever got cheated at O'Connor's Package Store. If your father traded on public trust, it was because he earned it."

"True enough, Ray," Warwick said. "The store wasn't the first business my father tried to open, but it was the first one that worked. Lenny reminds me of my dad a little bit, back in the day. Passion plus big ideas seasoned with desperation. Not always a good mix for the business world. I, for one, hope Lenny figures it out. He's bailed me out of a number of jams over the years and always comes in to spend a few days with the students. He teaches them how to use tools and how to sand things down. He is great at giving refinishing tips that are easy, but effective. Lenny is a good guy, I hope he gets a break at some point."

"How did you vote?" Ray asked Warwick.

"I didn't," Warwick said. "Neither did Lilly, I noticed."

"No, I took the coward's way out," Lilly said. "I didn't go on the record as for or against. I'm wondering if we shouldn't try and help Lenny come up with a better business plan for next time." She looked around, and, secure in the belief that she had all the coffee cups, she took her half-empty bag of trash and tied it closed.

"Oh, heaven help us all, Lilly is going to help somebody else," Tamara said. She finished typing up the notes from the meeting and closed her laptop.

"Oh stop, I was thinking—"

"Tell you both what," Warwick said. "If we're going to be thinking, let's do it over dessert. Who wants to go over to the Star Café? I told Ernie and Roddy to save us seats. Delia went with them."

"I'm afraid I'm going to have to take a raincheck," Ray said. "Megan's waiting dinner on me."

"You've got yourself a raincheck, Ray. See you Saturday?" Warwick asked.

"Wouldn't miss it. You all good closing up?"

"Absolutely," Tamara said. "I'll send you these notes as soon as I get home, so you can check them. Thanks, Ray. And thanks for the conversation before the meeting. Apologize to Megan for me, I didn't mean to have you miss dinner."

"No worries, Tamara. Next time we'll have you and Warwick over for dinner, so no one goes hungry. See you all Saturday," Ray said. He shook Warwick's hand and went out the side door.

"How about you ladies? Can I tempt you with dessert?" Warwick said.

"Dessert sounds perfect, but can we try to save

Lenny's business another day? I could use some small talk," Tamara said. They walked to the edge of the school gym, and Warwick turned the lights off. They let themselves out of the side door and double-checked that it locked behind them.

"I'm going to check the building, make sure it's secure," Warwick said. "I could meet you there—"

"No, we'll wait. I parked right beside you," Lilly said. "We'll meet you in the parking lot."

Warwick went around the back of the building, and Tamara and Lilly walked along the side and turned the corner to the front. Under the lights in the near empty parking area they saw Lenny and Gladys arguing. Someone tapped a car horn lightly, and Lenny and Gladys stopped arguing and looked around.

"Are you happy now?" Lenny yelled at Tamara. "Never thought I'd see the day with the two of you on the same side. Trying to shut me down. You'll be sorry, that's all I've got to say." Lenny turned and got into his pickup truck. No one tried to stop him.

Gladys got into the passenger side of a car that had been idling nearby. As it drove past, Lilly noticed Alex Marston in the driver's seat.

They all drove over to the Star Café and parked behind the store. It was crowded back there, which didn't portend well for a quiet night. They walked around to the front of the building and opened the door. Sure enough, when they walked in, the joint was jumping. Most of the town meeting participants had ended up at the Star. Stella Haywood was working the coffee bar, and the line was long.

Lilly looked to the left, but she didn't see Ernie or Delia in the café. They made their way back towards the restaurant, and Stan Freeland bustled over to them.

"Your team is over there, in the corner booth. They've ordered pie and coffee, decaf, for the table. Do you want anything else?"

"Could you pick out a nice red wine to go with the pie?" Tamara asked.

"I have the perfect one. Anyone else?"

"I'll take a glass," Lilly said. She smiled a thank-you at Stan, and they went to the corner booth. As a little girl, she'd spent hours in this area of the Woolworth store, which used to be the lunch counter. When Stan redid the old five and dime, he kept enough of the original architecture so that folks could remember what it used to be, while adding enough modern conveniences to make it a hip-and-happening place in Goosebush. Never mind that it was one of three restaurants in the entire town, and the only one open past nine o'clock. It was still a hot spot, and Lilly was a frequent customer.

"What took you so long?" Ernie asked as he got up and let Lilly slide into the seat beside him. Warwick and Tamara slid into the other side of the half-moon booth. Roddy sat beside Delia on chairs at the table edge. This was their booth, large enough to invite others to join them if need be. Nevertheless, they all sat in the same seats every time they ate together. Habit was a funny thing. Six months ago, Lilly could not have imagined so many regular meals out with this group. Now she was forever grateful to each and every one of them for helping her get her life back.

"Warwick had to lock up," Lilly said. She was about to tell them about what they saw in the parking lot, when Gladys and Alex walked into the restaurant. Gladys made a beeline over to Tamara.

"Let's get one thing straight, Tamara O'Connor," Gladys said. "Tonight was it. We'll never be on the same side of an argument again. Not ever. I wouldn't do business with you—"

"Gladys, as I indicated earlier today, you and I won't be doing business together. Ever." Tamara looked at the other woman and didn't break her gaze. Everyone else had the same thought—what did Gladys and Tamara talk about earlier? Why hadn't they heard about it?

"Who do you think you are? Everyone's on to you. Anyone else in the world would have sold the Dane house in a day. You keep coming up with excuses for being terrible at business, being stuck in the past."

"I'm not going to discuss my business practices tonight—"

"The thing is, you'll have to discuss them sooner or later. If not with me, then with the real estate board. As far as I'm concerned, you shouldn't have your license."

"Gladys, stop. I've been dealing with your ranting and raving a lot lately and I'm done. Leave us in peace. Please."

"Or what?"

"Or I'll ask Stan to remove you."

"He wouldn't dare—"

Stan stepped over towards the table. The younger man looked pale and swallowed hard.

"Who are you to—"

"Gladys, you are one of the references that Lenny used for this proposal tonight," Tamara said. "I don't know why you turned on him at the meeting, but you double-crossed him. Who knows what game you're playing, but I've had enough. Leave me and my friends alone. We're going to have a nice dessert."

"Well, aren't you something—" Gladys stepped back from the table. Everyone else in the restaurant had stopped talking but was pretending not to listen.

"Stop playing games with people's lives, Gladys. It's going to catch up to you at some point, and it's not going to be pretty."

"Are you threatening me?" Gladys said.

"No, I'm making an observation. Watch yourself."

At that moment Regan Holland walked into the restaurant and walked over to Alex Marston. She gave him a peck on the cheek. Alex, who had been trying to disappear into the woodwork, blushed. He spoke with Stan, who showed them both over to a table in the corner.

"Go join your friends, Gladys," Tamara said.

Gladys turned and walked over to Regan and Alex, sitting down noisily, her back to Tamara.

Lilly heard a smattering of applause in the restaurant and saw the color rise slightly in her friend's cheeks. Warwick took Tamara's hand in his, lifted it to his lips, and gave it a kiss.

"You okay, babe?" Warwick asked.

"No, not really," Tamara said. "I never speak as harshly as that. What's the matter with me? Was Regan in here watching that whole scene?"

"Tamara, Gladys has been pushing your buttons for weeks now. I'm not surprised she finally got a rise out of you," Ernie said. "She is such a miserable woman. Honestly, when she comes into my store the flowers wilt."

Everyone giggled. A waiter came over with a tray of pie slices, and Stan brought two wineglasses over and a bottle.

"This is on the house, from an anonymous fan, grateful to you for shutting down the Gladys drama. Should I bring over a couple more glasses?"

"Please, and thank you Stan," Tamara said. She took a sip of the wine he poured for her, nodded, and smiled.

"She was one of Lenny's references?" Ernie asked Tamara. "Who else did he list on his application?"

"I'm not sure," Tamara said.

"You were listed on his first application," Delia said to Ernie, "but he updated the application this week. You weren't on it."

"Good, I wanted to make sure that the public record was clear," Ernie said.

"You withdrew your reference?" Lilly asked.

"Not publicly, but yes. PJ Frank withdrew as well. It was a tough decision, but we told Lenny last week and asked that he take our names off his website."

"Do you mind me asking why?" Tamara asked quietly.

"Lenny's work was excellent when he was doing restoration work. But his flipping and building work hasn't been up to the same standards. PJ and I have both gotten complaints about his work from folks we recommended him to. So, we decided to step back. Lenny said he's trying to hire more folks to bring the work back up. I hope he does that. I don't wish him ill, you know that. By the way, this stays at this table. I don't want it public."

"It won't be public," Delia said. "The original application won't be part of the public records."

"Good, thanks," Ernie said.

"Lilly thinks we should help Lenny with his business model—" Warwick said.

"That's it, enough," Tamara said. "Let's talk about anything but houses, building permits, Lenny Andrus, and Gladys Preston. Go. Someone. Tell me a story about—"

At that moment Braden Dane walked into the restaurant. He looked around the room, and Regan waved at him. He walked over to the table.

"I'll be damned," Warwick said. "What's Braden doing meeting with them?"

"We both know what he's doing," Tamara said. "Regan's been trying to get his business for weeks. Promising him that the wonders of the Internet will sell his house in a hot minute."

"You'd sell his house in a hot minute if someone wasn't sabotaging your open houses," Warwick said.

"Sabotaging open houses?" Roddy asked. "What's going on?"

Tamara sighed. She looked all her years tonight and bit her lower lip gently before she spoke. "I've tried to hold three open houses," she said quietly. "Each has been a disaster for one reason or another." She told them the stories, ending with the mice catastrophe from the last weekend.

"That's terrible," Ernie said. "Why didn't you tell us what was going on?"

"I thought it was just bad luck at first," Tamara said. "But that meeting over there indicates that something fishy is going on. Fishy—did I mention the dead fish I found in the attic right before the brokers' open house? That makes four open houses ruined."

"No, you didn't mention that," Lilly said. "Have you told Bash Haywood what's been going on?" Bash Haywood was the Chief of Police of Goosebush, and a friend of Lilly's.

"I have," Tamara said. "But there's not a lot he can do. Braden hasn't wanted to call the police in, so he won't file a formal complaint. Bash said he'd do drive-bys, but since the house is at the end of a private drive, having someone drive by to check on the house takes some doing, so he hasn't caught anyone."

"What did Gladys say to you—" Ernie asked, but his question was cut off by a loud banging on the other side of the restaurant. They all turned to see Alex standing up, trying to put a hand on Gladys's arm. Gladys was standing, her chair overturned.

"You have a hell of a nerve, that's all I can say. A hell of a nerve. Stop telling me to calm down, Alex. I've had it. I'm only here because you begged me to come. I'm done. Take me home. Now."

"Now, Gladys—" Regan said loudly, "no need to make a scene over nothing."

"Nothing? Nothing?" Gladys picked up a glass of water and threw it at the younger woman. "Well, looky there. The witch didn't melt this time."

Gladys turned and stormed out of the restaurant. Alex threw some bills on the table.

After a few seconds, Regan left as well, wiping her face, keeping her head down. Braden followed after her quickly. He stopped when he saw Tamara. She lifted her wine glass and gave him a silent toast. He turned pale and ran out of the restaurant.

"Stan, I think we're going to need another bottle of wine," Ernie said.

CHAPTER FIVE

"Tell me again why we have to be here so early?" Delia asked Lilly. Delia was usually an incredibly even-keeled person. But at seven o'clock on a Saturday morning—after she'd been up until the early morning hours cataloging some of the archaeological finds so that a library exhibition could open— that tipped her over into surly. Lilly was tempted to tell her she didn't have to come, but that would've been a lie. In early August, getting good volunteers to spend several hours at a dump was tough. Next to impossible. Warwick and his students brought folks out, but Warwick needed a steady stream of adult volunteers to keep the operation running smoothly. Lilly didn't mind helping, but she was not as young as she used to be and lifting furniture was not on today's docket for her.

"We're here to help Warwick get things set up so that when the students all get here, there's a system in place," Lilly said. "Apparently there's an issue with clearing Dorothy's House that may take extra time."

Dorothy's House was a garden shed that resided in the town dump. When folks had to bring something to the dump because they no longer needed it or had room for it, they could do one of several things: immediately recycle, put in the area that was saved for the "good for parts" pieces, or leave it in Dorothy's House for folks to take home. A lot of people left children's toys, car seats, dishes, and other household items that still had a lot of life in them. All sorts of folks went "shopping" at Dorothy's House; people from all different economic situations. There were a few folks who ran secondhand shops who frequented it often. Since the dump was only open on certain days and at certain times, access to Dorothy's House was tightly controlled by a group of volunteers who went through the donations to make sure they were still useful. On Recycle Day Dorothy's House was only available for drop-offs, and all donations that could be used for Recycling Day went there first to be checked in. Delia was going to be stationed there since she knew the system and would be able to keep track of the comings and goings.

"I'm surprised there's anything left," Lilly said. "I know there are a lot of people who went to Dorothy's House yesterday afternoon to clean it out in anticipation of today's activities."

"Won't everything be given to the students today? I'm not sure why they felt as though they needed to clear the space entirely."

"It was a good excuse to clear it out. Most of the

stuff in there had been there since last Recycling Day, so things were recycled or tossed. Lots of donations will come in today, so a clean slate was called for."

"Good idea," Delia said. "It's easier to do the tracking if the space is clear, otherwise my system gets confused." Delia looked down at her beeping phone.

"There's a text from Ernie. He said he saw the volunteer list, and Gladys Preston is on it. He wants us to let Tamara know so she can stay clear."

"Gladys always volunteers. Maybe she won't show up this year. Tamara's going to be here to let us in, so we'll warn her," Lilly said.

"You know I've been spending a lot of time in the library lately, right?"

"Yes, getting ready for the exhibition—"

"Also doing some work for the town. There are a lot of deeds and old papers in the archives. I'm finding that I need to go back a few generations in some cases to undo what was done to property lines in the 'official' record. It is as much to educate myself as to change anything for the town itself."

"You're enjoying this aren't you? Getting the town records back into shape."

"I really am," Delia said. "It's using all my interests—research, historical context, academic rigor—but in a real-life setting."

"Maybe you should consider—"

"But I know that academia is my real career path. We both know that. I hope my new career is as much fun as this one has been so far."

"I'm sure it will be," Lilly said, continuing to

stare straight ahead. Lilly was trying very hard not to be selfish—to not ask Delia to reconsider working at the university, to stay living with her instead. "How did we get on this conversation? You were telling me you're spending time at the library—"

"Right. Usually when I'm in the archives I'm working alone. But the last few days Gladys has been in there with me, looking at old maps. I offered to help her look things up, but she wasn't having any of it. Told me to stay the hell away from her. She said that it was none of my business, or your business, what she was doing. She was loud and belligerent. I wanted to leave the room, but the librarian had asked me to stay to make sure that she didn't walk away with anything. She's a truly miserable person, isn't she?"

"Yes, she is. She's lived here for years. I honestly don't remember a time when she wasn't miserable."

"Really? I thought maybe while her husband was still alive—"

"No, she was miserable then too. As a matter fact, Bert, that was her late husband Albert Preston, was one of the sweetest guys around. He's actually her tie to Goosebush. His family bought the house when it was first built. Anyway, Bert was never a looker as they used to say. Terribly shy, not the best in social situations. But a lovely guy. Anyway, he met Gladys and asked her to marry him within a few weeks. I do think he loved her, bless him, but she didn't make his life particularly easy."

"How long has he been gone?" Delia asked.

"Heavens, let me think. Almost twenty years, can that be right? Gladys was miserable while he was alive, but his death made her mean. He left her a decent amount of money, but not enough to live high on the hog. She hasn't had an easy time of it, but she makes it very hard to want to help her."

"Did they have children, or is there any other family?" Delia asked.

"No, no children. I think Gladys is on her own. I've never heard her talk about any family. You know, it may be interesting, for curiosity sake, to know what she was looking at, or looking for. I don't suppose—"

"I could look at the sign-out book and see which maps she requested from the librarian. For these sorts of records, you have to fill out a specific request slip," Delia said. "You get to keep one copy, but the other copy goes into a book for perpetuity, so the people can find out who looked at what when. There's talk of getting it all into a database at some point, but it hasn't been a priority. Honestly, there aren't a lot of people who look at these old records. Or hadn't been until recently."

Lilly wanted to ask more questions about who else was looking at the records, but they'd arrived at the gates of the dump. Goosebush's dump, like the rest of Goosebush, was part quaint, part ridiculously old-fashioned, part quirky, but mostly functional. When Goosebush doubled down on recycling a few years back, a twelve-foot-high chain-link fence was erected around the dump in order to dissuade people from putting things in willy-nilly. Now people needed to get a dumping permit if regular trash pickup was not sufficient. The permit wasn't expensive, but it did limit which days folks could go to the dump. The fees from the permit helped with keeping the dump staffed. Volunteers helped as well. When people took things from Dorothy's House they could contribute to the suggested donation box. They often did. Those funds, and other funds raised through the different recycling streams, were part of how the town stayed ahead of its trash.

"Do you have a key to the padlock?" Delia asked. The gates to the dump were closed when they drove up. Very few people had keys to the gates of the dump. They had to be signed out and turned back in to the police station at the end of every shift. Bash Haywood regularly changed the padlock on the gates in order to thwart any attempts to have personal access to the dump. Lilly had never understood the reason for the high security. She made a mental note to ask Bash about it later since she didn't do well with unsatisfied curiosity.

"Is it locked?" Lilly asked. "The lock doesn't look shut."

Delia jumped out to check. Sure enough, the padlock wasn't clasped, so she took it off and pushed open the gate. Lilly drove in, and Delia went to close it behind her, but Warwick drove up behind Lilly. Lilly pulled forward, so Warwick could get past her. Delia closed the gate and got back in the car.

"Should I leave the lock?" she asked.

"No, we're all here now, may as well take it with us," Lilly said. They drove up the winding path and into the small parking lot to the left near Dorothy's House. Warwick was already out of his car, with the back hatch open. He took a six-foot folding table out, and walked it over towards Dorothy's House, leaning it up against the building.

"Good morning, ladies, thanks for being here so bright and early. Where's Tamara?"

"I haven't seen her," Lilly said. "The gate was unlocked, but closed, when we got here."

"She got on her bike early this morning and told me she'd meet me here. She was going to go by her office first. That was over an hour ago." Warwick stopped unloading tables and looked at Lilly. "Are you sure you were supposed to meet her here, not at your place?"

"No, we're supposed to meet here. You know how she can lose track of time when she starts answering emails or checking messages. Let me give her a call—"

A bloodcurdling scream ripped apart the early morning calm. Warwick, Delia, and Lilly all looked at one another. They heard another scream and all three of them ran towards it.

Warwick, Delia, and Lilly ran down the path towards the dump. The dump was actually several sites, and residents who brought their things there self-sorted into old clothes, computer parts, metal, household appliances, furniture, branches, composting, and garbage. The garbage pile was harder to access and was regularly tended to by folks to keep it healthy. In order to use the Goosebush dump a person needed to know what she was doing and where she was going; otherwise, she would get lost in pots and piles. The three of them stopped short at the access point to the dump. Another scream pierced through the morning haze.

"This way," Warwick said. Delia was able to keep up with him, but Lilly lagged behind. Her old arthritic knees couldn't carry her as fast as they once did no matter how much she tried. Another scream. This one felt closer to Lilly. She turned to the right, down the path between household items and computer parts. About fifty feet ahead she saw Tamara bending over. Lilly kept sprinting forward and called out to Delia and Warwick.

"I found her!"

Tamara looked up, tears streaming down her face. Lilly moved towards her, looking around to see if anyone else was there. She didn't see anyone else at first, but then she noticed the body on the ground. She got closer to Tamara and pulled her back. She heard a clang as Tamara dropped something. Lilly looked down. The old faucet had landed in a pool of blood. Lilly looked away, towards her friend. She pulled Tamara into a hug, and Tamara hung on. Lilly comforted her and glanced down to her left. She swallowed the bile that rose in the back of her throat. She barely recognized Gladys Preston.

Warwick came up beside Lilly and Tamara and took Tamara into his arms. Lilly leaned down and checked for a pulse. There wasn't one. She reached for the faucet, but Delia cried out to stop her.

"Don't touch anything," Delia said. "I'm calling 911 now. Try to walk out the way you came in. We need to preserve the evidence." Delia dialed her phone but kept taking pictures of the scene until the call went through. She held her phone up to her ear and turned away from Tamara to make the call.

Lilly sighed, frustrated by Delia's ability to be clinical at a time like this. Lilly had seen Tamara drop the faucet and would tell the police what she'd seen. She knew Tamara could never kill anyone, of course. But there she was, standing over Gladys's body. Would the police believe Tamara? Could Lilly trust that they would, especially with Delia securing the scene? Lilly took her phone out of her pocket and went to her starred contacts list. Bash Haywood's name was near the top. She selected it and hit dial. Bash picked up on the first ring.

"Bash, it's Lilly. You need to get over to the dump right away. Gladys Preston is here. She's dead."

CHAPTER SIX

Bash Haywood arrived at the same time the offi-cer on duty did. Bash wasn't wearing his uni-form. He had intended to come down to the dump today to help Warwick with Recycling Day.

Sebastian Haywood's father went to high school with Lilly. When he and his wife died in an accident, Bash was only a teenager and became responsible for his younger siblings. Bash's aunt moved in to help but didn't have the financial wherewithal to support the entire family. Lilly and Alan stepped in to help. Their support wasn't only financial, however. They did what they could to create a sup-port network for the entire family. Bash had inher-ited a sense of obligation and duty that brought him back to Goosebush after college instead of pursuing his dreams to be an artist. He started to work at the police station, eventually becoming an officer. When Ray Mancini retired, Bash stepped in to become the chief of police, the youngest in Goosebush history.

Goosebush was hardly the capital of crime, but it saw its fair share. Despite the small-town charm, there were still problems with drugs, crime, and other issues that required attention. Often, they took the ability to consider the issues from many sides. That ability did not come naturally to Bash. It was, however, Lilly's forte. Bash was secure enough in his own abilities to not feel insecure about asking for Lilly's help. Admittedly, at the beginning he sought her advice to make her feel needed and wanted after Alan's death. But lately? After what happened in May? Bash knew that Lilly could be his secret weapon.

Bash conferred with the officer, who began to secure the crime scene. Bash walked over to Lilly and took out his notepad, a sign that they were on the record.

"What happened?" Bash asked.

Lilly gave him all the details of what she'd done that morning. She told him that she and Warwick and Delia had arrived at the same time and heard the scream. That she'd been the first to find Tamara bending over Gladys. She also told Bash that Tamara had been holding a faucet, which she dropped into the blood besides Gladys. She added that the faucet had looked clean before Tamara had dropped it.

Bash jotted down a few more notes. "Were there any other cars in the parking area when you got here?" he asked Lilly.

"No," Lilly said. "Warwick said Tamara was rid-ing her bike over. Not sure where it is, maybe leaning up against one of the fences."

"Did you see Gladys's car?"

"No, I didn't. I don't remember seeing it on the road leading up to the dump either. The padlock on the gate was unlocked when we got here. I assumed that Tamara did that, but I'm not sure."

"Tamara must've, she's the only one who had the key," Bash said. "I changed the lock out myself yesterday."

"Then how did Gladys get in?" Lilly asked. She looked up at Bash, who was staring at her. Lilly inhaled a sharp breath. One could infer that Tamara let her in, but what would that mean? That Tamara had attacked her and then pretended to find the body? Lilly, of course, knew that couldn't be true because she knew Tamara. But still.

"Lilly, I'm going to ask you to stay here for a little while. We're not going to let anyone else in, but can you make sure that in fact happens? Also, write up what you saw this morning so that we can get your statement processed as soon as possible."

"Of course, I can help you with that; anything else?"

"That's enough for now," Bash said. "We'll let you go home as soon as we can."

"Do any of us need a lawyer?" Lilly said. Her calm voice belied her concern.

"I'm not sure yet," Bash said. "Always good to have one at the ready though, don't you think?"

"Indeed, I do," Lilly said. She walked away from Bash and took her phone out of her pocket. "Hello, Jim? Sorry for the early Saturday call. It's Lilly Jayne. I might need you today."

* * *

Lilly watched as more officers arrived at the scene. In situations like this other towns could and would offer help. In dire cases the state police could be called in, but Lilly knew that Bash preferred to keep things in-house as much as possible. She went over to Delia and asked her to make sure no one got in and out of the gate. She also suggested that Delia write down what she remembered from the morning.

"Already on it," Delia said. "I'm writing down what I remember and what Warwick told us. Trying to figure out what the facts are."

"The facts? The facts are that we believe what our friends tell us, right?"

"Not necessarily," Delia said. She was looking down at her phone, so she missed the look of anger mixed with exasperation that crossed Lilly's face. By the time Delia looked up, the moment had passed, and Lilly was back in control. "We all have our own truth, Lilly, but facts are facts. For instance—"

"Folks, can I ask for your attention for a minute?" Bash said. "Thanks. As you all know, this is a crime scene. Since we don't know what happened where, we do need you to walk us through your steps this morning. We'll get you out of here soon, I hope. In the meantime, if you could refrain from talking to each other, and answer the officers' questions as completely as possible. Thanks so much for your cooperation."

An officer came over to speak with Delia, so Lilly stepped away. She could get Delia's facts, as she called them, when they got home. She noticed Bash walking over to Tamara and walked towards them. Normally Lilly was a stickler for privacy. But this morning was far from normal.

"I'm sure you heard about the tussle between Gladys and me a couple nights ago. The one at the Star Café, after the town meeting?" Tamara said.

"I may have heard something," Bash said. "Why don't you tell me about it now." If Bash noticed Lilly standing nearby, he didn't say anything. Lilly stood behind Bash's shoulder and gave her old friend a smile.

Tamara told Bash about the town meeting and the conversation afterwards. "There's more," Tamara said. "Yesterday, I planned to have a realtors' open house at the Dane house. You know about the issues I've been having there with the other open houses. I thought if I dealt with this one on a Friday and kept it closed from the public, maybe it would go off without a hitch. I was wrong. There was rotting garbage left in every room. I was cleaning it up and noticed that mixed in there was some junk mail. I checked the labels and Gladys's name was on all of them. Anyway, I had to cancel the brokers' open house, for the second time. I went down to Gladys's house, but she wasn't there. I left her several strongly worded voicemail messages on her home phone. You should know that, since you'll probably find them. She finally texted me back this morning. She said she wanted to meet as soon as possible, that we needed to talk. I texted her I had to be at the dump to open the front gate since I had the key, and Warwick had already left to pick up the tables and other items for Recycling

Day. She said she'd meet me there, by the used appliance section. She texted that she had other ways of getting into the dump, and she was on her way. She didn't want anyone to know that we were going to talk."

"But she didn't mention what she wanted to talk about? Did that seem odd?"

"It was Gladys, so odd is part of the deal. Sorry, that was unkind. Poor Gladys. Bash, you don't think I—"

"Tamara, right now I don't think, I gather facts. Tell me the rest."

Tamara looked at Lilly, who nodded at her. "I rode my bike here. I opened up the padlock, came in, and locked my bike up on the other side of the fence, out of sight."

"What did you do with the padlock?" Bash asked.

"What did I do with it? I hung it back on the fence, but I didn't close it. There's that hole in the fence so you can reach your hand in. I figured once Warwick got here we could open officially. Then I closed the gate."

"That's how it was when we drove up," Lilly said. Bash shot Lilly a look, so she stopped talking. "Sorry, Bash, you want me to leave?"

"She may as well stay," Tamara said. "I'm going to tell her everything anyway."

Bash shook his head. "What did you do next?" he asked.

"I got my bike locked up, and then walked towards Dorothy's House. I always have to get my bearings when I come to the dump. I don't come here that often. Then I heard a scream. A really loud scream."

"How long was this after you'd closed the gate?" Bash asked.

"A few seconds, a minute at most. No one else came in behind me, if that's what you're asking," Tamara said.

"What happened next?"

"I looked around and grabbed the first thing I found, which was this old faucet that was laying there near the path. I picked it up and ran towards the scream. I found Gladys, lying there—" Tamara closed her eyes and shook her head. A tear ran down her face. "I tried to help her, but she was already gone."

"Did you hear anything else? See anything else? Anyone else?" Bash asked.

"I may have heard footsteps, but I can't be sure. I started screaming. I didn't want to leave her, you know? I honestly don't know how long it was until Lilly found me."

"Did you scream the whole time?" Bash asked.

"Pretty much," Tamara said. "It took me a little while to find her, so I don't know how long she'd been . . . there."

"How many screams did you hear?" Bash asked Lilly.

"One, then we started running. Then we heard a second one, but Warwick and Delia were up further than I was. That's why I found Tamara first. My knees are shot, I can't run as fast."

"How did you know where to run?"

"We could sort of tell that the sound was coming from our right."

"You didn't hear anything else?" Bash asked both Lilly and Tamara.

"No, I didn't. But I was running and breathing pretty hard," Lilly said.

"I didn't hear anything else," Tamara said. "Honestly? I didn't even hear Lilly coming towards me. I must've been in some sort of shock. I'm sorry I can't pinpoint the timing or what I did more precisely, Bash. There was no love lost between Gladys and me, but nobody deserves to die like that. Not even Gladys Preston."

CHAPTER SEVEN

Ernie arrived at the same time Warwick and Tamara finally got back to Lilly's house. Lilly had called and asked him to pick up some pizza. Ernie didn't just get pizza, though. That wouldn't do for a meeting of the Garden Squad. Not at all. Oven-baked pizzas, rolls, two kinds of salad, and some fresh cannoli. He also got a tray of ziti in case this afternoon soirée ran into the evening. Warwick went back out to the car to get the rest of the food while Ernie helped Delia set up in the kitchen. Delia told Ernie to put the food on the kitchen table, buffet style.

"Where's Tamara?" he asked.

"She went upstairs to rest for a few minutes and take a shower."

"Poor thing. I can always eat during stressful times, so I brought a lot of food."

"I'm glad you did. None of us have eaten since

breakfast. We'll eat in the dining room, but I want to leave some extra room at the table for laptops and notebooks just in case."

"Just in case we start doing some work?" Ernie asked. "I don't think there's a 'just in case' about this. All I've heard is rumors all morning, but my brain is perking. Tamara found Gladys Preston, is that right? Gladys had been killed?"

"Those are the facts so far as we know them, yes," Delia said. "Probably best to get the most gruesome parts out of the way before we sit down to eat."

Ernie stopped and looked at Delia. "Oh lord, there are gruesome parts?" He had a very weak stomach and didn't even like to talk about blood.

"Gladys was hit over the head, that's how she died," Lilly said, coming into the room. She was carrying three bottles of wine that she'd brought up from the cellar.

"Not necessarily true," Delia said. "We don't know how she died. We really need to stick with the facts if we're going to—"

Lilly put the bottles on the kitchen table and turned to look at her young friend. "All right, that's the second time today you've talked about facts clinically. Explain yourself."

Delia paused, and looked at Lilly, confused at the tone in her voice. "Lilly, I don't mean anything by it. It's just that, well, we talked about this the other day, didn't we? Facts are facts. Indisputable. Unarguable. The truth can be based on facts, but it's also a person's interpretation of the facts. A good example: the fact is that it is seventy-two degrees in this house. My truth is that I need to go upstairs and get a sweater. Your truth is that you'd like to turn it down to sixty-eight degrees."

"I can't help it if I'm always hot," Lilly said distractedly. "What you're saying is that we need to focus on the facts, and not our perceptions of those facts. Even if we believe them to be true."

"That's what I'm saying," Delia said. "We all believe, no, we know that Tamara didn't do this. But if the facts lead people to that conclusion, then we need to find some more facts that tell the rest of the story. If we get too focused on one truth, we're probably going to miss something."

Lilly looked at her friend for a moment and smiled. Alan would be so proud of his former student and the fine mind that she had. She wasn't sure if he'd be proud of the way Delia was using it now, untangling mysteries, gardening, and sorting through the minutiae of town history. But maybe he would.

"We'll follow the facts and dig for the truth. The question is where to start," Lilly said.

"Tell me what happened this morning," Ernie said.

"If we want to get to the truth, we'll have to go back further than that," Tamara said, coming into the kitchen. "Let's open the wine, shall we?"

Delia's best-laid plans of eating in the dining room were put asunder. Lilly opened the bottle of wine and poured everyone except Warwick a glass. Warwick took some plates out of the cabinet and put them on the kitchen table. Delia grabbed the silverware and set them on the counter. Ernie went to the refrigerator and grabbed Warwick a beer. He didn't bother to ask if Warwick wanted a glass.

Everyone had a slice of pizza and a drink. Tamara picked her pizza up and put it back down on the plate without taking a bite.

"Tamara, you should try to eat something," Lilly said. "It's been hours since you ate."

"I know, I will. It's starting to hit me, is all. Poor Gladys."

"I know," Warwick said. "Still, you've got to eat something. Want me to make you some eggs?"

"No, this is fine, thanks. I'm feeling a little guilty since I've been cursing Gladys up one side and down the other ever since I found her garbage yesterday."

"Wait, what? Explain," Ernie said.

Tamara told him about the garbage dump that thwarted her open house and how she'd found junk mail with Gladys's name on it.

"Do you think she was sabotaging the open houses?" Delia asked.

"I'm going to take a leaf from your book, Delia. I don't know. I guessed it was, but maybe someone was trying to make her look guilty. For all I know, Regan Holland was behind it all."

"Regan? What makes you say that?" Lilly said.

"That's not necessarily fair. I've been blaming Regan for a lot lately. Business has been off. It's been off for a while. I'm starting to realize that I rely on old school methods that may not work in this technological age. Maybe I'm out of step. Am I trying to hold onto a Goosebush that doesn't exist anymore—decent-sized lots for houses, the democracy of town meetings, the good for all outweighing the great for some? A couple of people came to me and told me that Regan has offered to sell their properties or their businesses for one and a half times as much as I've told them I could sell them for—if only zoning laws or some of the business regulations in town were relaxed. She's been implying that my being on the board of selectmen has been lining my pockets. I don't see how, but that's beside the point. She's been building up doubt."

"She's got a lot of chutzpah trash talking you, excuse the pun," Ernie said.

"The hell of it is, she's been undermining years of trust I've built up with folks," Tamara said. "What I can't figure out is whether she's a savvy businesswoman or a snake oil salesman. Maybe a bit of both."

"Do you think she could be the one who'd been undermining your open houses?" Ernie asked.

"I can't imagine she'd stoop that low, but I'm not sure. If I can't sell the Dane house, she'll probably get the listing. Braden has made that clear. At the same time, if she were caught doing something like that, it would be terrible for her business."

"That doesn't mean she shouldn't be on the suspect list," Delia said.

"What would be her reason for killing Gladys?" Tamara asked.

"I don't know," Delia said. "I don't know anyone's reason for killing Gladys, do any of you?"

"I hate to speak ill of the dead, but Gladys Preston was hardly the most popular gal in town," Ernie said. "But who had motive to kill her? Tamara, do you have any idea why she wanted to meet with you this morning?"

"I assume it had something to do with the open houses since I blamed her directly for the meddling. But I'm not sure. There isn't a lot of information in a text."

"Let's talk about those open houses, and who's undermining your business," Lilly said. "Who else would benefit from you not being able to sell the Dane house? Alex Marston? You said he was trying to buy the house at a lower price."

"Regan Holland," Warwick said. "I say she gets on the list."

"Miranda Dane?" Lilly said. "Should she be on the list? Do you think she has an issue with the house being sold?"

"Maybe," Ernie said. "I know, suspect, that Harmon was supporting her in a significant way over the years. Maybe she doesn't want the house to get sold? Maybe she's hoping delaying the sale will give her more legal grounds to get more money out of the estate?"

"Could be. Anyone else?" Lilly said.

"I can't imagine why he'd want to undermine the open houses, but let's put Braden Dane on the list," Tamara said.

"What about Lenny Andrus? Do you think he's trying to get the house at a discount?" Delia said.

"Maybe," Tamara said. "He also may be trying to get back at me for the vote the other night. He knew I was against him, even though I tried to remain neutral."

"You were neutral, but he did seem extremely

angry after the meeting. Put him on the list," Lilly said. "Let's try and figure out who's been messing with Tamara's business. I'm assuming that's what Gladys wanted to talk to her about."

"Do you think whoever that is killed Gladys?" Ernie asked.

"I have no idea," Lilly said. "But it's a place to start."

"Okay, so what do we do?" Warwick asked.

"In the short term, I'm going to work on getting some cameras installed at the Dane house, so we can see what's going on. Tamara, let us all know when your next open house is."

"It's tomorrow, but maybe I should cancel it," Tamara said.

"No, don't cancel it," Lilly said. "We can take shifts babysitting the house in the morning and make sure nothing happens to it during the day."

"Will that help us figure out who killed Gladys?" Ernie asked.

Lilly took a deep breath, reached over, and grabbed her friend's hand. She did not let go and looked around the table. "Let's leave that to Bash. For now."

"Are you sure?" Delia said. She sounded a little disappointed.

"Here's what I'm thinking. Tamara may end up on the suspect list for killing Gladys. If someone's going after Tamara's business, they may be going after her as well and trying to frame her. Let's look out for our friend and collect all the facts whether you think they're relevant or not. Then maybe we can put this puzzle together. What do you think?"

"I think I'm glad that Ernie got a tray of ziti, because we're going to be here for a while," Warwick said.

"I'm going to go grab my laptop, and the whiteboard from the library so we can keep running notes. Let's start figuring out what we know, what we don't know, and who's going to find out what," Delia said.

"Somebody should call Roddy and invite him over. I can't imagine he wants to be left out of this," Ernie said, looking pointedly at Lilly.

"Fine, I'll call him. Save him some pizza," Lilly said, pulling her phone out of her pocket.

CHAPTER EIGHT

On Sunday Lilly and Delia both packed what they considered provisions for the day. Lilly put her straw hat, a thermos of iced coffee, a novel, her traveler's notebook, and a stash of pens in her large, flowered tote. The tote's pockets were already packed for Lilly's ordinary needs, which meant that she could easily survive the day away from home. She could quite possibly survive a few days if it became necessary. She hoped it never became necessary.

Delia had insisted Lilly take a battery charger for her phone. She complied, to make Delia happy, but had no idea how or if it would work.

"It looks like you're going to try and hack into a bank instead of spend the day at the beach," Lilly said to her friend. Delia had agreed to spend the day at Swallow Point and to watch the house from afar. In addition to a backpack with two computers, solar-powered battery chargers, and an extra cell phone, Delia was packing a canopy, chair, blanket, food, and a bucket of sunscreen. Tamara's daughter Rose promised to come with the kids and their dog to visit Delia to help provide her cover story for a day at the beach.

Delia, Roddy, and Ernie had spent several hours on Saturday night coming up with an electronic surveillance plan for the Dane house. Getting cameras deployed and online was going to take co-ordination, and Roddy and Ernie put themselves in charge of setting up the cameras. Delia was going to coordinate with them from the beach and take pictures of them being installed.

"Is this legal?" Warwick had asked.

"Legal? What do you mean?" Ernie asked.

"We're installing surveillance equipment. That doesn't feel legal to me," Warwick said.

"We're installing a ring of protection around Tamara's client's house," Roddy said. "We'll keep the field of vision on the house, and only put the cameras in public spaces. Since we're not the po-lice we don't need a warrant."

"Lil, you don't have to worry about it," Ernie said. "Your job is to pay attention to the sanctuary. You'd said you wanted to spend some time looking at it anyway—"

"And hanging around during an open house isn't awkward at all," Lilly said.

"Having you hanging around during an open house may be a better deterrent than you know,"

Tamara said. "Especially around the Dane house. It will help folks know that you're involved. I can't imagine that wouldn't be helpful in the long run."

And so, the Garden Squad deployed around the Dane house. Ernie went over at five o'clock in the morning and did a sweep of the house. During the sweep, unbeknownst to Lilly or Tamara, Ernie set up small cameras outside each door at the house facing out to the yard. When he was done playing super spy, he sliced and baked some cookies to get the house smelling cozy. He was still staging the house when Tamara showed up at nine o'clock.

"You're good at this," she said to Ernie.

"My late husband and I flipped houses for a few years. I got very good at getting houses ready to sell."

"Any signs of dead fish, mice, locusts, or any other invasions?"

"None, so far as I can tell. What time is the open house set to start?"

"Eleven. We go until two. I've run a few ads about it, so hopefully we'll have a good turnout. This is a tough time of year for house sales, though."

"I saw one of the Facebook ads you did and shared it. It looked great. Are those from Lilly?" he asked, pointing to the large bag filled with brown paper wrapping.

"She told me you wanted some flowers?"

"I brought some small vases with me. I thought I'd pull some small bouquets together and put them around the house to brighten it up. I suspected it could use it, poor old thing. She's been empty awhile now, unless Braden's moved in?" said Ernie.

"The family lawyer suggested that wasn't in the best interest of the estate, so he's staying in an apartment in town. Harmon had paid his rent till the end of the year."

"I get it. You wouldn't want squatter's rights. But at the same time, this house needs someone to live in her. What a beauty. I had no idea she was in such good shape. The wood is incredible."

Tamara smiled. She'd seen people fall in love with houses before, so she recognized the signs. She'd fallen a bit in love with the house herself over the past few weeks. She watched while Ernie ran his hand across the wainscoting before laying the flowers out on the dining room table.

"Harmon was great at maintaining it," Tamara said. "Not easy, this close to the water. The kitchen and bathrooms could use modernization, but the plumbing and electrical system have both been updated in the past two years. The roof is also fairly new. The house is a steal for the price, that's for sure."

"Are all three of the houses in the same shape?" Ernie asked. He reached into the bag he'd brought with him and took out a pair of scissors. He laid them on the table, and then started to unwrap the flowers. "See that box? The vases are in there. Could you unwrap them?"

Tamara took out one of the vases and smiled. Ernie had several eclectic collections and frequented yard sales in search of treasures. He often lent table-ware to folks for different fund-raising events. She recognized the short-cut glass vase from the Beautification Committee cocktail party three weeks ago.

"Alex Marston completely renovated when he bought his house. The first floor is now completely open. The wood has been painted white—"

Ernie winced. "I'm sure it's lovely, but—"

"I know, I know," Tamara said. "Alex isn't the restoration sort. He's more of a new construction guy. But he couldn't resist the view."

"Can't blame him there," Ernie said. He put flowers into different piles and reached for a vase. "I'll get these sorted, then we can add water to the vases in the kitchen. Tell me, where does Gladys's house fit in the spectrum? Rehabbed or restored with historical accuracy?"

"Neither. I went by her house a few weeks ago, trying to get some of these routes of egress issues sorted. She let me in, reluctantly. She didn't have Harmon's resources, so the house hasn't been restored. It looks like this house, only faded. And full. Gladys had what I would consider a hoarding problem. I only got in as far as the living room, but the dining room looked packed."

"I'd love to see inside," Ernie said. He looked up at Tamara with a stricken face. "I sound like a ghoul. But you know what I mean."

"I do," Tamara said. "I'd like to see inside too."

"Does Gladys . . . did Gladys have any family?"

"I'm not sure," Tamara said. "I hope so. I'd hate for two houses on Shipyard Lane to be empty. Are you okay with getting the flowers put around the house? I have signs to put up."

"I'm fine. Is Lilly here?"

"She's out by the bird sanctuary," Tamara said. "She's taking pictures of the stairs."

"Why?" Ernie asked.

"I didn't ask. She went right over to them when we drove in. She had that look on her face, so something's amiss. But right now, I have to get those signs up."

"That was a bust," Ernie said, smearing a slab of cheese on a cracker, and topping it with fig jam. He took a bite, closed his eyes, and smiled.

"Speak for yourself," Tamara said. "It was the best open house we've had in weeks. Regan Holland had the nerve to show up, can you believe it? She's like a buzzard circling the carcass of my career."

"Stop being so dramatic," Warwick said teasingly to his wife. "Lilly, I'm going to start the grill. Is that okay with you?"

"That's fine," Lilly said. "Are you sure you don't mind grilling? It's so hot out."

"The ceiling fans out here keep the air moving, and we're having steak and chicken tips. They don't take any time to cook. I won't be out there long."

"Don't forget Delia's marinated tofu," Lilly said. She reached into her pocket and checked her phone for a missed message or email. She didn't have either.

"I won't," Warwick said. "Where is she anyway?"

"She's working in the breakfast room, making sure all of the cameras you put out are working."

"I hear you put a couple of cameras out yourself, Lilly," Ernie said. "Out by the stairs?"

"By Harmon's bird sanctuary," Lilly said. "I'm responsible for making sure that Harmon's request is met and the sanctuary is taken care of. When I got there today I noticed that the area near the staircase had been disturbed—"

"How could you tell?" Roddy asked as he came into the porch, carrying his laptop.

"Roddy, I didn't know you were here," Lilly said. "Let me get you—"

"Please, don't get up. I've been working with Delia on the camera setup. She's bringing us both a glass of beer now that the work's been done."

"I didn't know you were a tech guy," Tamara said.

"I used cameras like that in my last job," Roddy said.

"I thought you were a lawyer?" Ernie said.

"A full-service lawyer, as it turns out," Roddy said, sitting down next to Lilly.

"What does that mean?" Ernie asked Roddy. Ernie looked like he was going to ask another question but was interrupted by Delia's entrance.

"Did you all see Lenny Andrus at the open house?" Delia asked when she came out to the porch, carrying two frosted glasses of beer and handing one to Roddy before she sat down.

"I didn't see him at the house, but I think he was in the neighborhood," Tamara said. "Did you see him, Ernie?"

"I didn't. And between us we saw everyone who walked into the house."

"Maybe he walked around the house and didn't

go in. He showed up on a few of the pictures I took from the beach," Delia said.

"I didn't see him," Lilly said.

"I have him on camera seeing you and turning around. It's pretty funny, actually. What were you doing, anyway? Weren't we there to keep track of what was going on around the house?"

"That's exactly what I was doing," Lilly said. "Thank heaven I brought some more chicken wire with me. I thought I might have to patch it, but someone had taken it all out."

"Chicken wire?"

"You know, the fencing they use in chicken coops. Harmon used it to hold in parts of the stone wall, so that they didn't tumble down and hurt the nests. Anyway, a lot of the fencing has been taken out. Not carefully. I left a message with the professor I've been speaking with, asking her to come by and look at it with me tomorrow." Lilly's phone began to ring, and she reached into her pocket and hit a button. "Speak of the devil. Hello, Dawn! I was just talking about you." Lilly walked down the back steps and into her garden.

"Do you know what she's talking about?" Tamara asked Delia.

"Yes, she and I talked a lot throughout the day. She had me go over and check out the bottom of the stairs and see if the fencing beside the stairs had been removed. It had."

"What type of barrier was it?" Roddy asked.

"There was chicken wire underneath so that the birds were a little more protected. Also, the stairs themselves look like they've been damaged. Tamara, had you noticed anything?" Delia asked.

"No. I'll confess I hadn't looked carefully, and I haven't been down to the beach in weeks. What do you think that's about?"

"If the bird sanctuary gets destroyed, then the disbursements of Harmon's will can be contested," Lilly said, coming back onto the porch and sitting down. "I can think of two people off the top of my head who would benefit from that."

"Miranda and Braden," Ernie said.

"Exactly," Lilly said. "Roddy and Delia, do those cameras you gave me work at night?"

"They do," Roddy said. "Delia and I checked, and all of the cameras are functioning."

"Good," Lilly said. "I put up fencing and went back to put up No Trespassing signs. When Dawn and her team arrive tomorrow they can assess the damage."

"Dawn and her team?" Roddy asked.

"Dawn Simmons is a professor of ornithology. She has a team of students who worked with Harmon for years. He'd let them stay with him a couple of times each semester, and they'd do field studies. Anyway, we've been in touch since he passed. She was scheduled to come next week to do an assessment, but she's worried about the sanctuary and is going to come out with a student tomorrow."

"Where are they going to stay?" Ernie asked.

"At Harmon's house, of course," Lilly said.

"Will Braden and Miranda go for that?"

"Listen," Lilly said, "I'm the executor of Harmon's estate. I plan on talking to his lawyer tomorrow morning, but the reading of the will made it very clear about his wishes. If Braden or Miranda think they're helping their cause by getting rid of the birds, they're sadly mistaken. The way Harmon wrote the will, the entire estate could be used to protect those birds."

"Really?" Delia asked.

"Really," Lilly said. "I had no idea Harmon was going to make me the executor of his estate. Maybe he was going to tell me, but he died so suddenly. Anyway, I can't be certain where he'd want me to fall—on the side of his relatives or the birds. I thought I'd be able to navigate the two. But sabotaging the sanctuary? If Miranda or Braden had anything to do with that, well, let me say this: Harmon deserves a lot more respect than that. And he's going to get it."

"We have another mystery on our hands," Warwick said.

"Maybe more than one," Lilly said, looking around the table at her friends. "I can't help but wonder if the birds have anything to do with Gladys. Maybe she knew what was going on. I'm going to ponder that tonight. Now, all of you, catch me up on the cameras. I wonder if we should go back there tonight and reposition them? What do you think, Delia? Will we catch anyone who messes with Harmon's birds?"

CHAPTER NINE

Warwick was at the grill, and Ernie and Delia were in the kitchen pulling the rest of the meal together. Lilly and Tamara were in the dining room, setting the table.

"I don't think I've used this room as much in the past three years as I've used it this summer," Lilly said. She opened the side hutch to pull out a stack of napkins. The Jayne house was a cloth napkin house. Nothing fancy, mostly cotton. But because that had been a rule of Lilly's mother, Viola, there were many colors and sizes to choose from. Lilly settled on red, blue, and yellow flowered napkins. They would go well with the Fiestaware that Tamara was using to set the table.

"You and Delia may as well be running a restaurant. We've all been eating dinner here almost every night."

"I've been grateful for the company. It's not like

we've had to prepare the meals. Everyone has been pitching in. I've enjoyed it."

"I have too," Tamara said. "I like that this room is being used. I barely remember sitting in here when I was a little girl. We'd always eat in the breakfast room."

"The dining room was for special occasions. I never felt comfortable in here as a little girl, and decided to change that once Alan and I moved in. This house is ridiculous. There were so many rules around who ate where and when. I often wonder what my parents would think about the renovations I've been doing. Expanding the kitchen and making it eat-in. We never used the breakfast room any more. Plus, we had expanded the porch and the gardens so there are places to eat there as well."

"I think they'd be delighted, especially your father. He would have loved that kitchen."

"He would have used it more than I do, that's for sure. My mother would have too. That's another reason I'm going to miss Delia. I am not now, nor will I ever be, a very good cook. I suspect the freezer and microwave will get much more of a workout when she moves out." Lilly took a deep breath and started to set the silverware around the table.

Tamara turned to get the salad bowls from the sideboard. "We've got a couple of weeks before we have to deal with Delia moving, so let's pretend it isn't happening. Warwick and I are going to miss her cooking too. I hope she visits often." Tamara looked over and gave her friend a smile. She worried about how much Lilly would miss Delia. "Is Roddy going to join us, do you think? He ran out of here pretty quickly."

"Lenny Andrus texted him and asked for a meeting. Roddy had been trying to set one up for a while, so he didn't want to say no. Set him a place at the table."

"Will do. You know, it's ridiculous that he has to walk all the way to the front of your house to come visit when there's a garden gate between your houses. Had Delia had any luck with the lock?"

Lilly's house, Windward, had been built in the mid-1800s by a sea-captain relative of Lilly's. He'd bought a triple lot and eschewed all of the standards the rest of the town had set for houses on the main street in Goosebush. Most houses were Federal style. The captain built a large Victorian. Most houses sat close to the street with small front yards. The captain had purchased the lot behind him, so he pushed his house back while maintaining a large yard. Most houses had short fences, if any. The captain surrounded his house with large, thick, stone walls on three sides. He'd bought the house next door when his daughter got married, and put a doorway in the wall, with a thick-locked door that was double-locked. Both parties had to open their side in order for it to open. When the captain and his daughter had a falling out, she sent him back her key and told him she would never open the door to him again. So, the door had been locked for well over a hundred and fifty years.

Windward was almost lost to the Jayne family because of its size and the difficulty of doing the needed repairs, never mind keeping it heated in the winter. When George Jayne married Viola Evans, his father gave him the keys to the house, commenting that it was George's turn with the family millstone. George was thrilled since he'd always loved the old house. Happily, he married someone who loved it as much as he did. Together, he and Viola did their best to keep the house in working order, and they took great care to make the first floor a showplace. It wasn't until Lilly became a successful businesswoman that Windward started on its restoration path. Lilly's husband, Alan, had loved the house as much as she did, and he'd contributed a great deal to the plans.

One challenge, and opportunity, was that the Jayne family were collectors, and Windward had enough room for all of the collections. Delia had been cataloging them, and she'd also been actively searching for the keys to the garden gate all summer, to no avail.

"No luck with the keys, and there are two," Lilly said. "Delia has faith that when it's time the house will give them up."

"No doubt," Tamara said. "Interesting that Lenny reached out to Roddy. I wonder if it was partly to see how the open house went? I saw him up at Miranda's today."

"How could you see him at Miranda's?" Miranda's house was a couple of blocks away, up on the hill.

"Binoculars from the second floor," Tamara said.

Lilly stopped fussing with the table and looked at her friend. "Do you regularly check on Miranda's whereabouts?"

"I do. I also check on Alex. These open houses have been a train wreck, and I thought that they might be the culprits."

"But you'd settled on Gladys."

"I'd been checking on her as well. And yes, I did think she was the culprit. I wish I'd forced her to tell me what she wanted to tell me instead of agreeing to meet her at the dump. I'll confess, I wasn't anxious to talk to her, but I wish I'd picked up the phone."

"But you left her messages, right?" Lilly asked.

Tamara nodded.

"And she didn't mention the messages in the text? Doesn't that seem odd?"

"What do you mean?" Tamara asked.

"Gladys wasn't subtle. When she had something to say, she'd say it. Heaven knows she called me dozens of times over the years and laid me out in lavender on the phone."

"Me too," Tamara said. "You're right. To tell you the truth, I'd never gotten a text from her before. Why did she want to meet?"

"Maybe she wanted to show you something? Otherwise wouldn't she have called?"

"I can't imagine what she'd want to show me. But say that's true, what was it? Did she have it with her? How would we ever figure that out?"

"I have no idea, but it's worth contemplating. I wonder if whoever did kill her took whatever it was with them?" Lilly said. She took out her phone and made a note to talk to Bash in the morning. Maybe he'd have an answer to the why of the meeting. It wouldn't hurt to ask.

"I think—" Lilly started to say, but she was interrupted by the entrance of Roddy. She'd given him a key to the front door last week, mostly to save herself the time of getting to the front hall to let him in. He never came in on his own; he always texted first. She looked at her phone. Sure enough, he'd sent a text a few minutes before.

"I hope you don't mind me barging in—" he said. He had a pastry box and a bottle of wine in his hands. He put the wine on the sideboard next to the other bottle Lilly had laid out.

"Not at all, especially when you come bearing gifts," Tamara said. "How was your meeting with Lenny?"

"Unsettling," Roddy said. Both women stared at Roddy. Though they hadn't known him long, unsettled was not an emotion they would have tied to him.

"What do you mean?" Lilly asked.

"He had a business proposition. That I agree to tear down my house and then put a two-family house on the lot. Or reconfigure my existing house into a two-family. I'd get half of the house. He promised it would be in keeping with the architecture of the neighborhood. And that from the street the house would look the same."

"What an odd idea—" Lilly said.

"Not odd at all. If he could pull that off, next door to you, that would make some of his other plans more palatable to the board of selectmen. At least I assumed that's what he was thinking," Roddy said.

"You turned him down, of course," Lilly said.

"No, not at all," Roddy said. "I asked him to send me plans. Now, don't look so shocked, Lilly. I have no intention of going through with it. But there's something about the way he was talking about these plans. He had a mixture of desperation and renewed confidence. I'd like to understand where they both came from. Curiosity on my part, a bad habit from bygone days."

"Do you think that this idea had anything to do with Gladys's death?" Tamara asked.

"I don't think anything," Roddy said. "But I must admit, I'm curious. Let me do a little research and talk to him some more. I promise I'll keep you both informed. Now, these pastries should go into the kitchen with the other desserts. If you'll excuse me."

Tamara and Lilly both watched him go. "He is a mystery sometimes," Tamara said. "He makes leaps of logic that I can't keep up with. Delia can, I think. Do you have any idea what he's thinking about?"

"I don't, but I plan to find out. Hopefully before dessert."

"Pastries and garden plans, the perfect dessert," Tamara said. She hip-checked the swinging door into the kitchen carrying the last of the dinner dishes. She put them on the side of the sink closest to the dishwasher. Warwick gave her a smile and started to load the dishes.

"What are you talking about?" Lilly asked. She was loading the leftover chicken tips into a glass bowl.

"Delia brought out some plans for Roddy's gardens. Or rather the plans to plan. They're spreading them out on the dining room table."

"Ah," Lilly said. "She's been doing some research on the Winslow gardens in town. I'm glad she finally had a chance to show Roddy the research." Florence Winslow had planned several gardens in the 1800s but hadn't gotten the credit she deserved until recently. Delia was obsessed with giving Florence Winslow credit, and was thrilled that Roddy's garden was very likely one of her designs.

"Apparently, she has some old pictures of the house, and he wanted to see them," Tamara said. "Of course, being Delia, she said she wanted more time to pull it all together, but I told her to show them to him. He's thrilled."

"You've seen them?" Lilly asked.

"She's been showing me the Winslow research as she finds it," Tamara said. "My mother always said that Florence Winslow was a distant relative, but I'm not sure of that. I am sure that she did a lot of wonderful work in this town and should be remembered. You should go in and take a look at what Roddy's gardens used to look like. If he could pull that off he'd give you a run for your money." Tamara smiled and then closed her eyes, rubbing the bridge of her nose.

"Are you all right?" Lilly asked. "Here, why don't you sit down?"

"Should I take you home?" Warwick asked. He put the dishes down, and walked over to his wife, squatting in front of her. He took her hands in his and gave them both a squeeze.

"I'll be okay, Warwick. It's been a long couple of days. I was thinking about gardens, then about the Beautification Committee, and then I thought about Gladys. I'll never forget finding her like that. But as to the woman herself? I've barely thought about her all day. I thought about her, but I don't care as much as I should. I mean, I care, it's just that . . . it's just that . . ."

Lilly sat down next to her friend. "Of course. It's all terrible, and overwhelming. But I find that deep mourning has not been a focus of mine today either. Poor Gladys. I wonder how Bash is doing." She took her phone out of her pocket and texted him.

Lots of leftovers. Come over if you're hungry.

Lilly put some wrap on top of the chicken and walked the bowl over to the refrigerator. The plethora of leftovers was considerable. She moved some things around to make room. "Let me get the rest of these things put away—"

"Let us take care of it," Warwick said. "It will give Tamara and I a chance to catch up a bit. Tell you what, we'll get some decaf made and be right in with dessert. Sound good?"

Lilly looked at them both and nodded. She walked over to the swinging door to the dining room and opened it slowly. Delia, Ernie, and Roddy were all sitting on one side of the table. Delia had rolled out a set of plans, and there were stacks of books in several spots. Lilly walked over and sat at the end of the table, listening in on the conversation. Ernie made a motion to move, but Lilly shook her head at him. Delia would catch her up later.

Delia was explaining the challenges of some of the plants and suggesting that he should consider making decisions soon, so the seedlings could be started over the winter.

Lilly felt the phone in her pocket buzz and took it out.

Already ate. You know where Tamara is? I've been looking for her.

Lilly looked over at the sideboard and saw Tamara's and Warwick's phones. They had a no-phone-at-the-table policy no matter where they were. She picked them both up and took them into the kitchen. Warwick and Tamara were both at the kitchen sink, loading the dishwasher. She handed Tamara's phone to her.

"Bash is looking for you," she said. Lilly and Warwick exchanged a look.

CHAPTER TEN

"**S**houldn't you be with Tamara?" Delia asked Lilly.

Lilly looked around the basement of the town hall. It looked exactly as she remembered, which was both comforting and troubling. The previous town clerk has purposely kept the records mired in paperwork. What few records that were on the computer couldn't be trusted for various reasons, so part of Delia's charge was to look into old records and do what she could to assure they were accurate.

"Bash wants her to come in to answer a few more questions," Lilly said. "For that matter, he had a few more for me as well. She's probably back at her office already."

"You should know that the talk of the Star Café this morning was that she is the prime suspect," Delia said.

"That's ridiculous," Lilly said.

"I agree, and most folks were standing up for her."

"Most, but not all?" Lilly asked.

"Regan and Miranda were both there," Delia said.

"Did they start the rumor?"

"I don't know for sure, but I wouldn't doubt it, would you?"

Lilly sighed. "I wouldn't. Dreadful women, both of them."

"You sure it was routine, Bash calling her back in?" Delia said.

"I'm sure," Lilly said. She was lying and they both knew it. Tamara found Gladys and had had a public fight with her a couple of days before. If she wasn't on the suspect list, Lilly would have been surprised. "What are you doing there?"

"I'm looking at the town records for the Dane house," Delia said, looking down at the desk with the piles of old town records. Delia was wearing a smock and cotton gloves and had magnifying glasses on. "It's actually an official request from Alex Marston."

"Is he looking at property lines?" Lilly asked. She leaned over and looked at the documents Delia had laid out. She watched as Delia moved the mounted digital camera over and took a picture. There were two rulers taped down to the table to help provide scale for the picture. "That's quite a contraption."

"Do you like it? I made it. Putting these old records on the copying machine is dicey, so I got a wide-angle lens for my camera and I made this mount. I also ordered the remote control, which really helps."

"Don't they have these systems ready-made?" Lilly asked. Delia's contraption had bungee cords and duct tape and was attached to what looked like a desktop light. Other lights were focused on the pages being copied. It looked cumbersome and not very professional.

"Do you know how much they cost?" Delia asked. "The budget is stretched pretty thin as it is, and I decided that secure file storage was more important than a fancy-schmancy camera mount. This works just fine. Anyway, back to Alex. Yes, he's looking for property lines and the title history."

"Of his house? Wouldn't the title have been cleared before he got a mortgage?"

"He's looking for the title history of Gladys's house."

"Oh," Lilly said. "I wonder if he asked for her will while he was at it."

"He didn't ask for the will, but I have a source who says that a few folks have been asking about it."

"A source?"

"Yup. I don't want to say more. Those of us who work in public records have a code of conduct."

Lilly willed her smile into a straight line. "That's good to know. Not that I want you to breach that code, but I wonder if I could get copies of those documents as well?"

"I'm on it," Delia said. "I'm going to the copy center over in Marshton later. I need to have some large copies made and mounted on foam core for the Alden Park library exhibition. I can get some copies made there while I'm at it. I've got to get some school supplies too. Do you need anything at the office store?"

"I love office supply stores, but no. I'll stay around town. I'm going to head over to the Triple B to talk to Ernie about plant orders for the fall project we talked about. Then I have to go over to the Dane house to meet Dawn and her team."

"We both have a full day, then. Are you going to do any investigating?" Delia asked.

"No plans to," Lilly said. "That said, no plans not to. Will I see you for dinner?"

"Probably not. I have a lot of work to do at the library tonight."

"Good enough. Don't forget to eat."

"Like that's possible," Delia said. "Check your phone, and make sure to keep it charged. I'm creating a shared document for all of us. Anything you hear, see, or read, put it in there."

"Yes ma'am."

"And tell Ernie I said hello."

Lilly parked her Vespa by the Triple B's garden center and made her way to the front of the building. She opened the door and heard shouting from Ernie's office.

"How am I supposed to get my work done today?" Lenny Andrus's raised voice burst through the silence of the store. Lilly looked to her right and saw Lenny standing in Ernie's office. Someone, probably Ernie, closed the door. Fortunately, Bits, Bolts & Bulbs was fairly empty on a Monday morning. Fairly, but not completely. Most of the people in the store had the good grace to pretend they didn't hear the shouting, which was muffled when the door to the office was closed. Muffled, but not silenced.

Lilly walked over to the cash registers that were by the front door. She saw two carts of materials and a full dolly blocking the register. The cashier was fretting over his register with uncertainty, and a line was forming.

"Good morning. Just a thought, but maybe you should open another register until Ernie comes out. Can you do that? Is there a way for you to open that other register? I'm sure Ernie will be able to figure it out."

"Okay, right. I'll do that. Thanks," he said. "Folks, why don't you come over here."

Lilly took out her phone, and texted Ernie. *In the garden center.*

One of Lilly's favorite places was the Triple B garden center. She walked through the glass doors and took a deep breath. Warm, moist air that smelled of soil, some flowers, and a touch of dankness hit her. She loved that.

"You hiding out too?" a voice asked. Lilly looked over and saw Portia Asher looking at the perennials, or what was left of them at this point in the summer. Portia was a generation ahead of Lilly but had the energy of someone half her age. Like many folks, Portia was house poor. She owned her quirky old cottage, which was worth a small fortune for the location alone, but she wouldn't have been able to keep it without some creative thinking on her part and some help from her neighbors. Things were turning around for Portia, though. Her grandson was moving in for a while and would be able to help her do some needed repairs before winter hit.

"Hiding out? What do you mean?" Lilly asked.

"Avoiding the drama. Lenny Andrus was checking out, and his credit card was declined. He tried three others. He asked Ernie to extend him credit. Ernie said no."

"That's unfortunate," Lilly said.

"Ernie tried to keep it quiet, but Lenny lost it. They went into the office, and I escaped back here. He looks exhausted—did you see him?"

"Who, Ernie or Lenny?"

"Lenny. Man is a rumpled mess. What happened to him? I've known him all his life. I used to hire him all the time."

"He is expanding his business, from what I understand."

"Should have stuck to renovations. This house flipping business is risky, if you ask me."

"The real estate market seems to be booming here," Lilly said.

"Not according to that Regan woman. She's going around telling everyone who'll listen that the Goosebush real estate market isn't nearly as hot as it should be. She's a piece of work, that one. Who is she, anyway?"

"Who is she" was code for "she's not from here" and therefore wasn't to be trusted. Normally Lilly would push back against the automatic distrust of non-Goosebush natives, but in this case, she decided to make an exception. Regan had been going out of her way to make Tamara's life miserable, and that put her on the wrong side of Lilly Jayne. Not a good place to be.

"Hopefully it will all get sorted. Tell me, Portia, what brings you here? Are your gardens all right?" Portia's cottage wasn't far from Lilly's house. The house was small. But her lot was good sized. It backed up to a small park that was owned by Portia but maintained by the town, so that folks could use it for walking egress. Years ago the town elders had done that a lot, leasing back space for the public to control the building in town.

"The gardens are wonderful. It's almost like there are fairies tending them while I'm asleep." Portia paused, but Lilly didn't blink. "I thought I'd come down and talk to Ernie, catch up on the gossip."

"Gossip?"

"About Gladys."

"Is there gossip?"

"The woman gets hit over the head with a faucet, there's bound to be gossip."

"She wasn't hit—"

"'Course someone was trying to stir it up that Tamara killed her, but no one believes that. For a minute. Who do you think did it?"

"Me? I haven't actually thought about it," Lilly said.

"Lilly, please. We all know you have a Sherlock Holmes streak in you."

"Honestly, I have no idea—"

"Then what were you doing at the Dane house on Sunday if you weren't snooping around for clues?"

"Portia, really. You know I'm in charge of Harmon Dane's bird sanctuary. I was there checking it

out. In fact, I need to get back over there this afternoon. There are some scientists coming by."

"I still can't believe Harmon left all his money to
the birds," Portia laughed, and Lilly smiled.

"'Course who could blame him with the likes of
Miranda and Braden as family. I'm glad that Mimi
got the Florida house. With a son like Braden she
deserves a bit of good luck."

"Braden isn't that bad," Lilly said.

"Braden was born on third base and acts like
the world owes him a home run. He's too good-
looking for his own good. Harmon indulged the
boy, you know he did. How many colleges did he
go to? He never did graduate, did he? What a
shame."

"Maybe he'll find his path now," Lilly said. She
shrugged her shoulders. "He is a pleasant young
man, and that counts for something."

"He is pleasant, I'll give him that. That Miranda,
she's another one. Never done a day's work and
thinks the world owes her. I have no idea what's
going to happen to her, do you? Even if she gets
that cottage free and clear, the taxes and upkeep
need to come from somewhere."

"She has to have some sort of income," Lilly
said. "Doesn't she have some sort of business making tea? And essential oils? Is that what they're
called? Delia mentioned something."

"How can she make a living from that? What are
they, anyway?"

"I'm not sure, but Delia knows. She uses them in
her room. She says the specialized mix she uses
helps her with stress. I doubt she buys them directly

from Miranda. Miranda indicated Delia wasn't a customer, but who knows? Maybe Miranda has other distribution channels. I'll ask Delia."

"Maybe I've misjudged her business abilities. I've not misjudged her as a person, though. She's miserable. We need to get her off the Beautification Committee. Should be easier now that Gladys has passed. The two of them were quite the dynamic duo."

"An interesting duo," Lilly said.

"Well, they're . . . they were neighbors, technically. Miranda's house was right up the hill, and they visited quite a bit." Portia looked at her watch, and back up at Lilly. "Listen, I need to get over to the clinic and have some blood work done before I head home. I was going to ask Ernie to help me with something, but I may as well ask you."

"Of course, I'm happy to help if I can, or I can talk to Ernie."

"Alex what's his name—"

"Marston?"

"Yes, that's it. My memory is starting to go. Has that happened to you yet? Just wait. Anyway, he heard me talking to Stan about reverse mortgages and offered to come by and explain them to me."

"Are you thinking about getting a reverse mortgage?" Lilly asked.

"I am. I've got to get a new roof, and I'm thinking about adding solar panels. I'd rather not take out a loan, so I'm looking for options. That's what I wanted to talk to Ernie about."

"Options to a home loan?"

"I wanted him to happen to come by and listen while Alex was talking to me. That Alex is a charmer, and I'm a sucker for charming men. Not sure why, but my instinct is telling me another set of ears could be helpful."

"Always," Lilly said. "Tell you what, I'll come by. We can pretend I'm there to work on some plants for the Beautification Committee with you."

"Why pretend? Let's work on some list for what we'll need to get that started."

"I was going to do that very thing with Ernie. Tell you what, I'll talk to him, and then come by your house for more plans. What do you think?"

"Sounds good to me," Portia said. "He'll be by around two."

"I'll be at your house at one-thirty."

"Thanks, Lilly. Tell Ernie I said hello."

Lilly walked with Portia out to the front of the store. She looked into Ernie's office, but he wasn't there. She walked around a bit, looking down aisles. She found him in the paint department, putting paintbrushes back in containers.

"Ernie, how are you?" Lilly asked.

Ernie looked up at his friend and forced a smile. It wasn't the effervescent smile he normally gave her.

"What a day," Ernie said. "When did you get here?"

"A little while ago. There seemed to be a situation, so I escaped into the garden center. Portia Asher was in there too."

"Portia. Shoot. She asked me for a minute of my time. Is she still here?"

"No, but she told me why she stopped by. Alex

Marston is going to her house to talk about reverse mortgages. She wants someone with her." Lilly was leaning down and whispering in Ernie's direction. He stood up and leaned towards her.

"What time is the meeting? I can try to be there."

"Two. I told her I'd come over at one-thirty. We're going to talk about Beautification Committee lists. If you can make it over I'm sure we'll have lots to talk about."

"I doubt I'll make it. Someone called out, so I'm stocking shelves today. Restocking in this case."

"Is that the stuff Lenny was going to buy?" Lilly asked.

Ernie nodded. "I hate conflict," he said quietly. "But I needed to make a decision and stand by it."

"Lenny seems stretched thin these days," Lilly said. "Given that, the conversation he had with Roddy is interesting, don't you think? Where did he think he'd get the money—" Lilly stopped whispering when someone came down the aisle.

"Could you tell me where the stain is? The kind you use on decks?" a young woman asked.

"Next aisle over. Let me show you. There are a couple of different types." The woman walked towards the next aisle over, and Ernie held back for a moment.

"Lilly, there's a lot going on these days. Who knows if they are connected to each other. But we should start making more than plant lists." Ernie gave Lilly's arm a squeeze and went over to the next aisle where he started to discuss the different types of stain in great and exuberant detail.

CHAPTER ELEVEN

Lilly walked into the Star Café. She checked her watch. She had just enough time to grab something before she went over to Portia's. Now to decide on what to eat.

"Good morning, oops, afternoon, Lilly. How are you today?" Stan asked from behind the counter. "Can I get you anything?"

"Good afternoon, Stan. It's lovely to see you." Lilly stepped over to the counter and looked into the glass case in front. "Tell me, how are these pre-made sandwiches?"

"Made fresh this morning. We started to package them out front for folks who want to dine and dash."

"I'd rather dine and sit," Lilly said. "That beet relish and cucumber sandwich looks wonderful."

"I can't keep them in stock," Stan said. He was blushing slightly. Stan created a few of the signature dishes at the Star, and this was one of them.

"I'd love that, one of those kitchen sink cookies, and a big glass of that shaken tea concoction."

"Which one? Strawberry lemonade or blueberry rhubarb?"

"Surprise me," Lilly said.

"Great. It will be right up. There are tables in the café."

Lilly looked around. Her favorite table, the one in the corner by the stationery supplies, was open. That table was perfectly situated in Lilly's opinion. She could be sitting at it and not noticed by many folks unless they were looking around. Better yet, it gave her a perfect view of the comings and goings.

"I'll eat here. I don't suppose you could join me?"

"I was hoping you'd ask," Stan said. "Grab a table, and I'll bring the food right out."

Lilly went over and sat at her table. She noticed a small pile of postcards sitting on it and picked one up. Regan Holland was letting folks know that her office was opening in a couple of weeks. I'LL GET YOU A BETTER DEAL, GUARANTEED was flashed across the front on a yellow banner, with bright red lettering. Lilly sighed. She slid the card into her purse.

Stan came over with the tray. "I told her . . ." He put the tray on the table, and walked around, picking up the piles of postcards from the rest of the tables. He walked over to the trash can and tossed them in.

"There are more under the tray," Lilly said.

"I'll throw them out after lunch with the rest of the trash."

"I suppose you can't blame Regan for trying to advertise her business," Lilly said.

"I can blame her when I've asked her twice already not to leave them here. I showed her where the community board is at the front of the store. We don't allow advertising on the tables, unless it's our own."

"Leaving postcards strewn about without permission does seem a little rude," Lilly said. She took the food off the tray and put the tray on the floor, resting against the table leg.

"A little rude is her middle name," Stan said. "She sure can turn on the charm when she wants to, but when she doesn't get her way, watch out." Stan gestured to the drinks on the table. "I brought both of today's blends. You can sample both and decide which one you want."

Lilly took a spoon and sampled each drink. "That blueberry rhubarb drink is delightful."

"It's all yours," Stan said. "I like them both equally." As if to prove it, he took a long sip of the strawberry lemonade.

Lilly took a bite of her sandwich. Heavenly. The bread was fresh, a wheat mixture that added a nutty taste to the beets. The cucumbers couldn't stand up to the beet relish, flavor wise, but they did add a decent crunch. "Delicious," she said, wiping her mouth.

"Thanks," Stan said. "My grandmother would be thrilled that so many folks love her beet relish."

"Bless your grandmother for giving you the recipe," Lilly said. "How are things going around here?"

"Really well," Stan said. "Business is good, really good."

"You sound like you're trying to convince yourself," Lilly said gently. She took another bite of her sandwich to give Stan a chance to answer.

"It's Regan, again. How long has she been in town, anyway?"

"A few weeks?"

"Seems like longer, doesn't it? Apparently, she'd been visiting for months, scoping out how she'd launch her business. The Star was at the top of her list."

"What do you mean?"

"She tried to talk me into letting her buy it, throwing in with the other business owners, razing all the buildings, and reconstructing them into a better business model of spaces."

"You know, that was suggested back about thirty years ago. The town voted it down. Put some zoning laws in place to make sure it wouldn't happen."

"Delia told me about that. Regan said that I shouldn't worry about the zoning laws. She'd get the town to see sense in time."

"She certainly seems confident, doesn't she?" Lilly said. She was tempted to laugh it off but reconsidered. Regan was stirring up real estate discontent. Maybe she had a bigger game plan than Lilly understood. Yet.

Lilly finished her sandwich and took a bite of her cookie. "Stan, do you have a few more minutes? Tell me more about Regan's plans for the Star and the other businesses on the Wheel. I hadn't heard of any of them, but something tells me that was part of her plan." Lilly reached into her purse and took out a notebook. Ernie was right. It was time to start making some notes.

When Alex Marston rang the doorbell, Lilly was prepared. She grabbed the watering can she'd filled and told Portia, "I'll be out on the porch."

Portia nodded, and went to let Alex in. "I have a friend helping me with my plants," she said as they sat down.

"I could reschedule," Alex said.

"Oh no, no," Portia said. "Sit down. Can I get you a glass of iced tea?"

"That would be delightful," he said.

Portia's three season porch was open to the house with two doors, one from the living room and one from the kitchen. Lilly left the door wide open. She'd planned on sitting on the porch and listening but, when looking at Portia's plants, her fingers started to itch. She reached up into the higher plants and began to take off dead leaves and pinch back vines. She planned on putting some of the vines in water and rooting them.

Lilly opened her notebook to take notes. As she used a wet tissue to dust the leaves, she heard murmuring. Fortunately, Portia made it clear that Alex needed to speak up since she was hard of hearing.

"You really do have a lovely house here," Alex said. "Tell me, have you ever considered enlarging it?"

"Raised four children here, and it suited us fine. I never was one for a dozen bedrooms and twice as many bathrooms. Besides, these days it's only me here. My grandson will be moving in this fall for a few months, but for now it's me."

"But you've got some home repairs, I'd imagine," Alex said. "These New England winters are brutal. Roofs, heating systems. Expensive repairs."

"They are," Portia said. "I think I mentioned I was looking at solar as well."

"A huge investment, but worth it in the long run if not for you, then for your heirs."

"You're right. Didn't you mention that you're planning on doing some work on your house? Is it the heating system? I forgot what you said," Portia said.

"It is the heating system. I was also planning an addition up a floor and out a bit," Alex said. "But plans have changed."

"Yes, well, you are constrained by the deed for the three houses," Portia said. "I remember when painting them different colors, you had to go before a town meeting."

"Less constrained now, I think," Alex said. "I'm going to have new neighbors. Or, who knows, maybe I'll invest in the houses on either side of me and start thinking of them as one house instead of three. But I'm getting off track. I see these wonderful old gems in Goosebush and I can't help but think they could use a bit of a goose, if you'll forgive the pun."

"A goose?"

"You know. A bit of modernizing. Perhaps some rebuilding but as an homage to what was with modern conveniences."

"Is that what you wanted to talk to me about? Tearing my house down?" Portia asked.

"No, no, not at all. Please, this house is a gem. More than that, it's on the historical register. Can't be touched. No, I wanted to talk to you about a private loan some friends and I are underwriting. It's for folks like you—sitting on a mountain of money, but it's all tied up in your house."

"Is it one of those reverse mortgages? I looked into one of those and didn't like the sound of them."

"No, it's more of an equity line."

"I tried to get one of those, too, and was turned down."

"That happens more often than you know. That's why my friends and I are offering a loan program privately."

"Do you mind if I ask you who your friends are? Is Lenny Andrus one of them?"

"Lenny Andrus is a friend, but not on this part of the business. You know Lenny, don't you?"

"Of course. I've known him his entire life. I've tried to hire him a couple of times recently, but he's always busy."

"He is busy," Alex said. "Working on a new business model. I've agreed to partner with him on some new projects. We're still working on the details."

"My, you're busy. Sounds like you've got a lot of irons in the fire."

"I do," Alex said. "I like it that way. Anyway, I don't want to take up more of your time, but I'd like to leave you some literature about this program, if that's all right?"

"That's fine," Portia said.

"I'm delighted to have finally seen inside this charming house. It really is lovely. And what a great lot. You go all the way to the next street, don't you? What a great backyard. With healthy lots of land on either side."

"It is a nice lot, I'm glad you think so too. Most folks don't see the charm since I'm up against public lands. There are rules I need to follow about the house, and of course a lot of the backyard is technically open to anyone to walk through or use as egress. But folks don't overstep, and the open lot in the back sure makes it feel private."

"Charming," Alex said. "Thank you for letting me intrude. I'll let you get back to your friend now. Please, if you have any questions, be in touch."

Portia walked him out and came back into the living room. Lilly wasn't there, so Portia walked back into the kitchen, where she found Lilly putting some cuttings into juice glasses.

"My, that was interesting. What do you think?" Portia said.

"I think that he is offering an interesting service," Lilly said. "Like an equity line for folks who can't get them. What's he charging for that service?"

Portia walked back into the living room to get the brochure. She opened it up and scanned it quickly for a number. She whistled between her teeth and pointed the number out to Lilly.

"That's high," Lilly said. "Portia, would you mind if I borrowed these documents for a while? I'd like to look them over."

"I'd appreciate it. Please let me know what you think. I doubt I'm interested, but it's always worth looking into."

"Portia, I can find you a better loan if you need it. I'm also considering adding solar panels, and there are programs for that. Let me get you some numbers. I'll put it all in a packet for you," Lilly said. "By the way, you did a wonderful job asking him about his partners. I wonder who they are?"

"It was a bit unfeeling, if you ask me, when he mentioned that he may be able to make changes now that the houses on either side of him are empty. Harmon's been gone a few weeks, bless his soul. But Gladys isn't even in the ground yet, for heaven's sake. Granted, she was a miserable woman, but still. Usually you pretend to care about the dead for at least a week."

"True. It made me wonder. I hadn't considered who benefited by Gladys's death by having her house empty. May be something to consider."

"I leave it to you to consider," Portia said. "Now, before you leave, show me what magic you did to my plants."

CHAPTER TWELVE

Lilly hated being late for her meeting with Dawn Simmons, but she had to regroup. She'd stopped by her house to drink some water and sit down for a moment. Between age and the August heat, she wasn't up to popping around town today. She'd been tempted to change her dress but didn't see the point. She'd take a shower when she got home. She rinsed her face, put on fresh lipstick, and reapplied sunscreen. That was better. She may not love the heat, but she preferred it over the cold and was sure to soak up as much vitamin D as she could for as long as she could. She filled up her water bottle and got on her Vespa.

She arrived at the beach parking lot in short order. The smell of the sea lifted her spirits, and she breathed it in as she parked her scooter. She took off her helmet and ran her fingers through her short gray curls. Useless. She got off the Vespa and lifted up the seat. Her crushable straw hat and the bottle of water were waiting for her, alongside her traveler's notebook and favorite pen. She took them all out and put her helmet under the seat. Jamming the hat on her head she ran her eyes over the beach area, looking for Dawn. She saw her over by the stairs to the Dane house. She was on her knees, pointing excitedly. A very earnest young woman stood beside her, not looking at what she was pointing at because she was too busy furiously writing down notes.

"Hello, I'm sorry I'm late," Lilly said when she got close enough to not have to shout. She had no idea what they were looking at, but on the off chance it was something that could be startled she decided to keep her voice low.

"No worries, no worries," Dawn said, standing up. She reached her hand out to Lilly, who shook it. She'd met Dawn several times over the past few months, all Harmon's doings. Today Dawn's long curly hair was tied loosely behind her head. She was wearing jeans and short boots. Her button-up shirt was khaki colored, and she had a light safari jacket one tone lighter on top. She wore brightly colored beads and matching earrings. Her makeup was minimal, but she didn't need more. Her light brown complexion glowed.

"Lilly, I'd like to introduce you to Shi Wong. Shi is my graduate assistant this year and will be working with me on the Dane project. I've been trying to bring her up to date, but this is hardly a normal project. Shi, this is Ms. Jayne. This is the woman Harmon Dane left in charge of his wishes for this project."

"Nice to meet you, Shi," Lilly shook the younger

woman's hand. Shi looked like a deer in the headlights, so Lilly dug deep and turned on the charm.
"Please, call me Lilly."

"Nice to meet you," Shi said. She looked back at
her notebook and started to write.

Dawn looked over at Lilly. "How's that going, by
the way? Is the family still coming after you for
money?"

"How did you know about that?" Lilly asked.

"Because they've been after me, and I've been
sending them back your way," the younger woman
said with a laugh.

"Gee, thanks," Lilly said.

"They're a real delight, that's for sure. Especially that Miranda. She's a trip, that one. Does she
live near here?"

"Yes, sort of. She's a few streets up the hill, without a view. You can't see it from here, but you can
once you get to the top of the stairs."

"Tell Shi about the house situation," Dawn said.
"I can never explain that hot mess on Shipyard
Lane."

Lilly smiled. "Do you see how this beach is in a
cove? It's less of a beach, and more of an inlet actually. Anyway, there's this stone wall that goes up
quite a way. There's a ridge on top of this wall.
Years and years ago, almost a hundred years at this
point, there were three houses built on this ridge.
A lot of rules came with them, including the fact
that they all had to look the same from the outside. About thirty years ago one of the home owners got permission to paint their house a different
color. It was the scandal of the town." Shi and
Dawn laughed.

"Anyway, this neighborhood has access to the beach. There are lots of rules about keeping the trees and plantings in place since they help with wind and erosion. Plus, this beach is more for walking or for sitting on a chair, less for sunbathing and swimming. The rocks are helpful at keeping the beach intact, but brutal to feel. The houses on Shipyard Lane are coveted real estate because of the views, and the privacy. Honestly, they don't go on the market that often. Usually they get passed on to family members."

"Which is what Harmon tried to do, didn't he? He left it to his nephew, right?" Dawn asked.

"Right. The deal was, is, that if Braden took the house he'd need to have that appraised and put into the net worth of the estate for distribution. He decided he'd rather have cash, so the house had to be put up for sale."

"Has anyone bought it yet?"

"Not yet," Lilly said. "And of course, now there's going to be another house for sale."

"Really?" Dawn asked.

"Yes. Gladys Preston died last weekend. Did you meet Gladys?"

"I did, and since my mama raised me better than to speak ill of the dead, we'll leave it at that. May she rest in peace—wait. Was that who was found in the dump?"

Lilly winced. She hated it when Goosebush was in the news. She nodded, and then pointed to the stairs.

"Thank you for coming today," Lilly said, not even attempting subtlety in changing the subject.

"I was here yesterday babysitting the open house and spent some time up at the top of the stairs. It looked to me like the stairs were in worse shape than I remembered, and then I noticed that some of the plantings had been disturbed. I was concerned that someone had been disturbing the nesting areas."

"Looks like someone's been doing something," Dawn said. "See here? When I stopped by a few weeks ago, after Harmon's funeral, there were a lot more plantings. Plus, did you get a close-up look at these steps? Seems like someone or something has been hacking at them. They don't look very safe."

Lilly peered at the stairs closely. Indeed, they didn't look very safe. The weathered wood showed signs of being hacked and partially cut in a few places. "This isn't good," she said quietly.

"What do you mean?" Dawn asked.

"The stairs are for common use, even though they're on Harmon's property. Under the staircase Harmon asserted his rights to the area, but the stairs are deeded to all three houses. I know we'd discussed replacing them at some point, but an accident would move that timeline forward."

"A rush job wouldn't take the nesting areas into consideration," Dawn said.

"But since nesting season is over, wouldn't this be a good time to fix the stairs?" Shi asked.

Dawn bent down and pointed to the area under the stairs. "See that and this? The area's become home to a lot of life. The birds used to leave their nests, but now they come back here a lot more often. I think it's because it's safe for them. All of these rocks have nooks and crannies, and the vegetation has grown in to give them cover."

"Or had been safe for them," Lilly said. "Down here someone's been bothering the plants. Now that I'm looking closely, it looks even worse. Harmon spent a small fortune making sure folks don't climb the rocks, and they don't. It helps that it's a private beach."

"How do you make a beach private?" Shi asked.

"Here in Goosebush you post signs, and the neighborhood discourages visitors. As I said, this is a good sitting beach but not a good swimming beach. Goosebush has great swimming beaches."

Shi looked confused, but Dawn was moving past beach critiques.

"Should we try and go up the stairs?" Dawn said.

"No, I don't think we should until we have them looked at," Lilly said. "In fact, we should block them, don't you think?"

"Probably a good idea," Dawn said. She took out her phone and started making notes. "Shi, I'm going to send you a bunch of texts that are my notes. Don't act on them before we talk. But we'll want to do a roundup later this afternoon to figure out where we are with all of this. We were planning on setting up scaffolding next week and doing a stair project survey, but we need to do it earlier rather than later. Let's see if I can get the project moved up. Would there be any problems with that, Lilly?"

"None that I can't deal with. I'll talk to Ernie and see who we can get out to look at the stairs. Maybe we should have them redesigned to jut out further from the rocks, and provide more cover underneath?"

"Sounds like a plan. Shi, we may as well start some documenting this week to evaluate changes. We'll set up some new protocols." She typed for a few more seconds, and then Shi's phone started to ping over and over.

"What's the best way to get up to the house?" Shi asked, looking around.

"Driving. I'll meet you both up there," Lilly said.

"Come in the car with us," Dawn said. "I want you to point out Miranda's house. Just so I know where it is. I'll drive you back to your car afterwards."

"My Vespa."

"That sweet red ride over there? I love it. Lilly, you've got style."

"Thank you, Dawn. That's the nicest thing anyone's said to me this week. Why don't we take a short ride to get to the Dane house, and I'll tell you a bit more about the neighborhood and the neighbors. No gossip, mind you."

"Gossip? Me? I'm a scientist doing research, Lilly. Shi, put your notebook away."

Dawn rolled up to the parking space of Harmon's house. The three of them sat in the van while Lilly pointed out the peculiarities of the trio of houses. The oyster shell drive, with carved-out parking for two cars, no more. Each car needed to line up beside the mudroom entrance. If someone had a boat trailer, that took up the other space. No one was allowed to park on the road itself. If a resident had extra visitors, they needed to park them over by the beach. Lilly also pointed out the cliffside path in the front of the houses, only wide enough for single-file walking, and only accessible by the three houses.

"The path leads to the staircase, which was their route of egress to the beach."

"No one else wanders up?" Dawn asked.

"Sometimes, but once you're up there there's nowhere to go except through the yards. Then you'd have to walk up the hill, over two streets, and back down to the beach," Lilly said. "As I said, most of the folks who use this beach live here, and they know better than to climb the stairs."

"Did you ask Braden and Miranda if it was okay if we camped out here?" Dawn asked.

"I told them you were going to stay in the house," Lilly said. "If Tamara needs to show it, you'll need to clean up and clear out, but having someone in the house will be good. You can keep an eye on things." Lilly briefly explained the problems with the open houses.

"Will it be safe?" Shi asked. The three women were walking around to the front of the house. Lilly could have let them in the back door, but why deprive Shi of the view from the front.

"Oh yes," Lilly said. "I doubt anyone will do anything once there are people in the house. Also, we've set up some—" She stopped short and stared.

Miranda Dane was up on the porch, trying to open the windows.

"Miranda, can I help you with something?" Lilly asked coldly.

"Lilly, you scared me. Don't sneak up on someone like that."

"Are you trying to break in?" Lilly asked.

"My key doesn't work."

"Oh, good. The new locks must have finally been installed."

"New locks? You can't lock me out of my—"

"Miranda, it's not your anything. The house belongs to the estate. Braden was given the opportunity to buy it, which he turned down."

"I left a teapot in the house, and I need it back," Miranda said.

"I thought you went through and took all of your things," Lilly said. She walked up to the porch but made no move to unlock the door.

"I did. Listen, it's brown earthenware. If you see it, bring it up to me, alright? It took me years to season it. I brought it down to dear Harmon, so I could make him some of my special teas. I'd like it back."

"I'm showing Dawn and Shi the nesting area, and then they're going to get set up in the house."

"They're staying here?" Miranda asked.

Lilly took a deep breath. "They are. Dawn, as you know, was working with Harmon on the bird sanctuary. Shi is her graduate assistant. I was concerned about some activity I noticed around the sanctuary—you don't know anything about that, do you?" Lilly noticed Dawn and Shi walk to the other end of the porch.

"What are you asking me? Are you inferring . . . ? How dare you?"

"How dare I?" Lilly said. "Miranda, you were trying to break into this house. Don't even start with me."

"Who said that they could stay here?" Miranda said.

"I did. I suggest you remember that I am the executor of Harmon's estate. According to his will, taking care of that bird sanctuary was his primary concern. I'm trying to work with you and Braden, to get you some money out of the estate. But know this. Under the terms of the will I could sell everything and give it to the birds. Don't forget that."

"I can't believe you're threatening me," Miranda said.

"I'm not threatening you. I'm pointing out the reality of the situation. Now, if I find the teapot I'll bring it to you," Lilly said.

"I really need it—"

"I'll look for it, Miranda. Now, please. I don't want to be rude, but I have business with these women."

Lilly and Miranda had a brief staring contest. Lilly won, and Miranda turned on her heel and stomped off the porch.

Dawn walked over and stood next to Lilly. "She's a delight, isn't she?"

Lilly texted Tamara to remind her that Dawn and Shi were moving into the house for a few days. She also mentioned that they'd make themselves scarce if there was a showing.

No worries. No bites on the house. Suspect it will be slow until after Labor Day.

"When you don't have the listing anymore," Lilly thought. She moved into the living room and sat down on the settee, putting her feet up on the footstool. The view of the water did what views of the water always did, calmed her down. Not for the first time Lilly thought of her friend Harmon and felt a constriction in her chest. What a mess he left. Of course, bless him, he didn't think he was dying. No one did.

"Sorry, Lilly, are you resting?" Shi asked quietly.

"No, I'm thinking."

"I hate to bother you, but Dr. Simmons wanted to check and see if it was all right if we set up an office in Mr. Dane's study."

"That makes the most sense," Lilly answered. "I know that Harmon had the power upgraded in there. I don't know if the Wi-Fi still works. I doubt it, but it may. All of the utilities are still on."

"Thank you," Shi said. "I don't mean to intrude, but could I get you a glass of water or a cup of tea? I was going to try and make some tea for Dr. Simmons and myself."

"Tea would be lovely," Lilly said. "There's nothing in the refrigerator, but there are dry goods and tea. While you're at it, could you look for an earthenware pot? Supposedly it belongs to Miranda."

Shi walked towards the kitchen, and Lilly got a text from Delia.

Can you come by the library on your way home? I'd like to walk you through the exhibition.

Lilly sighed. She'd been hoping she could fit in a nap, but that didn't seem likely.

Of course. I'll be there in an hour or so, okay?

Great, thanks!

"Lilly, could you come in here?" Dawn called from the kitchen.

Lilly hoisted herself off the couch. "Is there no tea?" she asked as she walked through the dining room.

"Oh, there's tea," Dawn said.

Lilly walked into the kitchen and saw that the women had several small jars lined up on the kitchen table. "Shi found these and decided to make the 'Pick Me Up' brew. I took a sip and thought my heart was going to come out of my chest. Then I noticed this on the label. A MIRANDA D. MIX. Did you know that she made teas?"

"I heard that, yes."

"There are a few of these jars. 'Heart Health' and 'Stress Relief' are two other jars. I didn't dare try them. I need to pay more attention to labels. I'm going to stick with the regular tea for now. Should I throw them out?"

"Don't toss them. Here, let me take two jars with me. Then why don't you box up the rest and put them away."

"Away so that someone who wanders in doesn't take them with her," Dawn said.

Lilly looked at Dawn. "We're both being paranoid, but yes, put them away where folks can't find them. By the way, did you find the teapot she was looking for?"

"Yes, it's right here," Shi said. Lilly noticed it set off to the side.

"Put that away with the teas. I'll tell her I couldn't find it, but I'll promise her to keep looking."

"What are you thinking, Lilly?" Dawn asked.

"I'm not sure," Lilly said. "But I'm thinking."

"Watch out, world," Dawn said. "Now, how about if we make some regular old tea, maybe put ice in it, and go and look at the bird space from up here?"

CHAPTER THIRTEEN

Lilly showed Dawn and Shi around downstairs, and then she showed them up to the bed-rooms on the second floor. It still felt odd to ma-neuver herself around Harmon's house as if it was her own, but she felt confident her old friend would be pleased that Dawn was there.

"Oh, wait, let me show you the camera loca-tions," Lilly said.

"Camera locations?"

"Yes, we installed a few outside, and there are a couple trained on the nesting area. They're there for security. I can ask Delia to get you access to them if you'd like," Lilly said.

"That would be great," Dawn said. "Never know what you're going to see."

"Indeed," Lilly said. She texted Delia about let-ting Dawn know the website for the cameras.

Dawn offered to drive Lilly back to her Vespa, but Lilly turned her down. It was a bit of a walk but not terrible. Besides, Lilly needed to think. About a lot of things.

She put two of the tea jars in her pockets. Thank heavens her dresses had pockets. That was a must. The jars made her look more hippy than normal, but her blue seersucker dress had a very full skirt, so there was already volume in that area.

She left through the front of the house and paused to look at the view again. The wonder of a water view was that it always changed. The wonder of being Lilly's age was that she had stopped taking views like this for granted. She took a deep inhale and walked around the house to the back lane. She didn't take the cliff walk. Narrow paths and no guard rail made her nervous.

The houses on the bluff were fairly close together but not right on top of one another. As she neared Alex's house she saw him drive into the road. She sighed and readied herself. She stepped onto the grass, so he could park more easily.

"Lilly, nice to see you. What brings you by?" he asked.

"I was at the Dane house. There are a couple of scientists in, and they're going to stay at the house."

"Checking on Harmon's birds, are they?"

"They are. Someone's been disturbing the nesting areas," Lilly said.

Alex looked concerned. "Really? That's a shame. Especially since he left all that money to take care of them. Where would the money go if the birds aren't there?"

"The money would all go to bringing them back," Lilly said. She held back a smile when she saw a flash of surprise on Alex's face.

"Really? Could you do that?"

"I could. His will was fairly clear in its intentions. He wanted part of his legacy to be the study of the habitats in Goosebush, starting with the one he controlled, near his house. That much was clear, so that has to be honored."

"Braden and Miranda won't be happy with that. I think they're both counting on a windfall. Didn't he have a sister somewhere?"

"Mimi. Braden's mother. His legacy to her was also clear and will be honored."

"Well, Braden and Miranda benefited from Harmon's generosity in life. I'm not that generous with my own kid, never mind my ex-wives. He was smart to put you in charge, that's for sure. All of this reminds me to look at my will again. I haven't updated it since my most recent divorce. That would be a disaster if I kicked off unexpectedly."

"Not leaving a mess for folks to clean up is a good motto. I spent a lot of my career helping folks avoid messes. That's probably why Harmon named me executor."

"What line of business were you in?"

"Finance," Lilly said.

"Makes sense. You've got that look. You understand money, and what it will and won't do."

"Thank you, I guess. Not sure what that look is."

"Assurance. You put your money to work for you, but don't chase it. More folks could learn from you. 'Course I hope they don't, otherwise I'll be out of business."

"I thought you were retired?"

Alex shook his head. "I tried, I really did. But it turns out, I'm not suited to retirement. Too many ideas rolling around in my head. No, I've decided to go back into business."

"What sort of business?" Lilly asked.

"Real estate. I've actually got my fingers in several pots. I'm using my architecture background, which is a muscle I haven't used for years. I'm also working with a few folks on some investments. But I'm boring you. Where are you heading?"

"Back over to the beach. It looks like the staircase has been compromised. I'm going to have someone come and take a look at it. I'm worried about the safety of it, so don't use it until I do."

"Compromised? On purpose? It's a pretty old staircase."

"I'm not an expert, you understand, but the cuts look fresh. They're down towards the bottom, so someone would get hurt, but not necessarily killed. Still, I wonder who would do such a thing?"

"Lilly, I hate to speak ill of the dead, but Gladys Preston comes to mind. She was always looking for an angle. Since we're the only ones who are supposed to use the stairs, she may have been looking for a quick buck by suing the estate."

"That's quite the accusation," Lilly said.

"And very unkind of me," Alex said. "Especially now. But I was Gladys's neighbor. Probably as close to a friend as she had. She'd had a difficult life. She was one of the folks in life who was always chasing money."

Lilly didn't say anything. She didn't want to agree with Alex, but his perception of Gladys was astute. She was always chasing money. Her husband had left her some, plus the house, but that could only go so far. Would Gladys have feigned an accident for financial gain? Sadly, Lilly suspected she would.

"I wonder what's going to happen to her house?" Lilly asked.

"The folks she owes money to will want to be part of any decision making," Alex said.

"Do you think she owed a lot of folks money?" Lilly asked.

"I suspect she did. I'm on the list, but it wasn't that much money. I'd imagine it's going to be a helluva mess getting her estate in order. I hope she has an executor like you to help."

"I hope she has an executor. And a will," Lilly said.

"True. If there isn't a will, boy, that will be a mess. The house should sell at a decent price, I should think, though it's in pretty rough shape. I think that Regan Holland is going to get the listing. At least she's trying to."

"I'm sure she is," Lilly said.

"Yeah, well, I don't like her tactics, but you've got to admit she's a go-getter. Speaking of which, has the Dane house sold yet?" To his credit, Alex didn't gloat or smirk when he asked the question. Alex was very good at playing to his audience. Lilly needed to file that away for later consideration as well.

"Not yet, but there have been some interesting developments of late," Lilly said. There had been some interesting developments, but mostly in Lilly's thoughts. "You know, Alex, several of Tamara's open houses were sabotaged."

"What do you mean?"

"Garbage left in rooms. Mice let out to roam. Fish left to rot in the attic."

Now Alex looked away and over her shoulder. Lilly saw him clench his jaw, but he soon regained his composure.

"I had no idea. That's terrible. Listen, it's no great secret that I put an offer in on the house. But I wouldn't stoop to that level."

"I wouldn't think you would. This feels like amateur attempts at disruption."

Alex laughed. "As opposed to professional? Lilly, I hate that you think so little of me, I really do."

"Alex, I meant nothing by it. Forgive me, I'm hot and tired. Much too busy on a beautiful summer day."

"I'm surprised you're not looking for clues over at Gladys's house. I hear Tamara's the likely suspect."

"Tamara didn't kill Gladys Preston," Lilly said. "I have no idea who did, but since I was one of the people who found her, trust me when I say that. Tamara didn't do it."

"I wonder who did, then?" Alex said. "For the record, it wasn't me. Listen, it is hot. Would you like me to drive you over to the beach?"

"No, thank you. I'll walk slowly. It's a beautiful day."

"Take care of yourself, Lilly. I'll keep an eye out on Harmon's place, and let you know if I see anyone lurking about. Aside from the scientists and the birds, that is."

* * *

Lilly slowed down while Alex went into his house. She waved at him and made sure he shut the door. That didn't mean that he wasn't watching her, but at least it gave her a semblance of privacy as she made her way down the lane. She stopped and took out her phone, opening a list app that Delia had shown her. She wrote down a few thoughts while they were still in her head:

Who is Gladys's heir?

How much did Gladys owe on her house?

What are Alex's businesses?

Who are his partners?

Would someone kill Gladys to get her house?

After a moment, she wrote one more note to herself: How did Harmon die?

She put her phone back in her pocket and took a shaky breath and looked back at Alex's house. If Gladys was killed for her house, might Harmon have been killed for the same reason?

The thought was farfetched, but it wouldn't leave Lilly's mind. Another thought was entering Lilly's mind.

Shame.

Two days ago, Lilly had discovered her best friend standing over a dead body. Her concern since then had been for Tamara. That made sense. Lilly would do anything for Tamara. But looking at Gladys's house she suddenly felt enormous shame for how little concern she'd given her death. She took her phone back out of her pocket and added some more items to her list.

How did Gladys and her killer get into the dump?

What other motives could there be for Gladys's death?

Who had what alibi?

Then she added one more note to herself: check in with Bash.

The phone went back in her pocket, and she adjusted her hat on her head. Onward to the Vespa. She was almost at the corner of Gladys's house when she saw Lenny coming out the back door.

Lilly took her phone out of her pocket and spoke loudly.

"Yes, Delia, I'm on my way. Heading back to the parking lot now." Two more steps, and suddenly she saw Lenny Andrus by his car.

"Oh, hello," Lilly said.

"Hey Lilly," Lenny said. "What brings you here?"

"I was at the Dane house," she said. "What brings you here?"

"Checking on the house, making sure the water is shut off and things are buttoned up. I have no idea when the place will go on the market, but there's a lot of work to be done. It's in pretty rough shape."

"Does Bash know that you were coming by? As far as I know this is still a crime scene, at least he indicated it was when we spoke earlier today," Lilly lied. She wanted to see how Lenny reacted.

"Yeah, I know." Lenny looked sheepish, or tried to. "I'd given Gladys some plans to look over and make notes on, and I needed them back. I couldn't find them, though. No harm done."

"You should check with Bash and let him know you were here. He'll want to eliminate your prints if he finds anything." Lilly stared at Lenny and he looked away.

"My prints are all over that place. I did a lot of

work in there over the years. When you see Bash let him know I'm happy to answer any questions."

"Maybe you should drop your key off at the station," Lilly said. "We all want to find out what happened to poor Gladys, don't we? I'd imagine once the will is read whoever she left it to will be anxious to get it sold, so the sooner Bash is finished the better."

"From what I hear, the bank owns Gladys's house. She was mortgaged to the hilt. Besides, she didn't have any relatives that I know of, and I would know. I spent a lot of time with Gladys over the years. I'm pretty fond of this house, as a matter of fact. Who knows, maybe I'll try and buy it."

"I don't think you could tear it down," Lilly said quietly.

Lenny laughed. "Probably not. Who knows? Maybe for this project it would be worth going back into restoration work. Anyway, I've got to get going. Tell you what. I'll give the key to you, and you can give it to Bash. I'd rather not go by the station. I reset the alarm, but he has the code. Sound good?"

Lilly nodded, and he handed her the key. Lenny waited until Lilly walked by his car and back out onto the road before he left. He stayed parked at the end of the lane and watched as she walked up the street. When she was halfway up, he finally drove out, swerving past her, beeping, and waving as he went by.

Were Lilly a younger woman, or a different woman, she would have doubled back and gone into Gladys's house, or at least peered in the windows. Gladys had an alarm? Whatever for? She wondered if she could get Bash to give her the code. She shook her head. Lilly was a smooth talker, but not that smooth a talker. Instead she called Bash and left a message on his voicemail.

"I've got the key, and haven't gone into the house, but I did want to let you know. I'm making my way back to the beach to get the Vespa, then I'm heading over to the library to see Delia. Call me or text me if you need more information." She hung up.

Lilly hesitated for a moment, and then sent him a text. *I have some questions. Actually, they're questions about Harmon's death. Talk to you soon.*

Lilly stopped and looked at where she was. One more street to the main road. But in the meantime, if she took this right she'd still get to the beach, but it would take her longer. Longer, and right past Miranda Dane's house.

Lilly turned to the right.

Lilly Jayne wasn't nervous about seeing Miranda, but she realized she needed to be prepared. On her way down the street she practiced her "I looked for the teapot and didn't find it" lie. Once she got closer to the house she realized that she probably wouldn't need it. The driveway was empty. Lilly slowed down in front of Miranda's, not sure about how to proceed.

Miranda's gardens were stunning. Her lot was tiny, but from what Lilly could see, she'd used every spare inch in interesting ways. Lilly let herself in the gate and looked around. By habit she started taking pictures of the gardens. The layout and the plants. Rosemary. Lavender. Was that fox-glove? Lilly took another picture, this one closer up. Yes, it was foxglove. Lilly looked around. Though lovely, the gardens were medicinal rather than decorative.

She walked up on Miranda's porch and rang the bell. While she waited, she looked around. Miranda's home used to be the gardener's cottage of a large estate. The main house was torn down years ago, but the cottage remained. The Cape style abode was very small but had a large wrap-around porch on three sides. She wandered to the right, and saw flowers and plants drying on a compli-cated system of lines that allowed for many levels of plants. Lilly walked over and took pictures of the drying flowers. She needed to show them to Delia. Delia had begun to dry herbs and some plants, and Lilly had little doubt that she'd be fas-cinated with this system.

Lilly rang the bell once more, and then walked back out to the street.

"You picking something up or dropping off?" a woman's voice called out from across the way.

"Pardon me?" Lilly asked.

A woman stood up from the garden across the way and rubbed her hands on her pants. "I was wondering if you're picking up or dropping off. Miranda isn't home, so if you're dropping off I'll take the package. If you're picking up, she didn't leave anything."

"I thought I'd stop by and pay a visit," Lilly said.

"I'm sorry you missed her then," the woman said. "Not sure when she'll be back. That's a shame. You would have enjoyed visiting her laboratory. It's always a trip."

"Laboratory?"

"That's what I call it. I'll admit, I thought she was nuts when she said she was going to start making oils and teas and such. Thought she was desperate for cash. But she's good at it. I'll tell you what, she made me an oil blend to help with stress. I put it in a diffuser and use it all the time now. I've gotta tell you, it's made all the difference. Ask anyone. I haven't been this relaxed in years."

"You're a great testimonial. I'm extra sorry I missed her now. Tell me, does she have an online shop? I'd love to go home and explore."

"Miranda D.'s Potions. It's one of those small, boutique online shops. She hasn't been selling much yet, but it's starting to take off."

"Well, thank you for the information. By the way, you have lovely gardens here. You have a lot of shade. I'd imagine it's quite a challenge, with the shadows of the other houses."

"It is, or was. But Ernie down at the Triple B, do you know that place?"

"Very well."

"He's a godsend. He's forgotten more about plants than I know. It wouldn't surprise me at all if he was the night gardener."

"The night gardener?"

"The person who's been going around Goosebush all summer, fixing gardens. Surely, you've noticed. It started with the flagpole down by the Wheel."

"I had noticed it has been gussied up."

"The flagpole isn't the only job they've done. 'Course, I keep hoping they'll deal with the rosebushes at the top of the lane, but it's not like there's a suggestion box for the midnight gardener."

"What's the matter with the rosebushes?"

"They're overgrown, so it's a hazard when you try and turn. Nobody will take responsibility for cutting them back. Mostly because they're so overgrown that cutting them back and not killing them is a tough call. There's a persnickety old trout who lives up there, and when I go up to look at them he sticks his nose in. The bushes abut his property, and I think he likes the privacy. Anyway, the problem is getting worse and worse. I'm surprised no one's been killed, frankly. But as I said, there isn't a suggestion box for the mystery gardener. Would that there were."

"Would that there were indeed," Lilly said.

CHAPTER FOURTEEN

Lilly was tempted to go home before going to the library. She was hot, tired, and her mind was buzzing. Much as she desperately wanted to sit on her porch and make notes while drinking iced tea, she knew that she had to push forward and go to the library. Delia would be waiting for her.

To say that the town library was the pride and joy of most residents would not be an overstatement. For this small town, the library was a statement of priorities.

The Goosebush Town Library was moved into an old elementary school twenty-five years ago. For a time, the library was only given half of the space in the old three-story building. But over time the library encompassed the entire building. A series of fierce librarians, led by Dot Robie, the head librarian, programmed the space well and kept up with the modern needs of the community. Computer stations were everywhere. There were

study areas interspersed throughout the building.
The library lent books, art, music, audio equipment,
projectors, assistive listening devices, and other
needed technology. A corner room on the top floor
held town documents dating back hundreds of
years. The documents were under lock and key,
and only certain people had access to them. Delia
Greenway was one of those people, and she volunteered once a week to help answer questions.

Delia spent many more hours in a windowless
room in the basement of the building. That room
had housed the Goosebush Historical Society for
years. There was talk of the group getting a be-
queathed home, but that legacy gift was tied up in
miles of red tape. The society made do, hosting bi-
weekly meetings of volunteers. There was a dedi-
cated space on the first floor for historical displays
curated by the group, which were rotated out
every couple of months.

Delia had never been in charge of a display before, but since she'd been working on the Alden
Park project, she was tapped. At first, she balked.
As an academic, she didn't like the idea of showing objects that hadn't been closely studied yet.
But then she began to understand, thanks to Lilly
and Tamara, that by keeping folks informed of the
Alden Park project, she was doing a service to both
the town and the project. As Goosebush wrestled
with its history, finding pieces of it unearthed,
putting them in context, and letting folks understand the depth, breadth, and complexity of the
discoveries was a service.

And so, the first Alden Park exhibition was going
up, scheduled for a public lecture to the friends of

the library on Tuesday morning before the grand opening on Friday.

Lilly texted Delia once she arrived at the library. She'd parked her Vespa out back and entered through the basement.

I'm here. Where are you?

Main floor. Come see the exhibition. Be honest!

Lilly looked at the stairs next to her but opted to take the elevator instead. It had been a long day.

She got off the elevator and turned the corner to the display area of the library. She had to admit, even though she was a member of the historical society, more often than not she walked by the displays barely glancing at them. She would not be walking past these displays. No one would.

Delia had set up a number of renderings of Alden Park throughout the years. She recognized a couple of them easily—they were done by her mother and usually hung in the living room of Windward. She also had a montage of the photos of the park from the beginning of the cleanup to recently. Lilly noticed she'd skipped over the dead body in the shed in May. A good call, since it had little to do with Alden Park.

After Lilly had taken in the materials hanging on the walls, she went over to the display cases. Delia had taken the pieces found so far—mostly broken dishes and bottles—and laid them out. But she'd also added context where she could. Pictures of other items that matched the ones found, bits of information about the materials used, the meanings behind the different colored glass bottles, and more. Lilly knew about all of this—Delia had talked her through it a dozen times, but nevertheless she was fascinated. The hope was that by pinpointing when the items were in use, the age of the dump could be narrowed down.

"What do you think?" Delia asked quietly.

"Delia, you gave me a start," Lilly said. "I was so engrossed in this display I didn't see you there."

"Lilly, you don't have to lay it on thick," Delia said. Lilly smiled at the younger woman. Delia's smile belied her words. She was pleased by Lilly's praise.

"I'm not laying anything on thick. You have enough context for interest, but you aren't overwhelming. For the history buffs, you couch it all in 'we're still studying it' language, but you give them lots to consider. Well done. my friend. Really well done."

"Thank you. And thank you for all your help—"

"My absolute pleasure. You are very good at this, Delia. Making things clear, not talking down to anyone. You are going to be a wonderful teacher." Lilly cleared her throat. "Are you ready for the lecture tomorrow?"

"Do you remember when we first talked to the library about this whole project, and they thought no one would be interested? Well, it ends up they need to move the lecture up to the main lecture hall. They're going to livestream it, but I can't imagine who'd want to watch it online. They also want to tape it and use parts of it on the website. What do you think of that idea?"

"What do *you* think?"

"I'm a wreck, but I'm glad folks are interested."

"Of course you're nervous, but you'll be marvelous. Let's head home, if you're done here, and you can practice the lecture a couple of times tonight."

"You've already seen it a dozen times."

"You've changed it every time. I can't wait to see what you've added or taken out."

"Thanks, Lilly. I wouldn't have been able to do any of this without you."

"That's not true but thank you anyway. Are you ready to go home?"

"I am," Delia said. "Did you drive?"

"I have the scooter."

"I have my car. Would you rather drive that back home or your scooter?"

"I'd love to drive the car; how could you tell?" Lilly asked.

"You look tired and a little sunburned. We have a ton of leftovers, so we don't even have to stop for anything."

"Great. I've seen so many people today my head is swimming. Wait until I catch you up on my day."

"That sounds ominous."

"You know what, it feels ominous. Maybe you'll be able to help me figure this out and organize my thoughts. My brain is swimming."

"Do you want to give me a preview?"

"How's this? I am beginning to wonder if Harmon's death and Gladys's death are related."

"Harmon died of natural causes."

"Did he? Turns out Miranda is some sort of potion maker and had several teas that she served him. I caught Lenny Andrus coming out of Gladys's house. Plus, someone has tampered with the stairs down to the beach at the Dane house. And Alex

Marston is, I think, a money lender. Which makes me wonder who he's in business with. Can't be Lenny Andrus, because he is having cash flow problems. Oh, and Regan Holland thinks she's getting Gladys's house listing, but from whom? Isn't that awfully fast? The poor woman is not even in the ground yet."

"I think she's being cremated," Delia said.

"Whatever."

"Wow, Lilly, you have had a heck of a day. Let's go home. We'll have some dinner and start writing things down. Getting them out of your head and on paper will help you feel better."

"I hope so, Delia. I certainly hope so."

CHAPTER FIFTEEN

The lecture hall was full fifteen minutes before Delia was set to start. The library staff scrambled to set up a screen in another room for the overflow crowd, so they could watch the livestream. Part of the lecture was passing around artifacts, so Delia had to figure out how to make that happen in two places. Lilly decided she'd be in the overflow room, monitoring the artifacts.

"Are you all right if I'm not in the same room?" Lilly asked.

"I guess so," Delia said. "At some point, I'll have to do things without you in the room. I guess today's the day."

"Tamara and Ernie are both going to be there, so find them in the crowd before you start. You're going to be great."

"Thanks, Lilly. I've practiced this so many times, thanks to you, I'm ready. Wish me luck."

"Luck," Lilly said, giving Delia a brief hug. "Go get 'em."

The lecture was a huge success. Delia had included a lot of Goosebush history that was fascinating. She also discussed the process of digging things up and the involvement of the college students who had been working there for part of the summer and who would be there all fall.

"Isn't that a lot of effort for a dump site?" someone asked.

"Maybe, but we don't think so. Since the park is public land, this is a great opportunity for us to look at a time capsule in our history. Working with the local college is a great opportunity for students to get hands-on experience and for us to get the artifacts cataloged. I know it's hot out, but we're moving into fall. We will get back to building up the park next spring. There's no worry about taking some time and exploring."

"I had no idea that Alden Park was a dump. It wasn't always a park?"

"Public lands were used for different purposes throughout our history. Sometimes they were grazing lands. Other times they were used for community gardening. There must have been a time, and it looks like it was in the early to mid-1800s, when this part of the park was a dump site. I don't know if that was sanctioned or not, but none of my research indicated the town used it for a dump. For all we know, the contents of someone's house may have been dumped there for some reason. Because we're finding so many pieces that seem to have the same origins, that is one story that may be true. But there may be other reasons. That's why we need to keep exploring, to try and find out the facts of the dump site."

"Finding facts at the dump site sounds like a theme," someone else said. There was nervous laughter in the room.

"I want to say one thing about facts," Delia said. "When I talk about facts, they are undisputed. It is a fact that you are all here. I could say that the truth is you are all here because you are interested in Alden Park and Goosebush history, but that may not be true of everyone. Some of you may have been dragged here. Some of you may have wanted to cool off in the AC. Facts are facts. We need to find the narrative to fit the facts, not the facts to fit the narrative. That's what makes this exploration so exciting."

"Any other bodies so far?" someone else shouted. In the overflow room, there were gasps. Lilly wished she was in the main room and knew who asked that question.

Delia took a deep breath before she continued. "There are some animal skeletons, but that's not uncommon. We haven't found any human remains."

Delia kept answering questions but finally had to stop them since they were over the allotted time, and she knew the room was going to be used later in the day for another event.

"Tell you what," Delia said. "How about if we make the Alden Park updates a lecture series, every six weeks or so? Would that be of interest?" She got her answer with a huge round of applause.

* * *

"Are you sure it was okay?" Delia asked for the umpteenth time. She was standing out in the main area of the library. The historical society had provided some tea and cookies, and folks were hanging around looking at the display.

"You were fabulous," Tamara said. "Fascinating, but you avoided the dork factor. It made me think that the Beautification Committee and historical society should combine forces around Alden Park."

"That's a great idea," Ernie said. "This lecture series will be a great way to launch the planning process we need to go through for the park itself and the other projects we're trying to get off the ground. Especially the performance space at the beach. That's going to be a heavy lift."

"The lecture series is a terrific idea," Lilly said. "Are you sure you'll have time, Delia? You won't even be living in Goosebush." Lilly took a sip of tea to get rid of the lump in her throat.

"I'm staying involved though," Delia said. "I'll make the time. This is the work that makes me really happy."

Lilly nodded and walked to the cookie table.

Warwick was talking to a cluster of parents, but when he saw Ernie replenishing the cookie tray he made his excuses and walked over to him.

"Ernie, rescue me," Warwick said. "The teams are all starting to practice next week, and the parents are out for me."

"I'm not sure how you manage them all. Lacrosse, soccer, and football all at the same time."

"Don't forget field hockey," Warwick said. "There

are three of us, but we could use some extra coaches, that's for sure. It's one of the reasons we need to make the rehab projects work as a fundraiser. Losing last Saturday at the dump was unfortunate, but some of the parent volunteers set up an ad hoc drop-off spot at that parking lot across from the dump, so we're on track with donations."

"That's great," Ernie said. "Once I got the text from Lilly—"

"Which text from Lilly?" Lilly said.

"Hello, Lil," Warwick said. He leaned over and gave her a kiss on the cheek.

"The text Saturday telling me what happened at the dump. I went right over to your house. Warwick said that some of the parents set up an ad hoc donation center, so they actually didn't lose too much ground."

"That's wonderful," Lilly said. "I didn't even notice that."

"I didn't either," Warwick said.

"Not surprised," Ernie said. "It must have been pretty awful."

"It was," Lilly said, lowering her voice. "Delia and I started talking about it more last night. We should all meet."

"Tonight? I have to get back to work. We're still understaffed. We're so busy these days I think I need to hire an assistant manager," Ernie said.

"That's great," Lilly said. "Maybe what's his name who's been working will be able to fit the bill?"

"Roger. And no, Roger has trouble balancing his cash draw."

"I may have a couple of ideas for you, Ernie. Dinner tonight works for me too," Warwick said. His phone buzzed, and he reached into his pocket to look at it. "Braden Dane has been texting me like a madman. He wants to talk to me about a donation he made to the project. I don't know what he's talking about. I have to meet him at the school to clear it up."

"What would he have donated?" Lilly said. "If it was from Harmon's house, he shouldn't have moved it out without checking with me first."

"Yeah, well I checked the donation slips folks filled out, and he isn't on the list, so I have no idea," Warwick said.

"Do you think that one of the volunteers screwed up?" Ernie said.

"No, the parents who took over are old hands at this event. Some of them don't even have kids in school anymore, but they love helping out. The donation slips are old school. Carbon copies, numbers added to them and to the piece, and signed by the donor. Usually Delia helps us get everything organized online, but it's under control so far. A couple of folks are down at the school sorting, and so far there aren't any extra pieces." said Warwick.

"Curious," Lilly said.

"Very. Which is why I'm heading down to the school to meet him. I'll report back."

"You know what I keep wondering?" Lilly asked. "How did Gladys get into the dump? Tamara said the gate was locked when she went in. But Gladys, and her killer, must have been there already, since Tamara heard the scream as soon as she let herself in. Did Gladys and her killer come in together? If

Gladys was already there, and she obviously was, how did she get in?"

"Listen, all good questions. But we're in public, and folks are beginning to stare," Ernie said. "Tell you what, I'll drive around the dump today on my way back to the store and see if there's any other way of getting in. I'll report back tonight. But for now, let me get some more cookies out here. You'd think folks hadn't eaten for days, for heaven's sake."

Ernie reached under the table and took out another tray of cookies.

"You know what I'm worried about, Lilly?" Warwick said. "I'm worried that Tamara had the only key to the gate, according to Bash. If she were the only person who could let folks in, and she heard the scream right after she got there—"

"It doesn't look good, does it?" Lilly said. "We'll figure this out. I'm also reaching out to Bash. I don't want him to make a serious mistake."

"We need to—" Warwick was cut off by three parents who wanted to discuss the practice schedule and Labor Day weekend. Lilly squeezed his forearm and walked away.

She took out her phone and sent him a text. *Talk to you later.*

"What do you think the three of them are hatching?" Tamara asked Delia. She took a sip of tea, and pointed to Lilly, Warwick, and Ernie clustered by the cookies.

"Lilly and I started making lists last night. Maybe they're talking about that?"

"Lists? About what happened Saturday?"

"Lilly also went over to the Dane house yesterday and her brain is whirring. You know how that is. She starts making different lists, and at some point, the holes in the lists get filled and cross-referenced, and somehow she figures it all out."

"She's always been like that. Able to connect dots and draw a picture no one else sees. That's what made her good at her business. And solving the occasional puzzle," Tamara said.

"She's really smart, but she's also intuitive. I don't have that skill. I wish I could be more like her."

"You are a good team. You both think alike, frighteningly so, and have very complementary skills," Tamara said. "You know, she's going to miss you. A lot."

"I'm going to miss her too," Delia said. She took a deep breath and looked over at the older woman.

"Tamara, can I tell you something? Between us?"

"Anything."

"I'm not sure I want to leave."

"Delia, that's—"

"I really should, though. That has always been the plan, you know? Alan trained me to follow in his footsteps, and I've tried, I really have. Even today, I liked giving that lecture. I think I'll be a good teacher. But—" Delia took a deep breath and blinked back some tears.

"But?" Tamara said, moving closer to Delia and taking her hand.

"I like working at the town hall and doing the research. I even like working with the historical society and on all the other projects around town.

I'm not a joiner, so that's a big deal. I know I can still do them, but it won't be the same if I'm living in Burlington."

"Do you want to live in Burlington?" Tamara asked quietly.

"I'm not sure," Delia said.

"You know, Delia, nothing is written in stone. You can change your mind. Make sure you're changing it for the right reason. That it's not because you're afraid. It's because you really want to take another path. One thing I know is that Lilly would love to have you stay. She's never going to say that aloud to you, so I'll say it for her."

Delia smiled. "Thanks, Tamara. Do you mind if maybe I call you later to talk some more? I need to mingle with folks a little."

"I don't mind at all," Tamara said. "And Delia? You'll be great no matter what you decide."

CHAPTER SIXTEEN

Lilly took another cookie and nibbled on it. It would be much healthier to go home and make a nice lunch, but Lilly hated leaving a party early. People were poring over the exhibits. A few of them asked Lilly questions, all of which she was able to answer. Not because she was especially smart, but because she lived with Delia and had heard about the project every day.

The head librarian came over to talk to Lilly about a potential fundraiser for the fall. Dot wondered if Lilly would be willing to host it at her home. An invitation to Windward would be a thrill for a lot of folks and would help ensure that the event would raise enough for the new reading room.

Lilly sighed. The reading room. Alan's will had left a small bequest to the library to create a reading room that included technology for small lectures. The bequest had been spent, and the room was booked solid. It was such a success that the library wanted to create other salons in different parts of the library. Meeting rooms with community access were the future.

But hosting a fundraiser? That felt like the seventh circle of hell closing in. Lilly looked over Dot's shoulder towards the front entrance. She saw Regan come in. A minute later she saw Lenny come in and walk over to the maps on the wall on the other side of the entrance.

"Dot, can you send me an email with a couple of dates and what exactly you're asking of me? I promise I'll get back to you by the end of the week," Lilly said.

"Thanks for considering it, Lilly," Dot said. "I've been working up the courage to ask you for weeks."

Lilly smiled at the other woman. Dot Robie had worked at the Goosebush Library for the past fifteen years and had been a huge reason the library had turned itself around. Lilly had been on the hiring committee and was one of the people who convinced the group to take a risk on a young woman with bold ideas.

"Lilly, I want some other people to start stepping up and supporting the library. Right now, we have you and a few other folks who are very generous. I'd like to expand that pool."

"Smart plan. Send me the email. Now, please excuse me, I need to go over and speak to someone."

"The email is in drafts, I'll hit send as soon as I get back to the office."

* * *

Lilly walked over to Lenny, who was still looking at the maps on the walls.

"Hi, Lenny," Lilly said. "I saw you looking at this map and couldn't resist the temptation to point out the person who drew it."

"Hi, Lilly. Person who drew it? Of course, there had to be an artist. I never really thought about that. Who drew it?"

Lilly pointed to the initials on the corner of the map. "My mother drew it."

"Your mother? I thought this was from way back in the day. I knew your mother, but I didn't know she was an artist."

"She loved drawing maps, gardens, and ground plans. Landscapes, but from the point of view of a bird."

"How accurate is this?" he asked. "Border wise?"

Lilly looked more carefully at the map. It was of the area near Swallow Point.

"I'd imagine it is pretty accurate. My mother prided herself on accuracy. I'd check with the assessor's office to be sure."

"Yeah, I was hoping to skip that step. Look at all that land. Those lots. One house per. It's really a shame."

"A shame? This area is one of the most densely populated in Goosebush."

"Could be more so. A couple of condo units could easily fit on each lot."

"Condo units?"

"Yes, or townhouses. Tasteful, but more people being able to live in the most coveted part of town. More people with a view. You've got to admit, that wouldn't be such a terrible thing."

"Are you thinking about building condos near Swallow Point, Lenny?"

"I'm always thinking, Lilly. Good to see you."

Lilly watched as he took his phone out and snapped a few pictures of the maps on the wall. He turned and smiled at her, and then headed back out the front door. Lilly waited until he was out of sight and then took her own camera out and took the same pictures.

The crowd had begun to thin and Lilly was helping clean up.

"Delia, go sit down and take a deep breath. Ernie and I can do this. You must be exhausted. You've been on for several hours now, and I know that isn't your normal mode of operation," Lilly said.

"You're right, Lilly. It's starting to hit me. How could you tell?" Delia asked.

"I've gotten to know you pretty well over the past few years. I can recognize your overwhelmed look pretty easily by now."

"I'm going to go down to the historical society office and put these artifacts away. I may hide out there for a while. Come find me when you're ready to go."

The artifacts had been put in four different exhibition boxes, all compartmentalized to protect them, and stacked on a small-hand trolley. Delia went over and double-checked that the boxes were secure before guiding it towards the elevator to the basement. It was a short trip but a long wait. The elevators in the building had to be retrofitted and were not sufficient to the demand. Dot Robie had plans to build a larger elevator shaft off the back of the building, which would protect its historic façade but modernize the infrastructure. Delia hoped that project happened sooner rather than later. As the Alden Park project grew in scope the need for more space to store and protect the artifacts was growing exponentially. Carrying things up and downstairs was taxing even for somebody as young as Delia.

When Delia got down to the office she was surprised that the door was open. She walked in and called out "Hello?" Normally the door was locked unless somebody was there, and since it was a volunteer-run organization staffing the office was not a priority. Still, most of the volunteers had been at the lecture so it was entirely conceivable that somebody was in the office catching up on some of the duties.

The office itself was large and generous in size even though it was getting cramped full of various sundry items. A large bookcase ran through the middle of the room blocking the back half from view as you walked in. An old library desk sat about six feet in front of the bookcases and ran the length of the room, blocking access to folks who walked in. That was where volunteers worked when during public visiting hours. The front part of the office was for visitors, with a large library table set out with several chairs where people could sit and browse. The table contained books about the history of Goosebush and a large portfolio with maps of the town from throughout its history. The maps were all replicas but were closely treasured, nonetheless.

Regan Holland was sitting at the table. She'd

taken a map out of the portfolio and was taking pictures of it with her phone.

"Regan, what are you doing?" Delia asked. She set the boxes down gently and walked over to the table. She wiped her hands on her skirt and picked up the map that Regan was looking at. She moved over towards the portfolio, turned it towards her, and put the map back while glaring at Regan. She flipped through the portfolio and noticed one map was missing.

"Where's this map?" Delia asked.

"What map?" Regan said.

Delia flipped to the front of the portfolio and looked at the table of contents. She flipped through again to make sure she was certain and then looked up at Regan.

"The map of Swallow Point."

"I have no idea what you're talking about. If a map's missing anyone could have taken it. Why are you blaming me?"

"Maybe because you're here and nobody else is, which shouldn't have happened—"

"The door was open."

"The map was there this morning. I saw it."

"Anyone could've taken it."

"It's also a very small map with torn edges. It looks a lot like the piece of paper that's sticking out of your planner." Delia gestured to the executive-size, leather-bound planner that Regan always carried with her.

Regan stared at Delia as if daring her to look in the binder. Regan's problem, and she couldn't really be blamed for this since she was new to Goosebush, was that she didn't understand that

Delia did not back down. Especially when she felt she was in the right.

Delia took her phone out of her pocket and scrolled through contacts.

"Who are you calling?" Regan asked.

"Security." Delia found the chosen number and hit call.

Regan blinked and looked down at her planner. "Oh my, you may be right." She slid the map from between the pages and tossed it towards Delia. Delia winced and picked it up protectively.

"Aren't these all replicas? Some of them are available to be ordered if folks want to have a print of them, right?"

"Some of them are, yes. But as you probably know this map isn't one of those."

"I can't imagine why not. Who makes those decisions anyway? You?"

"I don't know if it's as much a decision as it is a request. If you had come in and asked for a copy of this map, chances are really good we would've made that happen. But stealing it—"

"I wasn't stealing."

"It was in your planner and if I hadn't come down you would've left with it. That's stealing. Stealing isn't the way to get what you want, Regan."

"I wasn't stealing. I made a mistake. Prove otherwise."

"Here's the thing. I don't have to prove anything to you."

"Such a rule follower, Delia. Can I get a copy of this map of Swallow Point?"

"No. Besides, as whoever let you look at them

would have explained, these maps are not accurate in property lines or lots. They are artist interpretations, usually created to enforce someone's point of view."

"Dammit," Regan said. Delia watched as she took a deep breath and collected herself. "Listen, I'm really sorry about the map. It was a mistake, truly. I'm trying to find out information about Gladys's house, and more information about Swallow Point. What other information do you have on that area?"

"Regan, I'm not a resource librarian. The historical society isn't open. And I'm not on duty as the town clerk. Go upstairs and talk to somebody up there. I'm sure the library has information."

"They sent me down here."

"So, you decided to let yourself in and help yourself."

Regan stared at Delia. Spots of color were raised on her perfectly made up face and her neck was getting splotchy.

"I'll come back when you're open," Regan said.

"I'll let everyone know to expect you."

"Such a do-gooder, Delia. It must be exhausting. Would you mind a word of advice? You don't get far in this world by following the rules."

Delia watched her leave. After closing and locking the door, she scanned the room. How long had Regan been in there? Had she taken anything else? Delia noted with satisfaction that the gate to the pass-through of the old library reception desk was closed and locked. Of course, Regan could easily have scaled the desk but then she would've needed to know what she was looking for in the stacks, files, boxes and other assorted detritus that was the Goosebush Historical Society.

Delia put the Alden Park artifacts back where they belonged and took a deep breath. She went over to the computer, logged in, and typed "Swallow Point." She printed out the list of materials that came up and started to gather them.

"Whoa, Lil, let me get that for you." Warwick took the large trash bag out of Lilly's hands and picked up the second one by the tables. "Where do these go?"

"Out to the dumpsters in the back, if you don't mind," Lilly said. Ernie had gone back to his store and the volunteer ranks were getting more depleted.

"Be right back," Warwick said.

The security guard helped Lilly stack the last of the chairs on the dolly and then he took over closing down the rest of the tables. Lilly took the pile of tablecloths and put them in an empty trash bag to bring home and wash. Anyone else would've left them for the library to deal with, but that wasn't Lilly's way.

"What else?" Warwick said when he came in.

"I think we're done," Lilly said. "What do you think? Does it look like dozens of people were here eating cookies?"

"No, it looks pretty good," Warwick said. "Where's Delia?"

"She went down to relax for a minute. I'm going to go get her soon. Where's Tamara?"

"I'm not sure. There were a couple of folks who are interested in a house and Tamara was going to show them some of the information about the neighborhood that the library has."

"Is it one of her listings?" Lilly asked.

"If it isn't now it will be by the end of the day if she has anything to do with it. That is if Regan Holland hasn't gotten to the owners already."

"Regan is starting to have a presence here, isn't she?"

"Yeah, she is. At home I spend most of my time trying to convince Tamara that it's all going to be okay. That another real estate office in Goosebush isn't the end of the world."

"But?" Lilly asked gently.

"But. I've known people like Regan Holland my whole life. She thinks that the best way to move forward is to make everyone discontent with the status quo and then set herself up as the only way to change things for the better. I think she's dangerous, Lilly. I'm not sure what I mean by that yet. But I see her with Lenny Andrus all the time. I look at the way he's running his business now as opposed to how he was running it before she got here, and I have to shake my head. She's convinced him that he shouldn't be happy with the status quo and it's ruining his business."

"I'm not sure that's fair. He seems to be doing a good job of ruining his reputation on his own. If only he had stayed with renovation and hadn't gotten into new construction—"

"See, that's what I mean. Who put the idea of new construction into Lenny's head? He wasn't good at renovation, he was great at it. And from what I could tell he was making a decent living and supporting a few other folks at the same time. Now he's ruined his reputation with his existing customers by overextending himself in this new business."

Lilly nodded. "It would be interesting to see who put that bee in his bonnet."

"Tamara's reputation is solid. But even there, with Gladys's death Regan has been asking if Tamara is too distraught to do her work since she's the one who found the body. One of the assistant coaches came to me and told me that Regan was at the Star last night implying that Tamara may have had something to do with her death."

"Not really?" Lilly asked.

"Apparently she was trying to pass it off as a joke, but it perked up the coach's ears. Seeds of discontent. I'm telling you, she's bad news. What are we going to do about it?"

"Which part? There are a lot of seeds of discontent being sown around town," Lilly sighed. "I spent yesterday over at the Dane house and my brain is whirling. Delia and I talked about it last night and we'll talk about it some more today. Who killed Gladys is a mystery that needs to be figured out soon for everyone's sake. Especially if Regan is going to use the death as a lever against Tamara."

"I'm worried about her, Lil," Warwick said.

"So am I. As you said, Tamara's got a lot of goodwill in this town. I'd hate to have her spend it defending her honor because of rumors."

Warwick looked down at his watch and sighed. "I do need to get back over to the school and deal with Braden Dane, but I'm glad we had this chance to talk. Tell me what you need me to do, and you know I'll do it."

"Let me know how the conversation goes with Braden. If he says anything that gives you pause, make sure to text me."

"Thanks Lil, I will. I feel better knowing that you're taking everything in and processing it. The Lilly Jayne perspective is what this town needs." Warwick leaned over and gave Lilly a kiss on the cheek. She returned it and watched him go out the front door.

"Time to get to work," she said softly under her breath. She walked over to the elevators, hit the button, and waited.

CHAPTER SEVENTEEN

"**A**re you sure we should do this? Take all of these materials home?" Lilly asked. She put the bag of tablecloths Delia had handed her on the dolly. It was heavy, and Delia was fumbling with the locks on the historical society door after having set the alarm.

"No, I'm not. Maybe this is a reaction to Regan calling me a rule follower."

"You are a rule follower."

"Nevertheless. Can you believe Regan tried to steal that map?"

"I hate to think so little of somebody, but yes, I absolutely can believe it. You know, Lenny Andrus was looking at a map up in the lobby earlier today and asking specifically about Swallow Point and if I thought the map was accurate. I saw him and Regan both come in, but they came in separately."

Delia finally finished with the locks and looked up at her friend. "That could mean a couple of different things. One is that they were together but didn't want anyone to think they were together. The other is that they're both interested in Swallow Point but for different reasons."

The two women made their way down the hall, towards the elevators. Delia was pushing the handcart which was again piled high with exhibition boxes. Lilly was carrying her purse and the bag with the tablecloths.

When they got to the car Lilly sorted the boxes in the back, tossing a blanket over them while Delia returned the handcart and climbed into the driver's seat.

"Should we stop and get something for lunch?" Delia said, pulling out into traffic.

"I don't know about you, but I'm exhausted. We have so many leftovers, and I don't feel like talking to anyone. Let's go home, what do you say?"

"I agree. Stan asked me to stop by the store and let him know how it went, but I'll text him and see him later."

"I'm sorry he couldn't get anyone to cover for him at the café, so he could be there," Lilly said. Lilly tiptoed around the subject of Stan and Delia, never exactly sure where the relationship stood.

"I am too, but he made me promise I'd do it for him later." Delia smiled and a blush rose on her cheeks. "Besides, it sounds like there may be other lectures he can come to."

"I almost fell off my chair when you suggested more talks. Ernie and I had such a hard time talking you into delivering this lecture, I'm surprised you offered to give more."

"You've been a good influence on me, Lilly. I'm starting to think of others. The lectures may be a good way to start some fundraising for the park or the historical society or both."

"I think it's a wonderful idea, I don't want you to overextend yourself, particularly since you'll be living a good hour away. But we can talk about that more later. Tell me about what's in these boxes. You said you did a search on Swallow Point. What did you take with you?"

"Everything I could find," Delia said. She hit the button to open the gate and turned into their driveway.

After some discussion, Lilly and Delia decided to convert the dining room into a war room for the time being. Lilly put the thin board with the felt backing on top of the table to protect it. Her mother had kept the board on the dining room table all the time except when it was being used, which was on Sundays and holidays only. The breakfast room had been used for all other meals. Lilly had gotten out of the habit of putting the table protector on and made sure the room was used regularly. Boxes were not normal wear and tear for a dining room table, however, and Lilly felt certain her mother would haunt her if the table was scratched.

Lilly was in the kitchen heating up some left-overs while Delia unpacked the boxes. She knew better than to rush Delia in her process. Even though she insisted she was comfortable with bor-rowing the materials, Lilly knew that Delia was going to worry about them, so she left her to her own devices.

Her phone buzzed, and she looked down at the text. It was from Warwick. *Braden was a no show at the school. I gave him a call. He said he'd written a check as a donation, but he put a stop payment on it for now.*

Did he mean to write the check? Lilly texted back.

Yes, he stopped by Saturday to help, and wrote a check instead. A few folks did. I told him I'd rip up the check, and he shouldn't worry. I don't want to embarrass him, so I won't mention it to anyone but you.

Thanks, I'll hold the information close. Lilly couldn't figure Braden out. She wondered if he knew the check would bounce, or if she'd expected that it wouldn't by the time Warwick deposited it. More to think about.

Lilly was putting spoons into the bowls of salads when she felt her phone buzz with another incoming text. She wiped her hands on her apron and pulled her phone out of her pocket.

The gate is closed. Can you open it? I'd love to come in.

The text was from Bash Haywood.

Of course, Lilly texted back. Before she walked over to push the button and open the gate she opened the swinging door into the dining room.

"Delia, Bash is here. I'm going to invite him to lunch. I'm going to close up the dining room and I'll tell him you're working. I'll turn up the AC, so you don't suffocate. We'll eat out on the porch or in the kitchen."

"You don't think he's here because—"

"Because you borrowed some materials from the library? Don't be ridiculous. I texted him yesterday. He's probably here because of that."

Lilly walked over to the panel by the kitchen door and hit the GATE OPEN button. She opened the side door into the kitchen so that he could let himself in.

"We need to talk," Bash told Lilly when he walked in to the kitchen.

"Nice to see you too," Lilly said. "I hope you're hungry. We've got a ton of leftovers and I'm gathering up an ad hoc meal. Delia's doing some research, so she's holed up in the dining room."

"I'm starving. Here, let me help you with that tray. Where's it going?"

"Your choice. Here in the kitchen, or on the porch."

"The kitchen is fine with me. In fact, it's the best place for you and me to talk business. I always feel like the porch is a more social visiting location."

"Business? What business?" Lilly asked. When Bash didn't respond, she went on. "Fair enough. Iced tea or water?"

"Water's great. Let me get it."

For the next few minutes Bash and Lilly worked side-by-side gathering plates, utensils, food, napkins, and a pitcher of water. Bash had visited Lilly countless times over the years and felt very much at home in her kitchen. In fact, when she was considering renovating it a year or so ago he was one of the groups of friends she conferred with about the layout. He'd advocated for the big kitchen table, and she'd been glad she listened. Her house had a breakfast room and a dining room, so her family had never eaten in the kitchen. But she found the informality of that space suited her more now as she got older. She was considering offering to make the breakfast room into another library area that Delia could use, but now that she was moving out the idea didn't seem to make much sense. Perhaps she'd go through the process anyway to keep herself occupied over the next few weeks after Delia moved out.

Lilly shook herself away from her thoughts and turned towards Bash.

"Let's sit," Lilly said. "I'm glad you're here. It feels like forever since we've caught up."

"Now, Lilly, don't play that game with me. I'm surprised I haven't gotten a dozen texts or even a visit from you since Saturday."

"I've decided to stay out of it." Lilly spooned some coleslaw onto her plate and passed the bowl to Bash. "Of course, I'd change my mind if you arrested Tamara."

"Not planning on it. Whoever hit Gladys would have had blood spatter all over them. And the faucet she was holding wasn't the murder weapon. We don't know what was. May never know, but they're working on it. Blunt instrument, like a baseball bat. Can't imagine there's a better place to get rid of a murder weapon than a dump. Never mind the woods and pond on the other side."

Conversations about murder and blood spatter did not curb Bash's appetite. He set the coleslaw aside and then took the potato salad from her and heaped it on his plate. Bash was a big fan of Lilly's potato salad and he considered making that his entire meal until he saw the tray of cold cuts and leftover barbecue that she passed to him.

"Did you ever figure out how Gladys and her killer got into the dump?" Lilly asked.

Bash took a sip of water. "That took us a while since the security of the dump was a project we'd all taken on. During a perimeter search we found a hole in the fence. Less of a hole, and more of a piece of fencing that had been cut out and was replaced so as folks wouldn't notice it. We also found Gladys's bike out there, so it seems reasonable to assume that's how she got in."

"What is it, like a hidden gate?"

"Yup. Seems like several folks use it to dump their trash or pick through recycling off hours."

"Really? Was Gladys one of those people?"

"More than likely. Have you been in her house lately?"

"No, why?" Lilly poked at her potato salad and took a small bite. She didn't like to discuss murder over lunch, but she didn't want to stop Bash.

"It's packed. Floor to ceiling. Stuff. Not magazines or newspapers. Stuff like potential valuables, or things she was trying to fix up and sell. Seems like a lot of it came from pickings at the dump."

"Who else knew about it?"

"The hole in the fence? No idea. But that's how folks got in. Past tense. We're closing it up."

"You know she had planned to meet Tamara there. I wonder why?"

"Another thing I don't know about. She didn't have a purse with her, and there wasn't one at her house or in her car. Her pockets were empty. No phone either."

"More questions than answers."

"That's for sure. Let me change the subject for a minute. I hear that you set up some cameras outside Harmon Dane's house. Any chance I could see the footage?"

"Of course. I'll have Delia send you the web links and passwords. But we only set them up Sunday, so I'm not sure how much help they'll be. What are you looking for?"

"Comings and goings."

"We didn't set the cameras up to see down the lane, only to see the house," Lilly said. Bash looked disappointed, so she went on. "They could be repositioned. Easily. I hate to invade on Alex's privacy, but I know that these are not normal times. Talk to Ernie, he can give you the exact locations. Or I can talk to him if you'd rather. Are you looking for anything in particular?"

"I'm not sure," Bash said. "I'm doing my best to make sure I have all my bases covered. In all areas."

"What do you mean?" Lilly asked. She picked up a roll and nibbled the corner.

"After what happened in May I decided to learn a little bit more about forensics. I've been sending some of my findings to the lab; in walking them through, I hope to see how the systems work for processing evidence. I want to understand how to detect a crime, in addition to how to solve them. We haven't had much call for a lot of lab work in Goosebush, so I needed to brush up," Bash said.

Lilly nodded and took another bite of the roll. She'd let Bash tell her things in his own fashion. If she rushed him or tried to get information out of him she knew that he'd clam up.

"I don't want you to take this the wrong way, but I had the lab run some tests run on Harmon

Dane," Bash said quietly. He stopped eating and turned to look at Lilly.

"Harmon? Why? Did you think something out of the ordinary had happened to him? That it wasn't a heart attack?"

"I didn't think anything, but since he died at home they had to do an autopsy and I figured they might as well run some other tests. I didn't expect them to find anything. I figured once I got the results I could go in and talk to a friend of mine who would walk me through them and explain what they found. You know me. I've never been good at straight book learning. I learn best when I've got examples in front of me. Anyway, they ran some tests and I got a call this morning. Some of the numbers were off."

Lilly took a large sip of water to wash down the bread that had turned into concrete in her mouth.

"Off?" she said quietly.

"Apparently, the ME compared the numbers with some blood tests he had taken a few months ago, to double-check. He was on a bucket full of medications, you know that. But it looks like the pills stopped working before he died. The test results don't make sense."

"Maybe they do," Lilly said. "I was there yesterday, at Harmon's house. This has nothing to do with Gladys, so far as I know anyway. I found some concoctions that Harmon had been drinking." She told Bash about her visit to the Dane house and included information about the teas in Harmon's house, presumably from Miranda.

"Do you have the teas?" he asked.

"I do. Dawn Simmons—"

"The bird professor."

"Right. Dawn made some and took a sip. It made her heart jump. She was going to toss it, but I stopped her. I'm still not sure what I'm thinking but I decided to take the teas with me. Dawn is boxing everything up for you. I also walked by Miranda's house and took some pictures of her gardens. Did you know that she's drying herbs and making different oils and tea blends?"

"That I did know. Stella's a big fan of her stuff. Our house smells like a spa these days." Bash took a sip and smiled. Bash groused about Stella as a big brother might, but Lilly knew that he was proud of her. He'd been more of a father to her since their parents had died, and he'd spent many hours talking to Lilly about his concerns, especially during her teenage years. Lilly knew he'd happily live with Stella's latest hobby as long as it made his sister happy. "She's got all kinds of contraptions tossing out different scents throughout the house. She's trying to get me to roll some oil on my wrists every morning, but so far I've resisted. She insists it's going to help me de-stress. Maybe I should give it a try, even if it makes me smell like your garden. No offense."

"There's a lot going on, that's for sure. What are you going to do about Harmon?"

"Between the tests and the teas, it seems like an investigation is in order, don't you think?" Bash said.

"I do, I definitely do. As the executor of his estate I'll do everything I can to support you in doing the investigation."

"Yeah, that's going to be helpful. I can't imagine

Miranda Dane is going to look kindly on this line of inquiry. We'll be opening a can of worms, but I say let's open the can. Harmon was a good guy. I hate to think anything bad happened to him on my watch."

"I'm not sure why this popped up in my brain, but do you think that his death had anything to do with Gladys's?"

"Normally I'd say no, but given those houses and the fact that a development company mentioned Swallow Point condos in a proposal recently, I'm not sure."

"A development company? Who?"

"I'm not sure," Bash said. "The project wasn't specifically for Goosebush but was bundled in a package for several interrelated projects. A friend over in Marshton gave me the heads-up this morning."

"It would be interesting to find out who is involved in that project," Lilly said.

"It would, and I'm looking into it. It's been surprisingly difficult to track the information, but I've got some calls in. Here's another tidbit, not for public consumption. I hear that Lenny Andrus applied for a loan and used Alex Marston as a reference. I started doing some digging around, and it turns out the two of them have started an LLC for a real estate development company. Not the same one associated with Swallow Point, but still. They're working on a project down in Providence and had to file a lot of paperwork. I made a couple of calls and a friend sent me the prospectus on their company. I can't help but wonder if their company and this other one aren't related somehow."

"Have you talked to Alex?"

"Not yet. Gathering facts. I hadn't planned on this particular path of inquiry, but it didn't take me long to follow it. I've got a couple of calls out to folks, looking for more background. I'm not sure what it has to do with anything, but I figure it needs to be added to the mix. Don't you?"

"I do, absolutely," Lilly said. Her fingers itched to grab a notebook and start writing things down, but she forced herself to stay still. She didn't want Bash to stop talking. "I'm changing the topic slightly. Do you know about the problems Tamara has been having with open houses at the Dane house? I've been wondering if Gladys was behind the problems, since the open house last Sunday went off without a hitch. But now I wonder."

"Do you think the sabotaged open houses had anything to do with her death?" Bash said.

"I don't know. Maybe Gladys found out something. At the last town hall meeting she voted against Lenny's proposal for turning two houses into four. I saw them having a huge fight in the parking lot and then she drove away with Alex Marston."

Bash took out his notebook and wrote. "I don't suppose you heard what they were saying?"

"I don't remember. I don't think I could hear them clearly. I saw her afterwards at the Star."

"Where she and Tamara had a knock-down-drag-out fight."

"It wasn't that bad, more of an argument. Tamara told you about it."

"I have other sources that told me it was a lot more than that."

"Let me guess who the other source is. Regan Holland?"

"I can't tell you that," Bash said, though the blush creeping up on his neck let Lilly know she was right.

"Regan has it out for Tamara," Lilly said.

"Now Lilly," Bash said.

"Don't you 'now Lilly' me," she said. "I'm not being paranoid, and neither is Tamara. There's something off about that woman."

Bash looked over at Lilly. He wasn't used to that tone in her voice. In fact, he wasn't sure he'd ever heard it before.

"She's always been nice to me."

Rather than dwelling on Regan's character or lack thereof, Lilly changed subjects. "Did you check on Gladys's house to see if Lenny took anything?"

"What are you talking about?"

"I called you last night. I walked by and Lenny was coming out of Gladys's house. I asked him what he was doing there, and he said he'd been looking for something. I didn't search him to see if he had anything, but I did let him know it wasn't a good idea to go to a crime scene without your permission. He gave me his key to pass on to you."

Bash pulled out his phone and looked at it.

"Dammit, I hate this phone. It doesn't let me know when I have voicemails, so I must have missed it." He dialed in and listened to the message now. Hers must not have been the only one since he listened for a while. He swore softly under his breath.

"At least you don't ignore my texts."

Bash blushed. "I'm going to go over and look at

Gladys's house. I was going to do it anyway. Do you still have that key?"

"I do," Lilly said. She stood up and got it for him.

"I'm surprised you didn't let yourself in and look around."

"Who do you think I am? Besides, Lenny told me he reset the alarm," Lilly said.

"What alarm?" Bash asked.

Lilly kicked herself for not taking the opportunity when it was in front of her. Maybe she shouldn't have mentioned the key. "If I'd known you were ignoring my call I probably would've let myself in and looked around."

"I'm sorry, Lilly. It will never happen again, I promise." Bash looked miserable, so Lilly took pity on him.

"I hate to think I'm a bother to you is all, Bash."

"Far from a bother. I don't know what I'd do without you being a sounding board, I really don't," Bash said. "Ray's great, but he quotes rules and regulations before I've fully formed an idea. Doesn't allow for a lot of creativity. Anyway, I'm really sorry I missed the call."

"You're forgiven, Bash. Always."

"Thanks, Lilly. I'll check in later, I promise."

Lilly smiled at the younger man, and she saw him relax in relief.

"Let me get you a bag of cookies. Don't say no. We have more cookies than the bakery does, and I hate to see them go to waste."

CHAPTER EIGHTEEN

Lilly sent Bash off with the teas she'd taken from Harmon's house. She also made him a care package of cookies to help him through the day. She stood by the kitchen door waving good-bye until he pulled out of the driveway. As soon as he was gone she hit the button again, and the gate closed. She wasn't certain why, but she felt the need for added security.

She walked into the dining room where Delia was still pulling things out of boxes and assembling them in her own specific way. Lilly had learned long ago not to try and help Delia when she was unpacking and going through materials. Everyone had their strengths and Delia's was sorting and culling through research. Lilly's was taking Delia's research and being able to make connections between disparate pieces of information. They weren't at the connection phase yet. Lilly was certain that Delia would find a place to start. She looked forward to Delia walking her through the research.

"I hate to throw you off even a little bit, but I'd like you to stop for second and let me tell you about my visit with Bash."

"Just for one second?"

"You're right, of course. When you have a moment come into the kitchen and grab some lunch. I'm going to go up and get my phone cable and my laptop. I want to download the pictures I took yesterday."

She went up and grabbed the two items from her bedside table. Web surfing in bed was a bad habit she'd gotten into. She knew that working on her laptop at night wasn't good for her sleep, but she also knew that if she didn't write things down or look things up when she thought of them, they'd bother her. That was worse for her sleep.

She and Delia had set up a system of files and folders so that they could add comments to their shared notes. That would ensure they were on the same page and not duplicating efforts. The conversations they had in the comment sections of some files were funny since often they added comments while they were both sitting in the same room. Delia insisted that the written record would be helpful when assessing their work. At first Lilly had regretted not having live conversations, but now she was grateful that they'd set up this system. It would be useful when Delia was no longer living at Windward, but they still wanted to collaborate.

When she went back into the kitchen Delia was sitting at the table, a notebook on one side and a plate on the other.

"You don't have anything to drink. What can I get you? I'm going to have some more water."

"There's some fresh iced tea in the refrigerator," Delia said.

"Is that what that was? The pale, yellow hue—I thought for a moment it might be lemonade, but I took a smell and it is definitely not lemonade."

"No, not lemonade. It's a mixture of some herbs I've been growing," said Delia. "All healthy, all natural. Dandelion greens boiled with some rosemary and—"

"I'll stick with water, but I'll get you a glass of your concoction. Speaking of which . . ." While Lilly got their drinks, she filled Delia in on what Bash told her about the tests he had done on Harmon.

"I gave Bash the teas I brought from Harmon's house. I'd hoped you'd taken some samples already."

"I did but I haven't had a chance to look at them yet. I wish I'd taken pictures of the labels."

"I did that before I gave them to him. Pictures and a video."

"Did he know you were doing that?"

"No, he was busy having seconds for lunch."

"What did he have to say about your finding Lenny coming out of Gladys's house?"

Lilly set Delia's tea down in front of her and sat down with her glass of water. "He missed my call. He's heading over there now."

"Missed your call? What the heck? Do you think he's ignoring you or he really missed it?"

"I'm hoping he really missed it. I hate to think he's ignoring me."

"Maybe he's not ignoring you intentionally. He may feel compelled to try to do this investigation on his own. You know, solve what happened to Gladys. Everyone knows you're the one who figured out what happened to Merilee. If it wasn't for you Pete Frank would be in jail right now."

"My intention was never, is never, to outshine Bash. It's only that if I see something not quite right I feel it's my civic duty to set it straight. Is that wrong?"

"Not at all. You're a fixer, Lilly. That's what makes you so wonderful."

"We're all fixers. You, Ernie, Tamara, Warwick."

"And Roddy," Delia said.

"I'm not sure about Roddy yet. He's a hard one to read."

"I trust him," Delia said. "You should too."

"Of course I trust him, but I can't imagine why. I've only known him for a few weeks. But he is a good neighbor, thankfully," Lilly said.

"He is. He's got interesting information to add to conversations, that's for sure. I'm glad he's part of the group."

"We're a team, and we work together. Splendidly, I might add. Speaking of which, I think we should have a team meeting here tonight. Should we invite folks over for dinner? I think we can make do with the leftovers."

"I'll defrost some sauce and make some pasta too."

"Don't you think it's a little hot for pasta?" Lilly asked.

"Tamara loves my sauce and given everything

that's going on I want to make sure she has access to a meal that makes her happy."

"That's an excellent thought," Lilly said. "I'll text folks and invite them over. We have a lot of catching up to do about the last couple of days, never mind anything they've been up to. What do you think the best way for us to proceed is?"

"I've been thinking about that," Delia said. "I think we should take a long roll of paper and put it on the wall. The whiteboard isn't big enough. That can be our timeline. We'll use Post-its for different pieces of information. Facts can be on yellow Post-its. We'll use other colors for information we need to verify or for what we need to determine where it fits in."

"Should we add the Harmon Dane questions to the mix?"

"Absolutely. I'm not sure how, or if, his death fits in with Gladys's, but we need to explore it all, don't you think?"

"I do. One factor that seems to tie into a lot of these conversations is money."

"We can write money questions on green Post-its. What kinds of questions are you thinking about?"

"Who's in business with whom? Who needs money? Does Miranda's herb work support her? Who did Gladys owe money to? Where is Lenny getting his money? Who, if anyone, is Regan in business with?"

"Sounds like a good place to start. Real estate is another thread we'll need to follow. Anyway, the dining room is going to be offline tonight with the Swallow Point information."

"Why don't you plan on using the breakfast room, so we don't lose the use of the dining room, but you can keep working. I can help you move items if that's helpful. We might as well turn it into a war room of sorts. We'll keep the kitchen for eating." Lilly took a long sip of water and reached for a cookie.

Delia looked to her friend and took a sip of her iced tea. She'd never admit it to Lilly, but it was terrible. She cleared her throat.

"Lilly, could I talk to you about something? I've been thinking—" she stopped talking when her phone buzzed at the same time Lilly's did. It was a text from Tamara to both of them.

Let me in. It's an emergency.

Lilly got up and quickly hit the gate button to open it again and stepped out the kitchen door to meet her friend.

"Are you okay?" Lilly asked anxiously as her best friend stomped up the stairs into the kitchen.

"I'm beside myself. I needed somewhere safe to go where I could let off some steam. You won't believe what happened."

"Sit down, Tamara. What happened? Have you had anything to eat? We haven't put lunch away yet. What can I get you to drink?" Lilly asked.

"I had a brokers' open house this afternoon. A sweet Cape over on the west side of town. The house will go fast on the market, but I was hoping to get some broker interest to help launch it. Anyway, I showed up an hour before the open house.

The owners are on vacation, which is why this was perfect timing. I walked in and the whole house smelled like rotten fish."

"Oh no, not again," Delia said. "Had the owners left some garbage and forgotten to take it out?"

"I was there early this morning before I went to the library and it was perfect. I'd even left one of the windows in the mudroom open to air that space out and then I turned up the AC before I left. Someone left rotten fish in one of the closets upstairs and in the china cabinet in the dining room. They'd also shut down the AC."

"Any idea who?" Lilly asked.

"None. I put an emergency call in to Warwick and he came over and helped me pull it together. I'm going to head back over in a while to make sure we've got everything. Maybe I'll try and ask the neighbors if they saw anything, but I doubt it. The lots are pretty private."

"Did you cancel the open house?" Delia asked.

"Almost, but I decided not to. I did my best to air it out and got the AC going and then I told everyone what happened. What's been happening. I asked if anyone else has had their open houses sabotaged, but they all said no."

"Was Regan there?" Lilly asked.

"She was. Butter wouldn't melt in that woman's mouth. Acted all shocked. I'll tell you what, though. I stared right at her as I was telling the story. She looked away. Everyone else was incredibly supportive and ticked off on my behalf. I noticed that Regan got a side eye from a couple of people. I hate to sound petty but that made me feel great. Ends up I'm not the only one who doesn't like her."

"Has she been stepping on other people's toes in other towns?"

"I got a sense yes, but no details. Yet. I suspect folks will be reaching out. Anyway, I thought I'd come by and talk to you both about this. Because you'd let me vent. Also, it seems like rotten fish on the west side of town is an important development, isn't it? Maybe it wasn't the Dane house that was being targeted, it was me."

Lilly pushed the plate of cookies towards Tamara and was happy when her friend picked one up.

"I'm not sure what to think, truth be told. There's a lot of different facts coming at us. Delia and I were talking about the best way to lay out everything and see what may connect to what."

"I'm going to try to have everything set up in the next couple of hours," Delia said. "Can you come over for dinner? You and Warwick? I'm going to defrost some sauce—"

"You don't need to say anything else," Tamara said. "If that sauce doesn't fix things I don't know what will. I'll text Warwick and tell him what the plan is."

"I'll text Ernie and Roddy and let them know as well," Lilly said. She took out her phone and sent a short group text.

"May as well have all hands on deck," Tamara said. She looked up at Lilly. "Lilly, would you drive with me over to the house? I know it's odd, but I don't want to go there alone."

"That's not odd at all. Let me go upstairs and freshen up a bit, and I'll be right with you. Delia, text me a shopping list if you think of anything.

We'll stop by the store on our way home. Will that be okay with you, Tamara?"

"Fine with me."

"Can we make one more stop while we're out?" Lilly asked. "I want to stop by one of Lenny Andrus's work sites."

"We can go anywhere you'd like. Why do you want to visit one of his sites?" Tamara asked.

"I haven't actually seen any of the houses he's building," Lilly said.

"Is that the only reason?" Tamara asked.

"I'll tell you on the drive over," Lilly said as she stood and put her glass in the sink. She walked over to the table to start to clear but Delia stopped her.

"You go upstairs, Lilly, and I'll catch Tamara up on what we've been doing" Delia said.

CHAPTER NINETEEN

"**Y**ou mind if we go over to the Cape first? I'm worried about getting that house back into shape," Tamara said. The two women sat in front of her very comfortable SUV, and Tamara pulled out of the driveway.

"Not at all," Lilly said. Delia had handed her a bag on the way out of the house, and Lilly looked into it now. "Delia sent us out with provisions. You want a bottle of water?"

"I'd love one," Tamara said. She took the glass bottle and pulled up the straw, taking a long sip. "Do you remember those cozies our mothers had back in the day that they put around those aluminum cups? That kept your hands dry when condensation built up?"

"I do, vaguely. Weren't they stretchy terrycloth?"

"Those are the ones. I wish they still sold them. I love that Delia sent us out with glass bottles, but I hate that they sweat. Puddles everywhere."

"You know, I bet I could knit something. Maybe with cotton yarn." Lilly took out her phone and made a note to herself to try it out.

"What else did she put in the bag? I'm suddenly famished. I should have eaten."

"Apples, more cookies, some almonds. And the shopping list, I think." Lilly took out the sheets of paper that Delia had included in the bag and unfolded them. They weren't a shopping list.

"What's that?" Tamara asked.

"I'm not sure if we should have this or not, but Delia included a list of all of the building permits currently pulled in town. Lenny's listed on what looks like half of them."

"That's handy. Where's the house site you wanted to visit?" Tamara said.

"Linda Lane. That's the site he was trying to get permission for to take two lots and change them into four at the last town meeting, remember?"

"I do. We'll definitely head over there. Read me the other addresses on the list."

Lilly did so, and Tamara pursed her lips and furrowed her brow in concentration.

"You know, most of those are pretty close by Linda Lane. We could drive by some of them on our way. We'll spend a couple of minutes mapping out a plan. But first, let's see if the fish smell has dissipated from my client's house."

As they drove up to the Cape house Lilly smiled. Tamara had been right. It was lovely. The gardens perfectly suited the house, with an English country edge that added to the charm. Lilly always admired gardeners who planned their gardens to suit their houses rather than themselves. She was not one of those gardeners. Granted, the gardens in the front of her house suited her house, but they had become Delia's domain. The back gardens were all hers and only matched the house in their scope and eclectic charm.

When they walked into the front hall they both stopped and took deep breaths through their noses.

"You smell fish?" Tamara asked.

"I'm sorry, I do."

"That's why I brought you with me. I've got the smell so stuck in my nose that I can't be sure. Let's do a walk through the house and make sure nothing else is hiding. I'll get the cleaners in here to do a deep clean. We'll leave the air conditioning on since that will probably help too."

"Are you going to tell the family?"

"I already did. I also told them that I'd pay for their electric bill this month since I am going to keep the AC running. They were very understanding. Happily, a couple of brokers showed real interest and I'm arranging tours before the official sale date Friday. If it all works out I may have the house sold before they get back from vacation."

"That would be nice for them."

"That would be nice for me too," Tamara said. "A real morale booster. The last few weeks have been tough."

The two women walked through the house. Lilly's keen sense of smell indicated exactly where the fish had been found earlier. They didn't find anything else amiss. They went down to the first floor and double-checked that all the windows were locked. Tamara triple-checked to make sure that the front door was locked before they got back into the car.

"Let me see that list," Tamara said. She took out a felt pen and wrote numbers on the houses. "We can go to these three houses on the way to Linda Lane, and then we'll see how we're doing on time."

"Do you have to get back to the office?" Lilly asked.

"No, Pete's in there watching over things. I told him to stay in touch and let me know if anyone called. My only time issue is that I'd love to get a nap in before dinner tonight."

"I'd like that too, so let's see how it goes."

They drove by the first two work sites. There were LENNY ANDRUS COMPANY signs in the front yards. For the most part, aside from a large hole somewhere in the property there didn't seem to be any activity. No workers, no piles of materials, no machinery.

At the third site, they noticed the owner out in the front of the house as they drove up. Tamara stopped the car and rolled down her window.

"Beth, how are you? It's Tamara O'Connor." Beth came over and leaned on the side of the car. Tamara introduced her to Lilly, who nodded.

"We're okay, how about you?" Beth said.

"Hanging in. Are you doing work on your house? I noticed the sign in the front yard."

"Oh Tamara, what a nightmare this has been. Back in April we hired Lenny to put an addition on the house. A family room and garage with a mother-in-law apartment over the garage. It all looked good. He dug the foundation right away, but then there were holdups. He finally got back to the work in early July and got the gas line and electricity conduits ready to go. He told us the work would need to be inspected. Since then we're stalled. He has one excuse after another. Inspectors cancelling. Work having to be done to bring it up to code. No workers. Supplies not in on time. He'll send a couple of people over every few days to measure and tweak, but nothing is getting done. Unless he's building it off site somewhere and planning on flying it in I don't how it's going to get done by Christmas. That's when we planned on my mother moving in."

"The addition sounds like a great idea. It will add a lot of value to your house. This neighborhood is hot, so it's a great investment. I'm sorry that the construction is delayed. That's always so frustrating. Maybe there's another builder you could talk to?"

"Would that we could. Lenny's got our money," Beth said.

"All of it, before the job was done?" Tamara asked.

Beth nodded. "We trusted him. We've known Lenny for years. Plus, there's a contract. We can't get out of it unless he doesn't deliver the project by November 1. So, we live in hope, with a huge hole in our yard."

Tamara dug a card out of the side pocket of her car and handed it to Beth. "Keep me posted. I'm not sure what I can do to help but I can check on things if you need me to."

Beth took the card and waved it. A genuine smile came across her face. "Tamara, thank you. This project almost caused a divorce. We're so frustrated that Fred and I fight all the time. I'll definitely keep you posted."

"Hang in there, Beth. These sorts of things are always stressful."

"You said it. It was great to see you. My best to Warwick. And nice to meet you, Lilly."

"When I've got more time, I'll come over and you can show me the plans. As I said it really sounds like a great idea," said Tamara.

The two women drove away. Lilly looked back and Beth gave her a wave. Lilly waved back.

"What do you think?" Lilly said.

"Hard to say. It's a pretty straightforward project. Conceivably he could get it done by November 1. But if he started in April it seems like there should be a lot more movement by now. Those other two sites didn't look any further along."

"If anything, the other two sites look less done."

"Who knows what the other two projects are, but those three projects alone will keep most companies hopping, especially a company the size of Lenny's. The next right is Linda Lane. Let's see what's up there."

On Linda Lane, it wasn't hard to figure out what the project was. The short dead-end street only had five houses on it and two of them had been demolished. The debris was still mounted on the two lots. There were no workmen at the site. No dumpsters. No construction trailers. Just two demolished houses.

Tamara had slowed down to look at them and then when they went around the cul-de-sac she handed Lilly her phone.

"Take some pictures, will you? This isn't right. From what Lenny said at the town meeting the lots were ready to go. Obviously, that's not the case. I can't even imagine what the neighbors think. This has to be a health hazard. I need to talk to the board of selectmen about this. If we're going to give folks permits it seems like there should be more follow-up."

"I agree. It feels like the town needs a couple more staff people to keep up with all of this, don't you think? Especially with Delia leaving."

"Yes, to more staff. In the meantime, maybe you should try and talk Delia into staying since she does the work of three people."

"Much as I'd like it, no," Lilly said. "She's got to have her own career and her own life. I can't stand in her way. I'm going to miss her. Given everything that's going on, it seems like Goosebush is going to miss her just as much."

Lilly and Tamara drove by one more site on their way back to Lilly's house. It looked the same as the others. Rather than go home Tamara accepted Lilly's offer to use the guest room at Windward. When they got home, Delia was immersed in research, and told them she wasn't ready for them yet. They both went up to take brief naps.

Lilly took a quick shower before she went back downstairs. August heat wore her out and she typically went through a couple of dresses a day. She'd never admit it, but she was grateful that Alan had talked her into putting air-conditioning throughout the house. They didn't use it often but this August they'd needed it to get rid of the humidity if nothing else. She ran a comb through her hair and put her earrings back on. That was the extent of her beauty routine these days.

When Lilly walked into the kitchen Tamara was already there. She was chopping vegetables and arranging them on a plate. Delia was making a spinach dip. Both women had a glass of wine in front of them. Lilly smiled. Tamara looked more relaxed than she had in days.

"Did you have a nice nap?" Lilly asked Tamara. She got herself a wine glass and went to the refrigerator to take out the bottle.

"I was telling Delia that the guest room bed is the most comfortable thing I've ever slept on. Every time I take a nap here I sleep like the dead. I need Warwick to go up and check it out. We need a new mattress. What we really need is a bigger bed, but we can't get one up those stairs in our house."

"That is a tough staircase," Delia said. "I love that your house is so historically accurate, but it does make it challenging for modern conveniences."

"That's one way to put it. You wouldn't mind if it was truly a historical house, but it isn't. It's a replica. It's charming and has served us well. We raised our kids there. But lately? It must be lovely to live in a house where you don't worry about hitting your head as you walk down the stairs."

"Well, you and Warwick could always move in here," Lilly joked.

"Don't kid around Lilly," Tamara said. "Warwick would love to have a place where he could entertain. Of course, that would mean we'd have to cook, so maybe we should focus on being guests for a while."

There was a knock at the kitchen door and Lilly walked over to open it. Ernie was standing there alongside Roddy. They both carried bags with them.

"I saw Roddy struggling down the driveway, so I gave him a lift," Ernie said. "Delia, let's look at that garden door lock again. I don't have a lot of time these days, but maybe I can reach out to some folks and see if they can help us figure it out. Not that I'm advocating an open-door policy, but when a man is bringing you bags of food, you want to make it easy on him."

"Bags of food? Roddy you're a man after my own heart," Tamara said.

"I eat here so often I felt it was time to help replenish your larder," Roddy said. "I went into Boston this morning and stumbled on an amazing cheese shop. I brought some of those with me and some nice fresh bread. I also brought a couple of bottles of wine. I don't know about all of you, but these days it's so bloody hot that wine, fruit, and cheese are all I want."

"One of my favorite meals. We think alike, Roddy. I brought some prosciutto and other charcuterie items," Ernie said.

"I was going to make some ravioli and sauce, but maybe we don't need it?" Delia said.

"Delia, we always need your pasta and sauce. Unless it's too much trouble?" Tamara said.

"No trouble at all," Delia said. "This meal will be easy. I'll wait to put the pasta on until Warwick's here, though."

"I'm here!" Warwick said, letting himself into the kitchen. He carried a bag as well. "I brought desserts."

For the next few minutes the six friends bustled around the kitchen putting cheese and meats on plates, cutting bread, making a salad, opening wine, and enjoying a few brief moments of inconsequential small-talk.

"Why don't we go out to the porch to eat?" Delia said. "I've commandeered the dining room and I've turned the breakfast room into an office of sorts. The fans are going out there and hopefully it will be cool enough for us to eat."

Everyone settled on the back porch, with plates full of assorted wonders. Ernie opened a bottle of wine and served.

"What's news?" he asked.

"Could we not talk about murder or anything else upsetting while we're eating?" Warwick said.

"I agree," Lilly said. "I have something else for us to talk about. This is in the Garden Squad realm."

She told everyone about the overgrown rosebushes that were blocking traffic over by Swallow Point. "We'll need to do some more reconnaissance and figure out who owns the roses, but we should plan on doing some pruning. They're a real hazard."

"Do you ever think we'll be able to do this work in the light of day?" Ernie asked. "Pruning roses at night on a main road sounds tricky, even to me."

"You know, we could make this a Beautification Committee project. We have that luncheon tomorrow. We can add that to the agenda," Delia said.

"I forgot about that," Lilly said. "Where are we meeting again?"

"Here," Delia said. "Don't worry, I've ordered sandwiches. I'll get the dining room cleaned out and move everything to the breakfast room tonight. We'll keep it locked. It will be fine."

Lilly took another bite of one of the excellent cheeses Roddy had brought. She was beginning to worry about herself. She'd lost control of her calendar, and her memory was slipping. The lunch had been planned for weeks. What was she going to do without Delia?

"What's on the agenda?" Ernie asked.

"There's less of an agenda and more of a chance to get folks together and thank them for being on the committee," Tamara said. "We'll talk about the projects that came up at the last meeting."

"Maybe we should also talk about the—"

"I can't wait anymore," Ernie said, interrupting Lilly. "Tell me what's been going on. I'm working so hard these days I feel out of the loop. What's everyone been up to?"

"Delia, I'm assuming you have some visual aids for the rest of the evening. In the meantime, why don't Tamara and I update you on our adventures this afternoon." They didn't mention how they got the list of the projects Lenny was working on, but they did tell everyone about driving around and looking at the progress, or lack of progress, on his projects. They ended by telling them about the demolished houses on Linda Lane.

"Just demolished?" Warwick said. "That doesn't seem very safe or sanitary, does it?"

"It doesn't. I called Ray Mancini and told him to go by. We may end up having an emergency board of selectmen meeting to talk about it."

"Does it seem odd that you didn't see any building supplies or workers on any of those sites?" Roddy asked. "Maybe they were on other sites?"

"Maybe. Or maybe there aren't workers or building supplies," Ernie said.

"What you mean?" Tamara asked.

"This can't leave this room. I've always thought the world of Lenny, but something's gotten into him lately. It's like he's playing some kind of shell game. Borrow from this project to pay for that project. He does have folks working for him, but they're stretched thin and it's a skeleton crew."

"I wonder if that has anything to do with—"

"Hold on, let me bring the board out. Ernie, will you help me?" Delia said. She opened the French doors into the breakfast room and Ernie followed her. Together they rolled out a large whiteboard and turned it towards everybody. On the board the roll of paper was taped up and folded in half. Delia carefully unfolded the paper and taped the right side to a tripod she'd put there for the purpose. Folks with their backs to it turned their seat around.

"I've put some weight at the bottom of the tripod, but it's still a little rickety, so be careful. I wanted to make sure we have enough room to work. I'm going to put a pile of Post-its and some markers in the middle of the table. The Post-its are going to be added to the board. Lilly, could you move that cheese plate? Thanks. At the top, you see a timeline. Anything written on a yellow Post-it is fact. Per Lilly's suggestion, anything written on a green Post-it has to do with money. We can add codes to the green Post-its to let us know if we can prove this as a fact or if it's rumor or something we surmised. Blue Post-its are for real estate issues."

"Why does the timeline start three weeks ago?" Ernie asked.

"That's why we needed the extra space. It starts with the death of Harmon Dane. Again, I remind you, friends, none of this can leave this room. Bash Haywood came to see me at lunch time." Lilly went on to tell them about her conversation with Bash.

"Are you telling me Harmon's death may not have been natural? That's horrible," Tamara said.

"It is awful. And it may not have anything to do with Gladys's death or Lenny's businesses or anything else. Or it might. I think it's worth us talking things through and seeing what goes where. What do you say?" Lilly asked.

"I don't suppose you have an extra pad of paper? I need to doodle while I think," Roddy said.

"Of course I do," Delia said, going back into the breakfast room. "Pens too. I'm going to suggest we talk through the timeline, what we remember, and anything else we remember that's happened in these last few weeks whether we think it matters or not. Tamara, include the open houses."

"Roddy, do you remember the dates when you talked to Lenny?" Ernie asked.

"I have them on my phone. On yellow Post-its they'll go."

For the next four hours everyone talked through dates, conversations, rumors, and the people involved. Lilly added information about Miranda's business and Alex's condo plans. Ernie added more details about projects he'd heard about and some of the conversations he'd had with Gladys about furniture restoration in the past few weeks.

The last thing they did was clarify the timeline on Saturday. Tamara recalled the phone call and took out her phone to check the time. Delia wrote it down on a Post-it. Tamara got up and walked to the edge of the porch, looking out on the gardens.

"Tamara, can you talk us through your texts and calls from Gladys?" Lilly said. "When did you get them?"

"I got the text from her Saturday morning," Tamara said. She took out her phone, scrolled, and read out the time.

"But you'd called her as well?" Delia asked.

"Yes, the day before. Friday. When I'd found the garbage in the house," Tamara said. "Here, check my phone. You can see the texts and when I placed the call."

Roddy picked the phone up and scrolled through Tamara's texts. "The text only shows a phone number. She identifies herself in the text, and says to meet you in the appliance area, but her name doesn't show up next to the number. I presume she was on your contact list," he asked.

"You're right. She said 'It's Gladys' and since she's the only Gladys I knew, I assumed." She held out her hand and Roddy handed her the phone. "You're right. Look, I had another cell number for her on my contact list. Usually I called her land line. Maybe she got a new phone?"

"Maybe she did," Roddy said. "Or maybe Gladys didn't send the text. I wonder . . ."

"I wonder what?" Lilly said.

"I wonder if Tamara heard Gladys scream? Or if

someone else screamed to get Tamara to the scene?"

"What are you saying? Why would someone do that?" Tamara asked.

"To make sure you were blamed for her death."

"Let me see your phone," Lilly said. She asked Tamara for her phone and sent Bash a screenshot of the text with a brief explanation that he should confirm it was Gladys's phone number.

Delia wrote a Post-it asking about the text and solemnly put it on the timeline.

"Next, let's write down the gaps that need to be filled in. The questions that need to be proven or disproven. Let's not make any assumptions about what we think so far," Delia said.

"Should we bring Bash into this?" Warwick asked.

"Let's fill in some of these gaps first. But we'll bring him in, soon," Lilly said.

CHAPTER TWENTY

The expected turnout for the Beautification Committee luncheon was ten. Delia had asked for RSVPs but had only gotten six. Nevertheless, she expected and planned for at least fifteen people. The fact that the luncheon was at Windward added to the cachet of the meeting. Add to that the fact that the entire Garden Squad was going to be in attendance and Delia woke up worried about the amount of food they'd have. She called Stan and added more sandwiches to their order.

The meeting the night before had broken up a few minutes before eleven. Roddy had stayed behind and helped Delia and Lilly clean up. He had also paused before the whiteboard every time he went out to gather dishes from the porch. Lilly caught him staring at one point but couldn't tell what he was staring at.

"What are you thinking, Roddy?" Lilly asked.

"This is quite the puzzle," he said. "If you take it

as an entire piece, it's very sinister. Not that Gladys's death wasn't sinister unto itself. But if there is a through line between Harmon's death and Gladys's, though that doesn't seem clear right now, it's very troubling. Yet I can't imagine what the reasons could be."

"Money. I suspect money is the reason for most of this," Lilly said. "By money I'm going to include real estate issues. We need to figure out who stands the most to gain."

"The nephew, Braden, interests me," Roddy said. "He's not on this chart very much but he did stand to gain."

"He did, as long as the house gets sold and there's enough money to support the bird sanctuary. His uncle had supported him a lot over the years, but there was always a desire for more. Still I can't imagine he would have done his uncle harm. But one never knows."

"Are you going to let him know about the tests Bash had run? Or leave that to Bash?"

"I'm going to leave it to Bash," Lilly said. "I hope he'll be supportive of the investigation, but these days nothing would surprise me."

"Good idea to let Bash tell him, though I'd love to see his reaction. We have a couple of more trips into the kitchen, and then I'll be saying goodnight. I'll be back for the luncheon. Would you mind if I took pictures of this board before I left?" asked Roddy.

"Not at all," Lilly said. She looked carefully at her neighbor as he photographed every inch of the board. She left him to it and went back into the kitchen with another tray of dishes.

*   *   *

The total number of people at the lunch was twenty-two. Fortunately, Delia had a contingency plan, and had borrowed ten folding chairs from the Star Café. The meeting got moved from the dining room to the living room and back porch. If it weren't so hot out Lilly would have had everyone move out to the porch, but since there were so many older members, she didn't want to risk heatstroke.

Lilly wandered through the clusters of people gathering for lunch. She didn't love entertaining, but she did like seeing how much people were enjoying themselves.

Portia Asher was holding court in the living room. There were several people gathered around her including three of the Girl Scouts who were part of the volunteer corps. They were discussing the merits of the different projects, and Portia was telling them about Goosebush when she was a girl. Lilly left them to it.

She walked towards the back porch where half a dozen people sat at the table and others were sprawled on the lawn furniture chatting. She looked out to her gardens and noticed Miranda and Regan walking through them, pointing at plants and whispering. Lilly looked back over her shoulder to make sure that the curtain was closed to the breakfast room, and it was. She walked over and tried the door. Locked. She walked down the back stairs towards the garden.

"I've never seen your gardens," Miranda said to Lilly. "They live up to their reputation. They are lovely. Tell me, what's that plant over there?" Lilly answered questions and was impressed by Miranda's knowledge. Regan pretended to be interested but had no knowledge of plants or gardens. She eventually went back into the house.

"I stopped by your house the other day, Miranda," Lilly said. "I wanted to tell you I couldn't find that teapot you asked about. I hope you don't mind but I peeked at your gardens a bit. They are also lovely. There were some plants I didn't recognize which intrigued me."

"My garden is more of a production garden. I grow things for my teas and for my oils. Some of the plants aren't native to this area, but I'm experimenting with growing them here. I really try not to get plants and herbs from places where I don't know the gardener. Unless I know the origin it's hard to make sure they are up to my standards, totally organic and all of that."

"Delia's been growing a lot of plants and herbs this summer. Perhaps she's been inspired by you. I didn't realize you were building a business. That's exciting."

"I'm not sure how much it's growing, but I'm pleased."

"Are any of your teas medicinal? Or the oils? What do you call them? Essential oils?"

"No, I don't do medicinal. I mean, I make blends and say that they may help with stress or with sleep, but if someone's looking for a homeopathic recipe, I'm not their person. I haven't done enough studying yet."

"There seems to be a call for that sort of thing these days," Lilly said.

"I'll get there someday. For now, I'm all about

the self-care home market. Come by the house again, Lilly. I'll be happy to show you around."

"Folks, can you come back into the living room? We're going to call this meeting to order," Tamara called from the back porch.

Lilly was the last person to enter the house. As she entered the back door she noticed that Regan was lingering by the library.

"The meeting's in the living room," Lilly said. "The front of the house on the right. I'll be right there."

The meeting had started when Lilly went into the room. Delia was standing by the door and took her seat when Lilly came in. Delia pulled out a laptop, so she could take notes.

Lilly barely listened to the conversations. Instead she looked around the room. She'd been surprised by her pleasant conversation with Miranda. The first in their lives. She filed that away, not sure how to process it. Maybe gardening was their common bond.

The idea of melding the lectures of the historical society with a beautification project was met with great enthusiasm. A subcommittee was formed to work on Alden Park. The committee also voted to work on the beach project with the understanding that funds would need to be raised by next spring to complete the outdoor performance space. Ernie volunteered to head that committee. The fall festival was also agreed upon, with a call out to folks with gardens to help make it work. Tamara mentioned that there would be a road race component to help raise funds, but those details were being worked out.

"There's one more thing we need to talk about," Tamara said. "Lilly, do you want to take the floor?"

"Sure. As some of you know I've been spending more time by Swallow Point than I have in a while. I've noticed that at the top of the hill there are a couple of overgrown hedges of roses. They're a real deterrent to visibility when you're trying to take a right or left turn. Now that's not exactly the busiest part of town, I'll give you that. But it's busy enough. As some of you know there are going to be some scientists working down at the Dane house taking care of the sanctuary space. I imagine there will also be some work being done on Gladys's house before, um, before it gets sold. That and the beginning of school mean there's going to be more traffic. I'm not sure if those hedges are town property or owned by somebody, but I'm going to suggest we find out; we need to trim them back in a healthy way so that they keep blooming but aren't such a hazard. Seems to me that there are probably other corners that could use some pruning too."

"Does that seem like overstepping?" Regan said. "I'm not sure what that has to do with beautification. It seems more like maintenance work to me. That doesn't seem to be what this committee was created for."

"Ultimately, I'd love to see the town be able to afford to hire somebody to go around to take care of these things, but for now we need to volunteer," Lilly said. "That's the way things work in small towns, Regan. We pitch in and take care of each other. Anyone else have thoughts on this project? I could do it on my own, but I thought I'd bring it up."

"We could wait to see if the midnight gardener takes care of it, but Lilly's right. We should clean up some of these hazardous corners," Portia Asher said. "I know that corner you're talking about. I personally avoid going out there because I can't see. I drive around it to an easier intersection."

"I'll find out whose land the bushes are on," Delia said. "I'll let you all know, and we'll figure out a time to take that on. Meanwhile, if you see anything else around town that needs to be taken care of, why don't we start a list. I'll send the link out to a document we can all share. I agree with Lilly. It would be good if we could hire somebody at some point. But for now, we can take care of it."

"Seems like this town's never going to get any bigger if you keep thinking like that," Regan said. "This mom-and-pop small-town-take-care-of-each-other mentality is going to keep Goosebush exactly where it is. Lost on the map."

"Exactly how we like it," Miranda said. "Folks taking care of each other, watching out for one another. It's one of the best parts about this town. I'm happy to help. I may be able to use some of the rosehips in essential oils."

"How quaint," Regan said. "Ladies, I'm not one for getting my hands dirty. I'll write a check though, happily. Tell me where to send the donation. In the meantime, thanks for lunch. It's been grand."

"Get that check quick, and cash it," Portia said after Regan had walked out the door. Everyone laughed nervously, and Tamara stepped forward to take over the conversation again.

"Folks, we all know that there are people new to town who don't understand it or who want to modernize it. Some of those changes may be good. She's not wrong in saying that we need to find a way to get a job for this position. Maybe that needs to become another one of the Beautification Committee's goals. To get a position staffed. Wouldn't that be a great thing? Once Regan's here for longer she'll understand the incredible value of living in a small town, especially in Goosebush. Give her time. In the meantime, her point about donations is a good one. Do we want to set up a fund or create a nonprofit for this committee so that we can raise funds, or do we want to think about being part of another organization like the historical society? I don't think we should talk about those questions today, but let's set up a meeting in the next couple weeks to address this head-on. I'll send out an email to everyone here and to everyone else who's shown interest, and we can get a date on the books."

"Tamara, I wonder if I could make a suggestion? I have a couple of friends who wanted to come to today's luncheon, but they couldn't because they work. Could we try to have meetings on weekends or in the evenings so more folks can come? Or could we change the times of meetings to hit different populations? I realize that no time is perfect for everyone, but I think there are a lot of people who would love to get involved but don't feel they can." Lilly didn't recognize the young woman who asked the question. She'd make sure to meet her before the woman left.

"Emma, that's a great point. I'll also send out a survey to see if folks have specific times of day that are better to meet, and we'll try to figure it out. We could use technology, if that helps. Maybe we could hold some meetings online or on a conference call. I'll add that to the email I send out.

"Is there anyone else who has anything they'd like to bring up? No? With that I move to adjourn the meeting and thank you all for being here today. Keep an eye on the email, and forward it to other folks who aren't part of the committee but may be interested. Thank you to Delia and Lilly for hosting us, and thank you all for coming," Tamara said.

There was a spontaneous burst of applause. Lilly couldn't help but notice how enthused everyone seemed about the projects they were taking on. She agreed that it would be good to have some of these tasks taken over by someone paid to do them to make sure they got done. But at the same time, this community spirit was growing for the better and adding more positive change in Goosebush. Lilly regretted that she never really thought about changing the time of a meeting from the middle of the day to an evening or weekend when more people could become involved. A sign of age and of privilege. She'd adjust that thinking.

She went over and introduced herself to Emma and then chatted with other folks as they left. Ernie apologized because he needed to get back to the store. Roddy did a walk-through of the house to make sure all the dishes were in the kitchen, then he bid them both adieux.

Tamara and Lilly were left alone in the living room.

"Good meeting," Lilly said. "Are you sure you're going to have time to take on all this coordination?"

"I'm not going to do it alone. Delia can help me with setting up the forms in email. I'm also going to draft a couple more people to include in the committee who will help with all of it. It's interesting. I'm realizing more and more that folks may not step forward, not wanting to overstep, but if they are asked they'll help. We keep asking the same people but that may not be the best thing to do. We need to be more inclusive about who we bring in on all these conversations and committees," said Tamara.

"Agreed. I used to worry that when our generation dies off no one would take care of Goosebush. But now I realize that there are generations of folks who care. It's heartening."

"It is. I hate to leave you with this mess, but I have to go and meet the cleaners. I also thought I'd drive by the rest of those locations and report back on anything I see. Ray asked me to take pictures. Does that sound good?"

"Sounds great. I'll see you later," Lilly said. Tamara gathered her things and went back to the kitchen to say goodbye to people and go out the side door.

"Is Tamara leaving?" Portia asked. "I was hoping I could talk to her about what she thinks the value of my house is."

"Why?" Lilly asked.

"Alex followed up with an email to me with a ball park of how much I could borrow for my house. I felt like he undervalued it and told him so. He offered to do a more official assessment yesterday. He dropped this off this morning." She handed an envelope to Lilly. "He says my house is worth $10,000 less than what he quoted the other day. It's disheartening. I wonder if I should sell it and move into one of those condos in Marshton."

"Don't do anything before you talk to Tamara," Lilly said. She put on her glasses and looked at the sheet Portia had handed her. "I agree with you. That number seems low."

"He makes a good point—that it's old and constrained by ordinances in town. One interesting suggestion he made was that I go to town hall and get the back part of my lot parceled off, so I could sell it. I told him the town ordinances precluded anything from being built out there, but he told me that ordinances could be changed. He's quite the operator," Portia said.

"That's one word for it," Lilly said softly. "Portia, would you mind if I made a copy of this? I haven't had an assessment done on my house in years, and I'd be interested to see what information they include."

"Sure. It's interesting if nothing else. While I have you I have another favor to ask, if you don't mind."

"Of course not."

"I don't know if you've heard about this, but the Goosebush Players are going to do a reading series this winter. We've got a show planned for the spring, but we want to build some more audiences. Anyway, we were looking at the Performing Arts Center, but it's pretty expensive. We want to start this series by doing *A Christmas Carol* in December, and I think that's their prime time for concerts. Regan offered to underwrite it, but I don't like the sound of that. I don't want to alienate Tamara or anyone else in town."

"I'm sure Tamara would understand, or she may be interested in underwriting it also."

"We talked about that. For now, we came up with another plan for the December show. We're thinking we could do it at the Star. I was wondering if you'd be willing to ask Stan if he's at all interested? I don't want to get the rest of the committee excited by this idea. I will be playing the Ghost of Christmas Past so I don't want my request to appear too self-serving or have him take pity on me. Would you run the idea by him?"

"I'd be happy to. I've got to go down there later today anyway, so I'll ask him and let you know what he says."

"One more thing. I was sitting at the meeting thinking how nice it was to not have Gladys harping on every idea and what was wrong with it. Then I felt badly. I wonder if we should set up some sort of a memorial garden at the beach project in her name? She was part of Goosebush for so long. And she was a good worker on these committees even if she was a pain in the neck."

"That's a lovely idea," Lilly said.

"It could be a patch of thickets. Wouldn't that be appropriate? I'm going to go and help Delia get these dishes washed. You go make a copy of that sheet and stay in touch. Thanks so much for helping me, Lilly. I'd forgotten how to ask for help. If there's ever anything I could do for you, please ask."

"Portia, I may take you up on that sooner than you know."

CHAPTER TWENTY-ONE

"That wasn't too terrible," Lilly said. "Some good ideas came out of it."

"Not too terrible. Damned by faint praise," Delia said. "What are you up to for the next couple of hours? I thought I'd go in and start pulling together notes from last night but if you need me for anything else—"

"I'm going to head down to the Star. Then I may stop by and say hi to Bash. My phone is fully charged so I'll stay in touch with you and let you know if I hear anything. Oh, one more thing to add to the mix." She told Delia about the appraisals on Portia's house.

"Do you think Alex and Regan are working together?" Delia asked.

"I have no idea. Honestly, there's a lot going on, but they all still seem like separate parts of a whole. When I go see Bash I'm going to let him know about this as well. Alex could be on the up and up. But I hate to think anyone's trying to bilk Portia out of her house by undervaluing it. I think it's interesting that one solution was to parcel off the back half of her lot, presumably for additional buildings. Lots of folks seem pretty interested in land, don't they?"

"Land is one resource that Goosebush does not have in abundance," Delia said. "That's one reason I'm so glad that Lenny's proposal went down in defeat. Building four houses on two lots may make sense in one way, but it is a Pandora's box that would change the face of Goosebush. Best to tread lightly."

Lilly arrived at the Star at the perfect time. The lunch rush was over, and most folks were back at work. That didn't mean there was no one there, but it meant that Lilly was able to order a pot of tea and sit at her favorite table right next to the bookstore. The challenge with her table was that she always ended up window shopping. Stan stocked lovely sundries in his bookstore, and since paper goods were a vice of Lilly's, the temptation was great.

She sat for a few minutes and let her tea seep. She took out a notebook and started to write her goals for the rest of the day. They included talking to Bash. Beyond that she was having difficulty seeing a path forward. Perhaps Delia's lists would inspire her.

She poured a dollop of tea. Perfect. She continued to pour herself an entire cup and took a sip. Delightful. This was the Star Café blend, and Lilly had become a huge fan of it over the summer. It was supposedly caffeine free, though it always revived Lilly. She'd never considered what was in it. Her palate wasn't sophisticated enough to discern it. She needed to talk to Delia about it and see if this mixture could inspire her next blend. That pale-yellow dredge had to go.

"What are you thinking about, Lilly?" Stan said. As the owner of the Star, Stan was always busy. But he made a point of always stopping by and spending a couple of minutes talking to Lilly.

"I was thinking about how drinking tea blends is a leap of faith."

"What do you mean?" Stan laughed.

"You could say a tea blend is caffeine free, but is it really? You could say the ingredients are organic, but are they? I'm not saying that you aren't sourcing things carefully, but I'm noticing a lot of blends of herbs and spices and plants are being bandied about. I can't help but wonder about them. Forgive me, Stan. An old lady's mind wandering into dark places."

"No worries. We all benefit from your mind wandering one way or the other."

"I'm not sure if that's true, especially lately. I feel more befuddled than ever. Thank you for coming over and sitting with me. I did have one question I wanted to ask you and I probably would've forgotten if you hadn't been right in front of me. Have you ever seen anything done by the Goosebush Players?" Lilly went on to explain the request from Portia.

"The theater is pretty booked in December, but there might be a day or two. It might also be interesting to do a few of the readings here in the café. The bookcases are on wheels, so we can move them around. Maybe we could even do one in the restaurant. I'd be happy to talk to the folks in the theater group."

"I'm not sure how big a budget they have. I know they're also thinking about this as a series, so they'll be looking at other dates throughout the winter."

"Winter is a tough time to get people in. If they're willing to help me with that, I'd be happy to talk to them about some favorable rates for the December events. Send them my way, and thanks." Stan got up and went back over to the counter.

Lilly took another sip of tea and took out her phone. She sent Portia an email encouraging her to reach out to Stan. She included his phone number. Lilly had adapted to using her phone for everything, but not everyone was on the same page. She wasn't even sure if Portia read her email without her grandson's help. She'd call Portia later to check in.

"You mind if I sit down?"

Lilly looked up and saw Braden Dane standing next to the second chair at her table. "Not at all. Would you like some tea? I could get a second cup."

"No, thank you. I was over at the police station meeting with Bash Haywood. I was too upset to drive right away so I was wandering around the Wheel and happened to look in and see you sitting here. I assume you've spoken with him?"

"He stopped by yesterday to talk to me. I haven't spoken to him today, but I was planning on stopping by the station."

"Has he told you about the tests he ran on Uncle Harmon?" Lilly nodded. "Were you as shocked as I was?"

"Absolutely," Lilly said. "I never thought it was anything but natural causes. It still may be. Perhaps they can explain the anomalies easily."

"He wants to exhume the body. I've already spoken to my mother and she agreed. I'm willing to agree to it too. I don't know where Miranda stands but as long as you're on board it can get done."

"I'm happy to support that. I've never been one to believe that lack of knowledge is a good thing. I'd hate to have all of us wonder. That isn't healthy."

"I know I didn't come to see him as often as I should have. Maybe if I had I would have noticed the changes and been able to get him to the doctor." Braden wiped his eyes. "I'll never forgive myself if he was . . . if someone, you know. I realize I've been coming off as a money-grubbing nephew, spending money I don't have to act like a big shot, but I really did love the old man. He was very good to me."

"He was a wonderful man. I wish I'd spent more time with him those last weeks. I took his being there for granted, and I miss my friend. You should know, I am pushing forward on the bird sanctuary. Dawn Simmons is staying at the house while she's assessing what's going on. She'll clear out if need be, for an open house or viewing, of course. But I'm happy to have somebody there using it."

"That's good. About the sanctuary. Uncle Harmon should be remembered, and that project will help. It's good to have someone keeping an eye on it," Braden said.

"True enough. Those open houses that were sabotaged are unfortunate, to put it mildly. I hope they find out at some point who was responsible."

"I do, too," Braden said. "I had assumed selling the house would be easier."

"You know buying and selling houses on that Shipyard Lane is tricky given the caveats around remodeling and building. There's got to be a special buyer, especially with the bird sanctuary issues. That said, I can't believe that there isn't someone out there who will love the house as much as your uncle did, even with all its quirky particularities."

"You know Regan Holland's been pushing hard to get the listing once Tamara's contract is up in September?" Braden asked.

"I'd heard that, yes."

"I'd been talking to her about it and she's been making persuasive arguments about the value of the land versus the value of the house. She's got an interesting perspective. I don't disagree with her necessarily. Rethinking what could be as opposed to what is not in the DNA of Goosebush. At least the Goosebush I know."

"But?" Lilly asked gently.

"I've been thinking of myself and not Uncle Harmon. He loved that house, for good reason. Some of my happiest memories are there. This news had really knocked me over. I think we should delay any decisions about the house until we know what happened to Uncle Harmon, don't you?"

"I don't think that's a bad idea. Tell me, were the conversations with Regan in person or over email? I'm intrigued by her point of view. I agree that rethinking is not a terrible idea. I'm not an advocate of rethinking without careful consideration however."

"She emailed me a proposal last week. I'll forward it to you," he said, taking out his phone and scrolling. "I should've done that as soon as she sent it." He scrolled for a few seconds and then punched his screen and put his phone back in his pocket. "I'm not sure about what the next steps are regarding Uncle Harmon."

"Neither am I. But as I said I'll go talk to Bash and keep you informed. Is it all right if I give you a call later?"

"I'd appreciate that. You think that Dr. Simmons would mind if I went by the house and learned about what she's doing?"

"I'm sure she won't. Take care of yourself, Braden. We'll figure this out." Lilly watched Braden leave the Star and took out her phone. She texted Dawn to let her know he was on his way over.

Enemy or friend? she texted back.

Friend. He has had a hard day. Help him understand why his uncle cared about the birds.

Will do.

CHAPTER TWENTY-TWO

"Hello, Lilly! Where are you off to?"

Lilly had stepped out of the Star and braced herself to face the heat. At the sound of his voice she looked to her right and saw Roddy coming towards her. She smiled at him. How could she not? Charming, handsome Roddy, an excellent neighbor and a good man. Lilly shook herself a bit. Thank heavens she was well past the age of thinking of men as anything more than a good friend. No, those days were past her.

"I thought I'd stop by and visit Tamara. I just read a proposal that Regan sent to Braden about turning the Dane house into a condominium, and I want to talk to her about it."

"Does that seem feasible?" Roddy asked.

"I shouldn't think so, but Regan referenced some code that could be stretched a bit. I'm also going to check in on Bash, if he's at the station. What are you up to?" she asked. They were both standing in front of the Star, which was awkward for conversation and close to everywhere you could want to be in downtown Goosebush.

"I'm heading home. Before you go over to Tamara's, let me catch you up on my last conversation. Shall we go in and have a cup of tea at the Star?"

"It's getting busy in there. How about if we head over to the Triple B? We can use Ernie's office. He has a tea kettle too."

"Twist my arm and show me the way," Roddy said. "What do you have in that bag?"

"Cookies for Bash. I could probably part with one if you're hungry," Lilly said. Roddy offered her his arm, and she took it.

The Triple B was almost straight across the Wheel, but to get there you had to walk around. They walked to the left, which had less foot traffic this time of day. They chatted a bit on their walk but didn't talk about the matter at hand. Too many prying eyes or ears.

They walked into the Triple B, which was bustling. Ernie was working on one of the registers. He saw Lilly and Roddy and motioned them into his office. Once they were in there Lilly turned on the electric kettle and went into the cupboard that held Ernie's tea stash.

"Caffeine or no?" Lilly asked.

"No caffeine, sadly. I'm finding I'm less and less tolerant of caffeine lately. I'm thinking about giving it up all together, but I'm not sure I want to go that far."

"I'm down to one cup in the morning," Lilly said. "If I drink tea past two in the afternoon I can't sleep. This aging thing isn't to be taken lightly, that's for sure."

"No, it isn't," Roddy said. "Though there are benefits. Anyway, that's another conversation. I don't want to hold you up too long. But I did want to tell you that I followed up with Lenny about working on my house. Purely as a research conversation. He asked me what my budget was, and I let him know that I was mortgaged to the hilt, so I'd need to look into another type of loan. All fiction, but I thought I'd try and bait the conversation."

"What did Lenny say?"

"He told me he had a friend who might be able to help me out and asked for my email, which I gave him. Alex Marston reached out an hour ago. We're meeting at my house in an hour."

"Interesting. Hear him out. He's gone back to Portia and suggested she parcel out her back lot and sell it for development."

"Lenny had suggested I do a tear-down or make my house a two-family."

"The building codes in Goosebush are strict. I wonder why people keep suggesting ideas that break the rules? Speaking of which, let me forward you the email Braden sent me."

"I've known people like these my entire life," Roddy said. "People who think that if they keep pushing their agenda, eventually it will break through. Problem is that they usually do such a good job challenging the norms that at some point they do break through."

"But how?"

"Imagine if both Portia and I, and who knows

who else, need money, and Alex is giving us a golden goose. Increase development on the land we own. Would that groundswell help change the rules? Even on a per case basis? It might. I'll take a look at this email. It may give me some more information for my conversation."

Lilly handed Roddy a cup of decaffeinated Earl Grey tea. She knew that it probably had some caffeine, but she couldn't abide chamomile tea, which was the only other choice. She was about to sit down when Ernie burst into the office.

"Please tell me you brought me something to eat," he said, flopping down on his chair.

"I did," Lilly lied. She took the bag of cookies out of her purse and handed it to Ernie. He chose a kitchen sink cookie, took a bite, closed his eyes, and sighed. She handed him her cup of tea and went over to pour herself one.

"I apologize for commandeering your office, Ernie. Roddy and I happened to run into each other, and we wanted to catch up in private."

"I saw you both at the meeting. What's happened since then? Have you been sleuthing?" Ernie asked.

"Roddy's been setting a trap, more like," Lilly said. They both caught Ernie up.

"Interesting," Ernie said. "You know, this may make me a heretic, but I don't think questioning the zoning laws in Goosebush is the worst idea in the world. I know of a few folks who'd love to build a freestanding guest cottage, for example, on their land, but they can't because of the rules. It's worth a conversation, as I said. But breaking up lots so that new houses could be built is a different way of going about it."

"I'll admit, I've lived in a large house on a triple lot for my entire life, so I have a different perspective. But why not have the conversation out in the open instead of using subterfuge?" Lilly asked.

"I wonder if it is because parts of this are under the radar? These loans that Alex is offering. I'd like to learn more about them and will take that on. Does he do them through a bank or through a private company? Who are his partners?" Roddy asked.

"And what, if anything, does this have to do with Gladys's death I wonder?" Ernie said. "For what it's worth, Gladys never had a lot of money. But last spring she seemed to come into a bit of cash. She ordered some cabinets and a countertop for her kitchen, for example. Didn't go low-end either."

"Do you remember when?" Roddy asked.

"No, but I'll look it up later. Right now, I need to get back out there. I don't suppose either of you know anyone who's looking for extra cash and would like to work here, do you?"

"Why don't you send that out to the Beautification Committee email list and ask them to forward it?"

"Great idea. I'll do that. Good meeting today, by the way. Thanks for the cookies. I'm going to meet Delia over at those rose bushes in a half hour or so; are either of you going to be there?" Ernie said.

"I'm heading home to meet with Alex. I'll let you know how that goes," Roddy said.

"Please do. I'm going to head over to talk to Bash, but if I can, I'll join you both at the hedges," said Lilly.

Rather than walking directly to the police station by going around the Wheel, Lilly decided to zigzag through side streets. She crossed the street and walked over to Alden Park. If she didn't have a mission, she would have gone in and talked to the folks working in there. Finding a specific dump site had been an unexpected thrill for everyone. At the same time, Lilly couldn't help but wonder about it. The land was always common space in Goosebush. It had been used for grazing and public parks. Since the items being found were consistent with the time line that had historical records, who would have used the park as a dump?

Instead of succumbing to her curiosity Lilly walked past the park and went down the alley. Once she got out the other side, she took a left and went over to Tamara's office. She hadn't crossed the street when she saw Alex Marston pull out of the parking lot and take a right. She hung back until he was far enough down the street that he wouldn't be able to identify her in his rear-view mirror.

Lilly walked into Tamara's office. Tamara was on the phone, so Lilly went back to the restroom. She splashed some cool water on her face and wet a paper towel to hold on the back of her neck. She'd done a lot of walking for an August day. Lilly wet her hands and ran them through her curls, trying to both tame and shape them a bit.

Lilly walked back into the office as Tamara was hanging up.

"That was the Cape family," Tamara said. "The brokers' open house got three tours set up for tomorrow. They're thrilled."

"How did the cleaners do?" Lilly asked.

"I'm going to check, but they think it's taken care of," Tamara said. "I hope so."

"Did I see Alex Marston pulling out of the driveway?" Lilly said.

"You know, just once I'd like to surprise you. Yes, you did see him. Guess what he came by to talk about?"

"I have no idea," Lilly said.

"Do you want to guess?" Tamara said.

"Not particularly. Roddy is meeting with him in a little while. I can't imagine the meetings were about the same thing."

"He came to me to ask my advice on prices. He says he's thinking about investing in a project over in Marshton, a unit with five townhouses. He wanted to know if, in my opinion, there was a demand for that type of housing."

"What did you tell him?"

"I said there likely was. It would depend on the specs for the townhouses, of course. But I'm finding more and more folks are looking for townhouses and condos as they get older. Some autonomy, but with help shoveling and raking leaves."

"Do you think there's a market for them in Goosebush?"

"Alex asked the same thing. I think there might be. But getting it through the permits and paperwork would be challenging. Mildly put."

"I'm forwarding a proposal that Regan sent to Braden about condoizing the Dane House," Lilly said, hitting forward on her email. "It's a similar conversation. What did Alex have to say about the paperwork issues?"

"He kept asking questions. I think he was testing me, not only as a real estate agent, but also as a member of the board of selectmen."

"Did he mention he had plans for a project in Goosebush?"

"Not a peep. I've been doing some of my own research on that. I haven't had much time, but there is a development company in Providence that Alex is involved with. They create condo and townhouse developments. They also offer interesting finance models."

"Really? Could you forward the information to me?"

"I already put all of the links on the document that Delia shared with us."

"Great. Tamara, is there any way you could find out how much Gladys owed on her house, and to whom? That might be interesting information to know," Lilly said.

"I'm not sure. I could try. What are you thinking?"

"Money is a good motivation for terrible things, don't you think? I wonder what it has motivated around here lately."

"Good question," Tamara said. "Let me see what I can find out. Meanwhile, if you don't mind me saying it, you look done in, my friend. Have you been walking around all afternoon?"

"I have been," Lilly said. "I'm going to walk over to the police station, and then I'll head home."

"Text me before you start walking home. It would be a good excuse for me to close up shop and give you a ride."

"I'll happily take you up on that," Lilly said.

CHAPTER TWENTY-THREE

The police station was busy, but that was par for the course in Goosebush. Like many small towns, a lot of business was conducted at the police station. Lilly sidestepped the folks who were paying tickets and getting permits and walked around back to Bash's office. She saw him through the glass panel beside his door, bent over his computer. She knocked on the glass and waved. He smiled at her and beckoned her in.

He started to stand up when she came in, but she gestured that he should stay seated.

"Lilly, what brings you down here today?" Bash asked.

"What doesn't?" Lilly asked. "Bash, I could beat around the bush, but to what purpose? I've got a ton on my mind and wanted to let you know about a few things in case they were helpful."

"I appreciate that," Bash said. "Would you like a glass of water or a cup of tea?"

"Water would be nice but only if you're getting some for yourself."

"I was planning on it," he said. He picked up a file on his desk and handed it to Lilly on his way out.

She took out her reading glasses and put them on. The results of Harmon's toxicology tests were on the top of the file. Lilly didn't understand them. She was tempted to take out her phone and take pictures, but she resisted. She didn't want to push her luck.

The next page showed a picture of one of the jars Lilly had given Bash. There were some preliminary results listed, with more tests pending. It showed a significant amount of foxglove, ginkgo biloba and St. John's Wort in the mix. The note said that the plants were easily identifiable, but their toxicity and other ingredients would need to be subjected to further testing.

The third page showed the second jar, with similar findings. Bash came back into the room and put Lilly's water down in front of her.

"If he drank the teas, they could have possibly induced a heart attack," Lilly said. She took a drink of water to get rid of the frog in her throat.

"From what I understand, the St. John's Wort could have had limited the effectiveness of his other medications. Do you grow any of these plants?"

"Do I? What are you asking?" Lilly said.

"Sorry, that came out wrong. I'm trying to figure out how common the plants are."

"I've grown foxglove. We may have some in the

greenhouse. Lots of folks grow these and other plants as plants, not as herbs to be used."

"Do you think Miranda grows it?" Bash asked.

"Some of them. But I don't think she uses it in her teas." Lilly told Bash about her conversation with Miranda from that morning.

"I've been looking at her website, and you're right. She doesn't list any of these plants as ingredients. Maybe she makes special orders, though."

"To kill Harmon?" Lilly asked. "What a terrible thought. I can't imagine she'd . . . even if she did, why would she put the teas in her jars?"

"To make him feel better about taking them? Didn't you tell me she'd come by looking for her teapot? She was probably trying to get rid of the evidence."

"Do you think Gladys knew about the tea?"

"Gladys and Miranda were friends. Maybe Gladys figured out what happened and confronted her. Or maybe she tried to blackmail Miranda."

"Blackmail?" Lilly asked.

"Gladys has had some influxes of cash in the past few months, and we can't figure out where they came from. They were all under the federal reporting limits, so they didn't get flagged until now."

"There could be several reasons for that," Lilly said. She told Bash about Alex Marston's private lending offers. Bash took notes and nodded.

"Yeah, I've heard about that. We're trying to lock down alibis for Lenny, Miranda, and Alex. Maybe Miranda didn't kill Gladys, but that doesn't mean she didn't kill Harmon. Or maybe Miranda was in cahoots with Braden."

"I saw Braden after he came to talk to you. He's shaken up. He may be lying, but I don't think so."

"I don't know what to think. I'm not going to assume all of these cases are connected, but I'm not ruling it out either."

"Did you talk to Lenny about going to Gladys's house? What was he looking for?"

"He said he'd left some tools over at her house that he wanted to get back and some plans as well."

"Do you believe him?"

"I don't believe anyone these days," Bash said.

"It is challenging, isn't it? It's hard to cut through all this murk."

"I'm trying my best. As, I'm sure, are you and your friends."

"We're minding our own business. By the way, did you get that text I sent you about Tamara's phone? Was that Gladys's phone number?" Lilly asked.

"Gladys used pay-as-you-go cell phones, so it might have," Bash said. "Good call on that, by the way. I assumed the text was from Gladys, but we haven't been able to find her phone to confirm."

"Tamara's cell phone number is on all of her business materials, so anyone could get it. You know, Tamara heard the scream and assumed it was Gladys. Maybe Gladys was already dead, and someone wanted to have Tamara found at the scene. I have to wonder if the goal was to frame Tamara."

"It seems like it might be," Bash said. "More murk. Listen, would you do me a favor? I want to go over and look at Miranda's garden, and I've got no freaking clue what I'm looking at. Would you come with me?"

"Of course," Lilly said. "Anything I can do to help, you know me."

The drive over to Miranda's house was a quiet one. Bash brought the reports on Harmon's death with him, and Lilly was reading them and trying to look up every minute or so to reorient herself. She didn't like reading in the car, but this was an emergency.

As Bash slowed down to turn right Lilly waved at Delia and Ernie, who were at the road-blocking rose hedge, taking pictures and measuring the hedge height. Lilly pulled her phone out of her pocket and texted them both.

Heading to Miranda's. Stay tuned.

Bash drove slowly down the hill and took the gentle left onto Miranda's street. He parked behind her car and walked around to open Lilly's door for her. Lilly walked slowly and looked at the garden. Now that she was looking at it, she noticed a number of plants that had poisonous potential. But then again, used in the right dosages, they could also be medicinal or have other benefits.

Bash stepped up on the porch and pushed the doorbell. There wasn't a sound, so he knocked using her Nantucket basket knocker. After a moment, she came to the door. She was wearing a smock, and she'd pulled her hair back in a messy bun. Lilly noticed that the glasses she'd put on top of her head had magnifying lenses on them.

"Good afternoon, Miranda. Mind if we come in to ask you a couple of questions?" Bash said.

"I'm in the middle of something—" Miranda said.

"We could always talk down at the station," Bash said.

"Oh, for heaven's sake. In that case, please come in. Lilly, I didn't know you'd joined the police force," she said.

"I haven't, but I speak plants. The chief asked me to come with him to help translate if need be."

They followed Miranda into the front door and stepped to the left. The house was a center-entrance Cape that had been expanded with dormers upstairs and porches on three sides. The rooms were small, and Miranda used every square inch. Lilly noted drying flowers, herbs, and plants hanging from the ceiling. Since the ceilings were taller than normal the plants didn't hit anyone on the head, but they still made the rooms feel oppressive.

Bash pulled one of the side chairs over and sat down. Lilly sat on a side chair and Miranda sat on the settee. Lilly looked around. All of the furniture was fairly new and had the boxed Swedish aesthetic that indicated it wasn't terribly high end. Lilly knew that Harmon had given Miranda several treasured antiques over the years, but from this vantage point she couldn't see any of them in the living room or dining room. Had Miranda sold them? For money or because she didn't like them?

"Miranda, do you recognize this?" Bash asked. He took the picture of one of the tea jars out of the folder and handed it to her.

"The label looks like mine, but it isn't from me. I don't make a tea blend called 'Heart Health.' "

"How about this one?"

"I don't make a 'Restful Sleep' either. Where did you get these? Is someone copying me?"

"We found these jars in your cousin's house."

"Harmon's? I didn't give them to him."

"We ran some tests on them and found that there were high levels of plants that may have caused Harmon to get sick."

"Whoa, wait a minute. What are you saying? Harmon died of natural causes."

"His cause of death is being reinvestigated," Bash said. "Tell me, do you use any of these plants in your work?" Bash listed several names, and Lilly looked around while he went through the list. She saw half of those plants drying in the living room.

Miranda didn't try and argue.

"I would never, ever have done anything to hurt Harmon," she said.

"Perhaps you didn't mean to?" Bash said. "You put some plants together that tasted good and—"

"I know what plants do and can be used for," Miranda said. "I may have some of the plants you've listed, but trust me, I wouldn't make a tea out of them, especially for Harmon."

"But you don't deny that this is your label?" Bash asked.

Lilly picked up the picture of one of the jars. "Could we see one of your tea jars with a label?" she asked.

"There are some in the kitchen ready to go out," Miranda said. "I'll get one."

"We'll go with you," Bash said. His phone buzzed as they got up, and he hung back to check the text.

While they waited for him to follow, Lilly stopped and looked around a bit more. Hundreds of drying plants combined with closed windows and a barely functioning window AC unit made it claustrophobic. Lilly saw a dehumidifier in the corner but wondered if it was up to the task. One challenge of living this close to the ocean was a permanent dampness and slight mustiness to everything. Drying flowers and herbs without them mildewing must be a challenge.

The three of them walked to the back of the living room and went through the swinging door. The kitchen ran the length of the back of the house. Unlike the modern vibe of the front rooms, the kitchen had clearly last been renovated in the seventies. The gold stove had four pots of simmering water. The brown refrigerator made a bevy of noises, none of which sounded good. The metal rim around the counters was popping off in places. The kitchen table was covered with packing materials. There were four card tables set up and they were covered with other parts of her business.

"Do you make everything in here?" Bash asked.

"I package things in here. I put stuff together upstairs. If business picks up I'm going to get more space somewhere but not if you start spreading rumors that my teas kill people."

"I don't spread rumors, I look for facts. Could you show me one of your jars?" Bash asked.

Miranda reached into a box and pulled out a jar. She handed it to Bash, who looked it over.

"Would you mind showing me one as well?" Lilly asked.

Miranda let out a loud sigh and handed Lilly another jar. Lilly turned it over in her hand. She ran her hand along the label. The lettering on the jar did look similar to the lettering on the jars she found. But the label was different.

"Miranda, do you have these labels printed for you, or do you do it yourself?"

"I have them printed. Then I run them through my printer to get the calligraphy printed lightly, then I go over it with a pen to give it the home-made look."

"They do look homemade, but now that you walked me through the process I can see the level of detail you add to them. Also, this jar has an *M* embossed on one side. Is that some sort of etching?"

"Hand done with stencils and etching paste. All of my jars have that," she said. "It's part of the branding. When you order high-end products, packaging details matter."

"Those details make your packaging unique," Lilly said.

"They are unique," Bash said. "Miranda, I need to ask you if I can take a look around. We need to make sure we investigate this thoroughly, so I can't take your word for it alone. I need to look into this."

"What happens if I say no?" she said.

Bash reached into the folder and took out an envelope.

"I was hoping I wouldn't need to use this, but

here's a search warrant. I'm going to have to ask you to wait in the living room." Bash pulled out his phone and sent a text. "Lilly, could you get home on your own?"

"I could, yes, of course," Lilly said. "May I have a word first?"

They walked to the front hall. Bash stood where he could see Miranda in the living room.

"Someone could have forged the label, and used a similar jar," Lilly said. "I don't remember seeing the etched *M*."

"They could have, or she could have changed labels. Listen, if we don't investigate carefully we'll never know. For her sake, if she's innocent, we need to make sure her name is clear. But there's one more thing. That call I just got? Guess who was a silent partner in this business?"

"Who?"

"Gladys Preston. I got a text from one of the people looking into Gladys's finances. She wrote a check to Miranda six weeks ago. In the memo, she wrote *partnership*. We found a few cases of these jars at her house too. I'll check on the *M*."

"Bash, this is getting more confusing all the time," Lilly said.

"Lilly, if you think that then I'm doomed. Sorry about getting you stranded out here, but I need to pursue this."

"You do what you need to do," Lilly said. "I'll text Delia to see if she can come get me."

CHAPTER TWENTY-FOUR

Lilly walked down the hill towards the Dane house. She didn't want to bother Dawn, but she also didn't want to wait out on Miranda's porch. She texted Delia to let her know where she was.

We're talking to the neighbor about the hedge. You okay for a while?

I'll find something to do.

Lilly looked down the lane. She didn't see Alex's car, so she walked over to Gladys's house. She wished she hadn't given Bash the key. She also wished she hadn't been such a goodie-two-shoes and believed Lenny. She should have gone to look around the other day.

She walked over to the mudroom. It was closed. She looked around but didn't see anyone. She walked along the side of the house and looked in windows. She couldn't see inside the house. Not because the curtains were closed, but because there were boxes piled in front of them.

She looked down at Gladys's gardens, the loveliest feature of the house. Say what you will about Gladys, but she was a wonderful gardener. Lilly reached down and pulled a few errant weeds. She took out her phone and made a note to herself. "Keep up with GP gardens till the house is sold," she wrote. It was the least she could do and would likely be the best-selling feature of the house.

She weeded along the side and then went out to the front of her house that faced the water. There was the large porch that the other two houses also have. But rather than the porch stairs leading out to grass, Gladys had a patio with various flower beds that led up to the path that ran along the front of all three houses. Lilly wasn't a fan of grass and enjoyed the choices Gladys had made. She wandered around and kept weeding. She looked at the cobblestones that were lining the paths and reached down. They were plastic. They looked fine, but Lilly took another look around. Gladys had used a number of household materials such as planters, and all sorts of materials to create separate spaces. The gardens were done on a budget, but they were well loved.

Lilly walked over to the other side of the porch and saw that Gladys had a compost bin. She went and gathered weeds and took them over. She kicked the bin to alert any critters that were nesting and opened the lid. She looked in and saw the rich dark compost. She tossed in the weeds. There was a pitchfork over to the side, so Lilly took it to turn it over. She put in into the bin and turned.

One more turn and Lilly noticed some white paper peeping through. Newspaper was good for compost, but this wasn't that.

Lilly reached in and took out the papers. There was a large pile of them, partially rolled at one end where they were bound together. She flattened the papers and pushed the compost aside. It was a drawing. SWALLOW POINT CONDOS was the name on the bottom corner. Lilly looked carefully and realized that the condos were a three-story set of buildings placed exactly where she was standing.

She rolled the sheet out flatter. A MAP DEVELOPMENT was written in the other corner, with the names Marston, Andrus, and Preston written underneath.

As if the plans themselves weren't interesting enough, someone had written across the front of the plans in dark marker: OVER MY DEAD BODY

"Lilly, where are you?" Ernie called. He was with Delia.

Lilly walked around to the side of the house to meet them. She wanted to stay out of Alex's sight lines in case he was actually home.

"Look what I found," she said to them both. She held out the drawings. "I wonder if this is what Lenny was looking for the other day."

"Where did you find it?" Delia asked.

"In the compost bin," Lilly said.

"What made you look in the compost bin?" Ernie asked.

"I was turning the compost and there they were."

"Anything else in there?" Delia asked.

"I'm not sure. I didn't want to dig anymore in case there was. I figured I should leave that to Bash."

Delia looked at the drawings closely. "MAP Development?"

"Marston, Andrus, and Preston," Lilly said, pointing out the names. "I wonder if that was a real company or part of the proposal."

"I'm assuming that Gladys wrote the 'over my dead body' sentiment?" Ernie said. "An unfortunate choice of words."

"What does that say?" Delia said, peering at a smudged part of the drawing where another logo had been.

"No idea," Lilly said. "I'd love to take this home and try to find the clues, but this does seem like evidence of something."

"You should probably call Bash," Ernie said.

"I know. He's up the hill, searching Miranda's house," Lilly said.

"He's what?!?"

Lilly let them know about their visit to Miranda's house. Ernie whistled.

"Do you think Miranda killed Harmon?" he asked.

"You know what, Ernie? I don't. Not intentionally. I hope she had nothing to do with it without meaning to, though," Lilly said.

"Without meaning to?" Delia asked.

"She's growing a lot of different plants for her teas and oils. Some of them could be poisonous if used improperly."

"Did you see foxglove?"

"I think I did," Lilly said. "But don't take my word for it. There are a lot of other plants up there. Someone could have made a blend and used one of Miranda's labels. She grows everything herself, so they might be able to test the plants to see if they're consistent with her garden and her soil."

"Someone could have set Miranda up?" Ernie asked. "Is that what you're saying?"

"I guess so. Bash is up the hill. I'll give him a call. This will require more than a text."

Lilly called Bash and told him about her compost exploits.

Bash said four words. "I'll be right there."

"Now, walk me through this again," Bash said. "Miranda has asked for a lawyer, and I've got two other people looking through her house, so I have a little time."

Lilly told him about weeding and then wanting to put the weeds in the compost bin. "Then I decided to turn the compost."

"Why?" Bash asked.

"It's August. You have to turn the compost pretty regularly this time of year," Delia said.

"Besides, I've also decided we're going to take care of Gladys's gardens until the house is sold," Lilly said.

"Who's 'we'?" Bash asked.

"The three of us. Gladys was not a pleasant person—"

"You can say that again," Ernie said.

"But she loved her gardens, and they are as close to a legacy as she's got."

"So, we're going to take care of them. It's the right thing to do," Delia said, reaching over and squeezing Lilly's hand.

"Anything else in the bin?" Bash asked.

"We haven't checked," Lilly said. "I called you. What do you think this means?" She pointed to the logo on the corner.

Bash looked around. "Let's go in the house for a minute," he said. He took a ring of keys out of his pocket and unlocked the door. He left it open, and the three of them walked up the porch and inside.

It was stuffy, but the lack of air flow wasn't what made everyone feel claustrophobic. As Lilly had surmised, there were all sorts of objects packed up against windows.

"Wow," Lilly said.

"That's one word for it," Bash said. "Gladys was buying and selling antiques and refinishing some of them. As you can imagine, we haven't been able to figure out what was coming and what was going. Haven't had a lot of time to look for it either. I had plans to go through things today but haven't had time."

"Could I help you?" Delia asked.

"I wish you could, but I worry about chain of custody in case you find something that's a clue. Like those plans."

"I called you right away," Lilly said. "I suppose I could have left them out there."

"No, it's good you found them," Bash said. "If you'd left them they may have disappeared. Ernie, where are you going?"

"Sorry. This house fascinates me. It's like Harmon's house, but with more potential for a fun renovation. And look at that view."

"I wonder who will inherit it?" Lilly asked. She tried to sound innocent but looked right at Bash.

"She was mortgaged to the hilt, and in debt, so there's not much for anyone to inherit. We haven't been able to find a new will. The old one left everything to her late husband. As far as we can tell, she didn't have any other relatives either."

"So, the bank owns the house?" Lilly asked.

"There are several folks who need to be paid back. Folks with bigger brains than I have are sorting through all of that. Wish I could tell you more, but there's a lot there."

The four of them paused to see if Bash would add anything more to the conversation. When Bash was still silent after a few seconds, Ernie broke off from the group and looked around some more.

"Okay if I go upstairs?" he asked.

"Don't touch anything," Bash said.

"I won't."

Delia walked over to look at some of the boxes. When she was out of earshot, Lilly unrolled the plans again and pointed to the names on the plan.

"Marston, Andrus, and Preston," Lilly said. "Was it a partnership or a promise? Or maybe it was a bribe if she were willing to sell them her house?"

"Lilly, you know I can't tell you—"

"You know she probably owed Alex money, right? He offers loans on houses. Maybe he was trying to pressure her and it got out of hand. You know he talked to Portia Asher? Did I mention that?" Lilly told him what she'd overheard.

"Lilly, I'm going to let someone know about that and they'll probably be in touch."

"Any names?"

"No one specific, yet," Bash said. He looked over his shoulder to make sure Delia was out of earshot. "Someone from the FBI may be in touch."

"The FBI?"

"Yes, and I want you to keep that close to the vest. Parts of this investigation have gotten bigger than me. Parts of Gladys's death are out of my hands, so I have been asked to step back. I don't love that idea, so I've been focusing on Harmon's case."

"This could be a clue, though. Maybe if you look into the logo, and see if it's registered—"

"Gladys's murder is still in my ball park, but every time I've tried to do deep research on a path, I've been blocked. I've agreed to keep the FBI informed of anything I find out while investigating Harmon's death."

"Does that mean you can't check into Lenny's and Alex's alibis?"

"Already done, with help. They were in Providence Friday afternoon till Saturday afternoon. They didn't kill Gladys."

"Do you think Miranda did it?" Lilly asked.

"I do. She has means and motive. But . . ." Bash took a deep breath and pursed his lips in concentration.

"But?"

"She's been crying for the past half hour. Maybe it's because she got caught, but I'm not sure. She was shocked by the idea that Harmon may not have died of natural causes. She did mention one thing. She said that Braden's been visiting her a lot. He's been staying in her guest room. He could have gotten his hands on the teas and added to them."

"Did she come up with the Braden angle?"

"No, that was my logic jump."

"Double-check the label on the jar," Lilly said. "I don't think it was Miranda's label. Someone may have created it on a printer. It wouldn't be hard to do."

"But wouldn't it have been smart for Miranda to make it look like a fake label was made?" Bash asked.

"That's too complicated. What sense does the label make? It doesn't have anything to do with Gladys's death. Or maybe it does." Lilly looked down at the plans. "I've got an idea I want to follow up on." Her hand reached into her pocket, but she didn't take out her phone.

Bash sighed and took a deep breath. "Lilly, I know that look. I'm going to go out and see if there's anything else in the compost bin. Keep an eye on this, will you? I'll be gone for a few minutes."

She waited until he was out of earshot, and then called out to Delia.

"We need to take some pictures," she said.

CHAPTER TWENTY-FIVE

"Are you sure you're up to this?" Lilly said for the fifth time. She got up from the chair in Roddy's living room and walked over to the fireplace to look at decorations on the mantel. The room was sparsely but tastefully decorated with mid-century furniture and antique rugs. She wondered if he'd chosen the décor himself, or if he had help.

Roddy looked over at his neighbor and smiled. "Lilly, trust me. I'm up to this. It reminds me of some of the work I used to do." He checked on the tea, which still needed a couple of more minutes.

"What exactly did you used to do? I thought you were a lawyer or a businessman?"

"I did what was necessary, and that, sometimes, used different skills. A conversation for another day. Are you ready for this meeting?"

"I am," Lilly said. "I'm not sure if it will come to

anything, but I thank you for indulging me on this whim. It does seem a little far-fetched, I'll admit."

"Lilly, I trust your whims more than I trust a lot of folks' perfectly thought-through plans. Besides, it was the only plan we came up with last night, despite our best efforts."

Lilly smiled, and moved to sit down on the couch. Dinner last night involved the entire Garden Squad and concerned all of the pieces of information people had been gathering. Lilly hadn't told them about the FBI involvement but did let everyone know that Lenny and Alex had an alibi. Suddenly Lilly saw another thread running through the information and talked it through aloud. That new avenue of thought required additional information to fully bloom. Roddy had volunteered to try and wrestle with the source, but Lilly insisted on being with him. Not that she didn't trust Roddy to ask the appropriate questions. If what she was thinking was true, she didn't want Roddy to be alone.

The doorbell rang.

"The game's afoot," he said to Lilly. He went out to the front hall and welcomed their guest.

"Lilly, I didn't expect to see you here," Regan Holland said as she walked into the living room. If she was surprised she didn't let on, instead leaning down to air kiss the older woman and then sitting down on the club chair by the French doors.

"I insisted, I'm afraid. I've been trying to talk him out of his plan, but to no avail."

"What plan is that?" Regan asked.

"Would you like some tea?" Roddy asked.

"I'd love some. I'm a tea fanatic," Regan said.

"This is nothing special. A black tea blend that I'm rather fond of. Low in caffeine, but not caffeine free."

"Caffeine is fine with me," Regan said. "I'm a bit of an addict, I'm afraid. I'm at the point where it barely affects me."

"Milk and sugar?"

"No, thank you," she said. She took the cup that Roddy offered her and took a deep sip.

Roddy handed Lilly her tea after he added a dollop of milk and some sugar. He added the same to his and sat down next to Lilly.

"Regan, as you know Tamara O'Connor is a friend of mine, so I'll be speaking to her as well. But I wanted to get your opinion on something I've been thinking about for the past few days. You might know that I spoke with Alex Marston yesterday afternoon?" Roddy asked.

"I don't think he mentioned it, no," she said.

"Really? I thought he said . . . well, no worries. I wanted to get your opinion. I'm concerned I bit off more than I can chew when I bought this old darling, and I'm not able to do all of the work it requires. I discussed some financing options with Alex, and he mentioned some nontraditional loans. He also mentioned the possibility of making this house into two or three dwellings, which would mean an influx of cash for me."

"Is Lilly here to talk you out of that?" Regan said.

"No, not necessarily. We've got a tall and solid wall between our houses, so it won't affect me," Lilly said. "I've also come to understand the value of more affordable housing in town. My concern is two-fold. One, that it be done tastefully, and that the house remains standing. This is, after all, the historical district of Goosebush."

"Of course," Regan said. "What is your other concern?"

"As you may know, I've been on the Board of Selectmen several times over the years, and I know the zoning rules of Goosebush fairly well. I don't think he could do this, not without town support."

"Support from people like you could make the difference," Regan said.

"Which is why I am being sure to keep Lilly in the loop," Roddy said. "I'm hoping to get her on board with the idea. From what I understand, you've done some work with this sort of thing before? Is that right?"

"I'm not sure what you mean," Regan said, putting her cup carefully in its saucer.

"I also met with Lenny Andrus, and he mentioned that he had a business partner with a development project in Marshton. I thought that was you."

"That project? I've got a small investment and a contract to be the lead agent on the new buildings. Lenny isn't one of our partners, but he has done some work on the buildings."

"Is it a condo development?" Lilly asked. She knew that it was. Delia had spent the last twelve hours researching.

"It is. We took an underused part of town and reconfigured three lots to house nine townhouses. The investment promises to pay out well."

"Marshton has built condos in the past, so it isn't as big an issue," Lilly said.

"The times are changing, Lilly," Regan said. "Goosebush is a lovely place, but it's time to modernize a bit and get some more housing stock in town."

"You don't mind if I'm a bit cautious, do you? I'd hate for someone like Roddy to get tied up in a project that doesn't have legs. Tell me, are you going to be investing in projects here in Goosebush?"

"I'd love to, if possible," Regan said. "Forgive me for saying this, but I do think some new ideas and new blood will be good for the town in the long run. I know you're friends with Tamara, but she's got very old-fashioned views."

"As do I," Lilly said. "Take, for example, this tea. Delia's been trying to get me to try new blends that include some of my plants, and frankly I'm not interested. Give me traditional blends any day."

"Now that Miranda's been arrested, you probably won't be changing your mind any time soon," Roddy said.

Regan choked on her tea. "Miranda's been arrested?" she asked. "For what?"

"For poisoning Harmon Dale," Lilly said sadly. She didn't need to fake the tears that pricked her eyes. "Roddy, I don't think Bash meant for Miranda's arrest to be public quite yet."

"Oh, dear, I am sorry," Roddy said. "But as you said, it will be public soon enough. I'm surprised that the plans you found at Gladys's house haven't been the lead story on the Goosebush gossip site."

"Roddy, please! Bash asked us not to say anything until they've finished searching the dump."

"Searching the dump?" Regan asked.

"Oh well, as Roddy said it will probably be on the gossip train by the time the sun sets. Apparently, Gladys sent a delayed email that got delivered this afternoon to Bash Haywood. She'd attached a picture of her bicycle and told him that she was leaving a flash drive in it in the handlebar. Gladys's email stated that the flash drive would help explain her disappearance, and it would include bank statements and legal documents he'd probably find interesting."

"A flash drive?" Regan said quietly.

"Very mysterious," Roddy said. "Do you think she'd intended to leave forever, or until something blew over?"

"Hard to say," Lilly said. "Gladys wasn't immune to drama, so it could mean a lot of things. Anyway, Gladys's bike is missing. They didn't find a purse or anything else with Gladys's body. Bash said it wasn't in her pockets. Perhaps her murderer took it or else it got dropped in the scuffle. They're going to do a search of the perimeter of the dump now. They're also checking inside."

"Of course, the bike could be anywhere by now," Roddy said.

"You're right, though it is certainly worth looking for," Lilly said. "Bash said they're going to do a wider sweep in the morning. Oh my, look at me, telling tales out of school. Who knows how Gladys got in there, anyway? That's a large area to search, but it's the best clue Bash has gotten so far."

"I wonder why Gladys sent the email to Bash? Do you think she was planning on leaving town?" Roddy asked.

"I don't know. Maybe she was using the email ploy to keep someone in line, and it backfired. Anyway, until they find the bike, presuming the USB exists, we can only guess," Lilly said, taking a sip of tea. "That's not why you're here, is it, Regan? Tell me, would you be willing to share more of your thoughts with us about Roddy's house?"

"Roddy's house?"

"Making it a multifamily house," Lilly said. "Funny, the abstract idea becomes more viable when your friend is looking for help. If you can show me this is a good idea, I'd be willing to consider backing it at a town hall."

"That's wonderful news, Lilly," Regan said. "I'll put together a report and send it to you. Now, if you'll forgive me, it's getting late, and I have another appointment. I'll talk to you soon."

Roddy walked Regan to the front door. When he came back into the living room Lilly was on her phone. She gave Roddy a thumbs up.

"What do we do now?" Roddy asked.

"We tell Bash we set the trap, and then we wait."

Lilly and Roddy finished their tea, and then they took a stroll around his garden as the sun began to lower in the sky.

"I think we should take a drive," Lilly said.

"Anywhere in particular?" Roddy asked.

"We'll stay out of the way," Lilly said. "We'll do a loop around the dump, and if nothing is happening we'll go to the police station. I'll drive."

She offered to help clean up, but Roddy waved

her off. She went over to get her car and pulled up in his driveway.

"Thank you for driving, Lilly," Roddy said as he climbed up into her car. "My car stands out a bit."

"Just a bit," Lilly said, thinking of his red Jaguar convertible. Her ancient Jeep looked like dozens of others that roamed around Goosebush.

"By the way, I don't think I've properly appreciated the long trip to get over to my driveway," Lilly said. "We really do need to deal with that garden gate door."

"It may be a moot point if I decide to sell," Roddy said.

"You're not going to, are you?" Lilly asked. She was surprised at how much the idea rattled her.

"No, of course not. Contrary to the story I've been telling, I have the funds to fix the old girl up and look forward to the project. Looks like I'll have to find someone besides Lenny to do the work, though."

"Sounds like," Lilly said. "I still can't believe he's involved with something shady. I've known him his entire life. I never thought I'd say this, but thank heaven his parents aren't here to see this."

"Lenny doesn't strike me as smart enough to do any of this on his own."

"He was looking for a short cut," Lilly said.

"And he met people who offered him one," Roddy said. "Where are you going? I thought we were heading to the dump?"

"We're going the back way. This is a bit past where the access point was. It's down there on the left. Can you see anything? Wait, what's that?"

"What?" Roddy asked.

"That shadow cutting through the woods."

"It's a person, a man I think," Roddy said. "Slow down a tick. Let's see what he does."

Lilly heard a sharp noise, like a firecracker going off. The figure broke into a run, dodged to the right, and ran into the road towards the car. It was Braden Dane. He broke into a run towards the car and let himself in the backseat.

"Lilly, get us out of here. She's trying to kill me."

Roddy used Lilly's phone to call Bash. He left a message and then sent a text letting Bash know they'd meet him at the police station.

"Can't we go to your house?" Braden asked.

"No, we need to do this the right way and take you to the station," Lilly said. "If someone's trying to hurt you, we need to keep this official. Who's trying to kill you, Braden?"

"Regan. It probably would have been better if I'd let her."

When they got to the police station there was only one officer on duty. The officer set them up in the conference room. Both Roddy and Lilly waited with Braden. The minute they'd gotten in the room Braden had put his head on the table and started to weep.

"You must hate me," he said after a few minutes.

"I don't hate you," Lilly said. "I will confess I'm curious about what happened, but you shouldn't say anything. I can be compelled to testify against you. So can Roddy. You need a lawyer, not a confessor."

"I didn't know they killed Harmon, you have to know that," Braden said.

"Who?"

"All of them. Gladys, Lenny, Alex. Gladys did the dirty work, brought him over teas that she said Miranda sent down."

"How do you know that?" Lilly said.

"Regan told me."

"Regan?" Roddy asked gently. "Did Regan know what Gladys was doing?"

"She said no, but she had to know about it. She did admit that she and Gladys were sabotaging the open houses, with Alex's help."

At that moment the conference door opened, and Bash Haywood came in. Lilly and Roddy got up to leave.

"Please, stay. I want you to understand. I didn't do anything," Braden said.

"Is it okay with you if we stay?" Lilly asked.

"It's fine, we're all talking. Just talking," Bash said. "We were at Gladys's house waiting, but no one showed up. We had a couple of officers at the dump as well, but they didn't see anyone."

"Braden was telling us that he didn't kill his uncle," Roddy said.

"Did he know anyone was going to kill his uncle?" Bash asked Roddy.

"He says no."

"No, of course I didn't. I didn't. You have to believe me," Braden said.

"What happened?" Lilly asked. Lilly hadn't been

sure if Braden was involved or not. She'd hoped not, but now? Now she needed to know the truth.

"After Uncle Harmon died, I thought that he was going to leave me some cash. But he didn't. He left me the house instead. So we all agreed to put the house on the market. Then I met Regan. She kept talking to me about how I was being ripped off. But if I got her the listing for the house, she'd make sure I got some cash."

"Did she try and talk you into selling the house to Alex?"

"No. She was pretty upset when I told her what he was offering. They argued about it at one point. Anyway, Regan and I started, you know, seeing each other."

"Really?" Lilly asked. Regan had at least twenty years on Braden.

"Yeah, I thought that too. What did this sophisticated, beautiful woman see in me, right?" Braden asked. He wiped his eyes with the back of his hand.

"Feeling sorry for yourself is counter-productive," Lilly said.

"Braden, did you kill Gladys Preston?" Bash asked.

"No, of course not."

"Do you know who did?"

"I didn't until a little while ago, I swear."

"But you do now?"

"Yes, because she told me. Gladys was threatening to give Tamara some information about the plans for Shipyard Lane and Swallow Point. She wasn't happy with the deal anymore and wanted more money. At least that's what Regan said. Maybe she found out about what happened to Uncle Harmon. She was so scary. Yeesh, she probably did that too."

"Who? Who told you she killed Gladys Preston?" Bash asked.

"Regan Holland. She came by and picked me up. She took me towards the dump and told me she needed us to find Gladys's bike. I asked her what she was talking about, and what was so important about it. She freaked out and kept asking me why Gladys was such an idiot."

"Idiot? What do you mean?" Bash said quietly.

"She said that Gladys lost her nerve, started to feel bad about Harmon dying. He wasn't supposed to die, just get sick. That's what Regan said. What sort of people poison an old man for a house?"

"Gladys lost her nerve?" Bash prodded.

"Regan said they had a plan, but Gladys wanted out. She told Regan that she made digital copies of everything and was going to give them to Tamara O'Connor."

"Everything?"

"Regan said Gladys knew about all the plans, and had been keeping records. Gladys said unless she got cash, she was going to turn it all over."

"Why give the information to Tamara? Why not go to the police?"

"Gladys wanted to buy herself time. She was planning on getting out of town that morning."

"How come Regan told you all this?"

"She was trying to talk me into looking for the bike.

"She said she'd make sure I would be blamed for Harmon's death unless I helped her. She told me she had proof that I'd given him the tea. I had, but I didn't know what was in it. You have to believe me."

"Did she tell you what happened to Gladys?" Bash asked.

"She told me she didn't mean to kill Gladys. She found a note that Gladys had left at Lenny's office, telling him she had proof of what they'd done. All of it. Harmon. The open houses. Lenny was out of town, so Regan decided to deal with it. Regan texted Gladys, and told her to meet her at the dump and she'd give her some cash."

"Why would Gladys agree to meet at the dump?"

"Gladys wanted the money," Braden said. "Regan probably made some excuse about them not being seen."

"How did Regan know how to get in there?" Lilly asked.

"Regan caught Gladys coming out of the hole in the fence one day, and Gladys admitted she went in to pilfer furniture. Regan collected information about people, stuff that seemed innocent enough but could get them in trouble."

"So why did Gladys text Tamara?" Bash asked.

"She probably didn't," Braden said. "Regan was pretty good at spoofing phones."

"Spoofing phones?" Lilly asked.

"Making a phone call or a text look like it came from one number, when it came from another," Roddy said. "An odd ability for Regan to have."

"She uses it for her real estate deals," Braden said. "She showed me one night. She used to love to show off what she could do. It's how she creates bidding wars for her clients."

Bash was taking notes, and looked up. "Tell you what, we'll talk more about this in a bit. Did Regan tell you what happened to Gladys?"

"She said that she gave Gladys some money, but Gladys wanted more. They got into a fight, and then Gladys fell and hit her head, so Regan ran."

"Gladys was killed by multiple blows to the head," Bash said. "And we didn't find any cash at the scene. So Regan's story doesn't hold up."

"What? Really? But she told me—"

"Regan lied to you, Braden," Lilly said. "Sounds like she lied to a lot of people."

"She called me this afternoon. She was completely freaked out, so I agreed to meet her. She told me about the bike and insisted I needed to help her look for it. We walked along the edge of the dump, but we didn't find a bike. I told her the police probably had it. Then she really lost it. She took out a gun and tried to force me to keep looking. I pretended to, and then when she turned her back, I made a run for it. I saw a car and jumped in. I'm so glad it was both of you."

"Lilly happened to drive by?" Bash said.

"Roddy and I were out for a drive on a beautiful summer night. What's wrong with that?"

"Nothing. Nothing at all," Bash said. "You didn't happen to see Regan, did you?"

"No, not at the dump. We did see her earlier in the afternoon. We heard the gunshot, but we drove away from it and didn't go looking for Regan. Maybe we should have," Lilly said.

"You absolutely should not have," Bash said. "Braden, I'm going to step out and make a couple of calls. I'll be right back. I'm going to ask Roddy and Lilly to leave. It will all be fine. I have a few more questions for you."

"Braden, you're going to need a lawyer," Lilly said. "I'll make a call and have someone come down."

Braden nodded and put his head back on his folded arms on the table.

Lilly, Roddy, and Bash walked out of the room, and Bash closed the door.

"Have you found Regan yet?" Lilly asked Bash.

"Not yet, but a lot of folks are looking for her," Bash said. "I'll keep you posted."

"One minute, Bash," Roddy said, taking a paper bag and handing it to the officer. "Regan used this teacup and saucer. You'll be able to get prints off the saucer, I made sure she grabbed it. It will also have her DNA. It may be helpful."

"At some point you'll need to explain this afternoon to me. For now I'll take that. Thanks. I'll talk to you soon," Bash said. He walked away and started dialing his phone.

CHAPTER TWENTY-SIX

"Knock knock," Roddy said through the kitchen door. The August heat had abated a bit, and Lilly opened the back door to clear the burnt toast smell out of the kitchen.

"Come in," Lilly said. "I was about to make myself some avocado toast which was, as Delia would say, an epic fail. I'm going to try again and make an omelet. Would you care to join me for dinner?"

"I'd love to. How about if I make the omelet? I'm pretty good at it, if I do say so."

"Well, I'm not, so I'll take you up on it. What do you need?"

"A glass of wine would be nice. I can find my way around your fridge. Where's Delia?"

"Some sort of emergency at Alden Park. Ernie's with her."

"Have you heard anything from Bash?"

"No, but it's only been an hour. I hope they find her soon," Lilly said.

"I can't believe Regan tried to get Braden to help her find the bike. She must have been waiting for Gladys inside the dump, and not seen the bike when she left. She must have been fairly secure in her control of Braden to tell him everything," Roddy said. "It's hardly proof, since we made up the story about the bike, but it makes her look guilty."

"I can't believe Gladys was blackmailing them all. Do you think she had anything to do with Harmon's death?" Lilly asked. She'd taken some cheese and bacon out of the refrigerator and put them on the counter.

"I don't know, I doubt it. If Regan was a regular visitor to Gladys's house, she may have put the jars from Miranda's supplies in her house."

"Hoping to frame Gladys."

"Exactly. I think there were a lot of terrible things happening and that Regan was the mastermind behind most of them."

"But she was smart enough to keep her name out of things," Lilly said. "Those plans we found had Lenny's, Alex's, and Gladys's names on them."

"But Regan was likely a silent partner."

"If Braden hadn't been rattled by the news about Harmon, she probably could have talked Braden into anything. I wonder where she is now."

"Probably looking for Lenny and Alex. I wonder where they are," Roddy said.

"I don't know, but I'd imagine Bash does. I may be naïve, but I can't imagine Braden intentionally being part of all of this, can you?"

"I think Braden is in over his head, likely because of Regan's influence. He may not have understood what he was getting himself into. She seems adept at keeping a lot of people involved with her plans to varying degrees."

"So now we just wait," Lilly said.

"We do," Roddy said. "It's a bit anticlimactic, but I'm not sure what else we can do."

Roddy intently cracked eggs into a bowl and started to beat them. "Perhaps some wine?" he said.

Lilly went over to the cabinet and took down two glasses. When her phone rang she smiled at Roddy and answered the call. He stopped beating the eggs and looked over at her.

"Lilly, do you know where Tamara is?" Warwick asked. "I've been trying to call her, but she isn't picking up. Is she with you?"

Lilly's hands started to sweat. "She isn't here," she said. "Have you checked at home?"

"I'm over in Marshton at a scrimmage."

"Tell you what, I'll drive over to her office and then the house and check in on her. For all we know her phone's off for some reason. I'll call you as soon as I find her, all right?"

"Thanks, Lilly. Call me."

"What's the matter?" Roddy asked.

"Warwick can't find Tamara," Lilly said. She dialed Tamara's office and her cell phone. Both went right to voicemail. "She's not answering her phones."

Roddy put the eggs into the refrigerator and turned off the stove.

"Let's go," he said.

"You don't think that Regan—"

"I don't think anything except that we should find Tamara. Home first, then office?"

"And then?"

Roddy shook his head. "One step at a time. Let's go."

Roddy and Lilly drove to Tamara's house. She wasn't there. She wasn't at her office either. Lilly felt her stomach clench. She called Pete Frank, but he didn't know where she was. He checked the company calendar, and she didn't have any appointments.

"Where else could she be?" Roddy said.

"I don't know—"

"Think, Lilly," Roddy said. "Maybe she is with someone?"

Lilly closed her eyes and tried imagining where her friend might be.

"Maybe she's at the Cape," she said.

"Cape Cod? Do you know where?" Roddy asked.

"No, the Cape she's trying to sell over near Linda Lane. She's got a couple of showings tomorrow and may have wanted to check on it."

"Is this the place where someone left the rotten fish?"

"The same. Let's check it out." Lilly pulled out onto the rotary and headed back over to the Cape house. "Roddy, text Delia and Ernie, tell them we're looking for Tamara."

"Let's not panic yet," Roddy said.

"I know, I'm not panicking. I'm just concerned."

Roddy reached over and patted Lilly's arm. "Who do you think left the rotten fish?" he asked.

"Regan may have done that, come to think of it. I know Tamara thought she did, anyway."

"To throw us off and make us think the open house incidents were not about the Dane house?"

"And to make us think they were about Tamara," Lilly said. "You know, the sabotage may have been about her after all. Braden gave the Dane house to Tamara to sell, but he wasn't going to renew Tamara's contract. Regan had a lot to gain."

"If Tamara hadn't had the listing they would have been able to sell the house more easily— maybe to a front or a trust that was part of the development deal," Roddy said.

"Also, because Tamara is on the board of selectmen, she's a stickler for the rules. She wouldn't have been willing to entertain ideas about tearing it down, so they needed to force her to recuse herself somehow. Or throw her under a cloud of suspicion about Gladys's death. Okay, here's the house. The second one in."

"Turn off your headlights and slow down," Roddy said. "There's a car in the driveway."

Lilly did as she was told. "That's Tamara's car. She must be inside." Lilly reached to open her door, but Roddy put his hand on her arm.

"Wait a minute," Roddy said. "I don't see any lights in the house, but there are some out back. I'm going to try and sneak around the house and see if she's in there. And if she's alone."

Roddy gave Lilly a long look, and Lilly nodded.

"Be careful," Lilly said.

"I will. You stay here, and I'll be back," Roddy said. He disappeared into the dark around the house. Lilly called and texted Bash and got no answer.

Lilly counted to one hundred slowly. Roddy hadn't come back, so she tried to count again. She only got to fifty before she decided she couldn't wait any longer. She called the police station, and told them that there was an emergency. They promised to send someone out as soon as possible. Lilly took a deep breath and she let herself out of the car.

Lilly walked slowly in the direction that Roddy had gone. She took her phone out of her pocket and turned on the screen, dimming it. She'd rather have used the flashlight app but didn't want to risk too much light. She hoped she was being overly dramatic, but why hadn't Roddy come back?

She finally got towards the back of the house and stopped. The moonlight was full in the backyard. Tamara was there, sitting on the back deck. Regan was standing beside her, holding a gun to Tamara's head. Lilly crept forward, and saw Roddy several feet away, a shovel in hand. He was digging. Lilly took a deep breath.

"You're much better at this than Tamara was," Regan said. "I think she was deliberately slow. She must have been hoping someone would show, and look at that. She was right. You came to her rescue. Frankly, I'm surprised you found me. Found us. And that you came alone."

"I told you, Lilly asked me to stop by and make

sure the house was locked up. She's down at the station with Braden. He's being questioned by the police."

"Braden. Lord, is he dim. Beautiful, but dim. Such a pity he started to doubt me. Still, he's got no proof," Regan said. She didn't move the gun, but she glanced over at Roddy.

"No one had proof, Regan. Though I will admit, I'm not sure how you're going to be able to talk your way out of this situation."

"This situation? I'm getting rid of the evidence, or will be soon. Keep digging, Roddy. If you stop, I'll shoot your friend. I can see you, so don't try anything. You're far enough away from me that I could shoot her and take you down before you got to me. So keep digging. I'm sorry you found us, Roddy. I hate killing handsome men. Seems such a waste of a limited resource. I wish that old bat was the one who'd found us. I wouldn't have minded planting that particular lily, let me tell you."

"You've done this before then," Roddy said.

"No, of course not," Regan said. "Whatever do you take me for?"

"You're having me dig my own grave, so that should be fairly obvious," Roddy said.

Regan laughed again. She leaned over and tapped her gun on Tamara's head. Lilly saw her friend flinch.

"Dig faster, handsome," Regan said.

Lilly squatted down carefully, which wasn't easy given the state of her knees. She held out her phone to scan the area. She found a couple of pine cones and a short, thick branch. She stood up carefully and slipped her phone in her pocket. She blinked a few times, and let her eyes get used to the moonlight.

Lilly maneuvered herself to the side of the deck. It was the type that led out to the patio, with no railings. Unfortunately Regan stood at the other side of Tamara, so Lilly couldn't rush her. Where were the police? She watched as Regan started to fidget, tapping the gun on Tamara's head. Tamara cried out in pain, but Regan only laughed.

Lilly took one of the pine cones and hurled it towards the front corner of the house. She stooped back down.

Regan turned and looked around. Lilly tossed another pine cone in the same direction. This time Regan stepped out to look over at the side of the house. Lilly picked up the branch and ran at Regan, screaming as she ran. Regan turned towards the noise. Lilly was afraid she wouldn't get to Regan before she recovered, so she threw the branch as hard as she could. She hit Regan on her left side. Regan stumbled slightly, but she didn't fall. She steadied herself, turned towards Lilly and aimed.

Tamara jumped up and threw herself at Regan's back. It threw Regan off, so she missed Lilly. Lilly kept moving forward, seeing Roddy moving towards them from across the yard, but not daring to wait until he got there. Regan twisted to try and get Tamara off her, and Lilly threw herself at Regan's side. That took them all down. Lilly grabbed at Regan's hand that was holding the gun, pushing it down with all of her might. The next thing she knew Roddy was taking the gun out of Regan's hand and pulling Lilly away. He held it on Regan and told her not to move. Lilly stood up and pulled Tamara up and away from Regan.

"Tamara, are you okay?" Lilly said. She took both her arms and put them around her friend.

"Oh Lil, I was so scared," Tamara said, and she started to weep.

"We're going to be all right," Lilly said, rocking her friend and holding her close.

CHAPTER TWENTY-SEVEN

Lilly brought Tamara back to Windward after they'd both been checked out by the EMTs. She'd called Warwick and let him know what happened. Lilly took Tamara upstairs with her and drew her a bath. Tamara had given Bash a statement at the scene, and he'd agreed that he'd talk to her more in the morning. Lilly went into her own room while Tamara was in the tub. She looked down at her ruined dress, her bloody knees, and bruised arms. Her entire body ached, and she wasn't sure if she had enough energy to get cleaned up. She heard someone in the hallway, and a knock on her door. Warwick stuck his head in.

"She's in the guest room bathtub," Lilly said. "She's had a tough time."

"Roddy told me. Thank heaven you knew where to find her."

"I know. I can't even imagine if—"

"You don't need to, Lilly. You found her. I'm

going to go in and take care of her now. Are you okay? Do you need help? Should I ask Delia to come up?"

"I'll be fine," Lilly said. Warwick came into her room and gave her a huge hug. He held on until she let go. "Go take care of your wife. I'm going to get cleaned up, and then I'll be downstairs. Roddy's making us omelets."

Lilly took a quick shower. She didn't spend a long time contemplating the bruises that were starting to appear, but she did put bandages on anything that was bleeding. She slowly made her way downstairs. Delia and Roddy were both working at the counter. Roddy looked disheveled but seemed in good spirits as he tossed vegetables in melted butter.

When Delia realized Lilly was in the room, she put down the eggs she was whisking and ran over to her.

"Oh Lilly, are you okay?" Delia said, giving Lilly a gentle hug.

Lilly hugged her back. "I'm fine," she said. "Not great, but fine."

"Roddy was telling me how you saved them," Delia said.

"I did no such thing. I'd called the police, so they were on their way. We all saved each other."

"You were brilliant, Lilly," Roddy said. "If I didn't know better I'd think you'd been trained."

"Hardly," Lilly said. "I did play softball when I was younger, and I was an excellent pitcher. Are you all right?" she asked. She walked over to him and put her hand on his arm.

He turned away from the vegetables for a moment and gave Lilly a huge smile. "You're going to think I'm a basket case, but I'm terrific. Very, very grateful that we all got out of there in one piece, but terrific. We really are quite the team, aren't we? How's Tamara?"

"She's shaky, but Warwick's with her," Lilly said. "When Tamara got home, Regan stepped out with a gun and made Tamara drive. Tamara decided to take her to the Cape house, hoping we'd figure it out."

"I wonder what the plan was?" Delia said.

"Regan seems to have gone around the bend from the way she was behaving," Roddy said. "Having Tamara dig her own grave was a time filler while she figured it out, I suspect. From what I could ascertain, her life was unraveling, and she placed most of the blame for that on Tamara."

"That's so scary," Delia said. "I'm so glad you're all in one piece."

"So am I," Lilly said. "We're not going to know many more details for a while, so let's change the subject. If you don't mind, I'm going to sit."

"Of course. Let me get you something to drink. Tea? Water?"

"Wine, please. Now, what was the emergency at Alden Park?"

"You know how everyone kept saying it was so weird that there was a dump site there, since the town history never showed the space being used for that?" Delia said.

"Yes," Lilly said, taking a sip of the wine Delia had handed to her.

"They found the rest of the dump site today. There was another six feet of items, including what might have been furniture. They found some draw pulls. The wood must have rotted."

"How do they know they got to the bottom of the site?" Roddy asked.

"Because buried under all the other debris were skeletons. Three bodies. A woman and two children."

"Oh no," Lilly said.

"Oh yes," Delia said. "It looks like this is a crime scene. It's terrible, of course. But it's also pretty interesting. Given the items we've found we can figure out a range of dates when they were likely buried. I'm going to do some research and see if I can find anything about a woman and two children disappearing."

"You're going to solve the mystery," Roddy said. "It must be something in the air in this house."

"It will be hard to solve the mystery from Burlington," Lilly said. "A lot of those old newspapers aren't online."

"Yeah, about that. I've been thinking," Delia said. "Since I am teaching two classes online, I only have to be at school three days a week. Would it be all right with you if I stayed here and commuted?"

"All right? I'd be thrilled."

"Thanks, Lilly. I'll move out someday, but not for a while. I'd hate to miss anything, you know?"

"Stay for as long as you'd like, Delia. You're always welcome. Always."

The shift from summer happens quickly in New England. One minute the air-conditioning is blasting, the beach is crowded, and sweat is omnipresent. But then the milky summer sky gives way to clear blue and the wind shifts a bit, adding a crispness. Lilly loved fall. It wasn't the best gardening season, but the color palette was magnificent. Lilly also had a chrysanthemum addiction that she fed every season.

The Beautification Committee projects were going well. Alden Park had actually been a mixed blessing. The news of the one-hundred-fifty-year-old bodies eclipsed the news of the con game that had been going on in Goosebush and had culminated in two murders.

And, as it turns out, it was a con game. Regan Holland had a history of them. Creating pyramid schemes that made a few folks rich but left most other people holding the bag—but too afraid of legal repercussions to go to the police. She'd been using Alex and Lenny. Gladys had gotten caught up in it, but then she got greedy.

Regan hadn't admitted to killing Harmon, but she'd been indicted as an accomplice to his murder, nevertheless. The ultimate goal had been to create condominiums on Swallow Point, and Regan had been orchestrating a lot of deals to make that happen. Apparently, Alex confessed that Harmon had gotten wind of the plans, and made it clear he opposed them. Alex insisted that Gladys and Regan had poisoned Harmon, but that would be tough to prove. What was certain is that they all were complicit, and that added to the charges they were all facing.

Tamara recovered, but it took time. When Warwick left town for conferences she'd go over to

Lilly's house and stay in the guest room. She always said it was because she preferred the bed there.

"What are you doing?" Delia asked. Lilly had stopped gardening and was sitting at the outdoor table.

"Enjoying my garden," Lilly said. "I love fall, but I hate it when everything goes dormant."

"I do too, but we'll keep the greenhouse hopping this winter. I want to grow more plants and flowers I can dry. I'm going to keep working on my tea mixes."

"You'd think after what Miranda went through you'd give that up," Lilly said.

"From what I understand her business is booming. I offered to give her some of the plants from our gardens we aren't going to use. Is that all right with you?"

"That's fine," Lilly said. "The Dane house is finally getting sold, but a lot of the money is going to be used for the bird sanctuary. I'm glad she has a steady income."

"She won't have to share the proceeds with Braden," Delia said.

"She won't have to, no. Such a shame about Braden," Lilly said.

"A shame? He isn't going to jail, which in my opinion makes him really, really lucky. I think he knew what Regan was up to."

"We'll never know," Lilly said.

"By the way, do you know who bought the Dane house?" Delia asked.

"Tamara's going to let us know when she comes over," Lilly said.

"I'm going to let you know what?" Tamara said. "You know, you really shouldn't leave the kitchen door open. Anyone could come in."

"Anyone with the code to the gate," Lilly said. "We had to leave it open today. The locksmith has been in and out all day."

"Locksmith?"

"We're trying to get the garden gate open," Delia said.

"That's nice," Tamara said. "It will make visiting easier for Roddy."

"He's going to use the greenhouse over the winter to get ready for the spring. It's much easier for us all if he can come through the gate and not have to come through the house," Lilly said. She turned away from her friend, who was smiling.

"So, Tamara, who bought the Dane house?" Delia asked. "I heard that Gladys's house got sold too. That's good. With all three houses being available at the same time, I was worried they'd end up getting torn down after all."

"Not likely," Tamara said. "Alex's house isn't going up for sale. His daughter is moving in."

"His daughter? I'm surprised his creditors aren't going after it," Lilly said.

"They've gone after everything else," Tamara said. "But it ends up the Shipyard Lane house was in her name. The condo he'd given to her was in his company's name, and she's been forced to move out."

"Awkward," Delia said. "Do we know the people who bought the other houses?"

"Which houses?" Ernie said as he came down the porch stairs. He handed Lilly three large keys. "These are the keys to the gate. One for you, one for Roddy, one in case the other ones get lost."

"Thanks for making that happen Ernie," Lilly said. "We'll wait until Roddy comes over and we'll give the gate a try."

"I brought some oil and other items that will help us coax the door open. The gate hasn't been opened in over a hundred years, so this will be a project. Now, what were you talking about?" Ernie asked.

"We're asking about Harmon's house and Gladys's house," Lilly said.

"I have some news on that front. Warwick and I bought Harmon's house," Tamara said. "I put a bid in as third party, and the estate accepted it."

"That was you?" Lilly asked. "It was a very generous offer."

"The house is worth it," Tamara said. "Buying it was Warwick's idea. He loves the views and doesn't mind sharing the house with the bird folks every once in a while."

"At least we know one end of Shipyard Lane is protected," Lilly said.

"So is the other end of the lane," Ernie said. "I bought Gladys's house."

"You did?" Delia said. "But your house is so cute, and you've done so much work on it."

"That's just it. It's done, and I need a new project."

"Gladys's house is quite the project," Tamara said. "It's in very tough shape."

"Which is why I got it at such a great price. That, and the fact that it was auctioned. When they took my bid, I figured why not."

"Why not indeed?" Lilly said. "It looks like we've got some winter projects to look forward to. It will help with the lack of gardening projects."

"Lack of gardening projects?" Delia said. "Did I mention that I'm growing a poison garden for Halloween? And that we need to get some holly and other decorations for the Star for their *A Christmas Carol* readings? No, Lilly, we're not dormant, not this winter."

Gardening Tips

I love gathering gardening tips from folks, since inevitably stories come with them. Thanks to my sister Caroline, my Aunt Carol and my Uncle George for help with these tips!

- Add instant drama to your patio and deck with tropical plants. They add height and lush-green color from spring to fall and can easily be over-wintered inside. In fact, add lights to them and they can be part of your holiday decorations.
- Fall is a good time to plant shrubs that bloom in the spring or summer. Make sure you do what is necessary to protect the shrubs over the winter.
- Use perennials in your containers and supplement with annuals for color each year. Different annuals can be added each season, and other decorations can help them last a long time.
- For containers, think thriller, filler, and spiller. Thrillers add drama and height, but don't overdo them. Fillers add mass. Spillers anchor the pot and add a beautiful counterpoint of color and texture. Don't be afraid of exploring your gardening artist when planting containers. If the design doesn't work, you can always redistribute the plants and try again.
- Good soil is the key to a successful garden. Add sand, compost, and peat moss to clay soil to aid in drainage, and humus, manure, and peat moss to sandy soil. Giving roots the ability to grow while balancing their water intake is the

key. Run tests on the soil, particularly if plants are dying. Make adjustments as needed and take notes about the mixes you're using.

- Speaking of manure, it can add a lot of nutrients to soil. Consider adding it, especially if your garden is downwind from your house.

- Don't use wet soil when you're planting. It will compact the roots and inhibit their ability to take in water.

- Plan out your gardens. Avoid planting the same plants in one large group. Instead, intersperse them with other flowers and plants so that pests will be confused and won't wipe out your entire crop. If you're planting a vegetable garden, some plants work well near each other and some don't, so do your research.

- Pay attention to the light in your yard. Choose plants that will work well with your sun exposure.

- Some plants seem like a great idea but end up being invasive or killing other plants. Do your research before you plant.

- Dig a hole twice the size of the plant's diameter. Loosen the soil below, but do not plant any deeper than the plant's surface.

- For perennial gardens, the goal is to intersperse your flowers and shrubs so that they bloom in stages from spring until the end of fall. Adding annuals for splashes of color can help fill in spots when the garden doesn't cooperate.

- Before you bring plants inside, do your research and make sure they aren't harmful to pets and small children.

Acknowledgments

There are so many folks who have helped bring this series to life and who support me in my writing career.

Thank you to John Scognamiglio and the team at Kensington. I'm thrilled to be part of the Kensington family.

Thank you to my agent, John Talbot.

Thank you, as always, to my family: my parents, Paul and Cindy Hennrikus, my sisters Kristen and Caroline, my brothers-in-law Bryan and Glenn, and my nieces and nephews Emma, Evan, Chase, Mallory, Becca, Tori, Harrison, and Alex. I am so, so blessed that you are my family.

I have wonderful friends who double as a cheering squad. A special thank-you to Jason Allen-Forrest, my first reader. And to Scott Forrest-Allen, who is always there for title help. Courtney O'Connor, thank you for helping me reframe and think of myself as a writer this past year. Thank you to Deb Brown, John Montgomery, Paul Weatherbee, Scott Sinclair, and all my other friends who come out to events and cheer me on.

A huge thank-you to my wonderful readers. I love meeting you at events and conferences or hearing from you on social media. Thank you for your reading support; it means the world.

I blog with five amazing women, the Wicked Authors (www.WickedAuthors.com): Barbara Ross, Sherry Harris, Edith Maxwell, Liz Mugavero, and Jessie Crockett are friends, mentors, cheerleaders, and wonderful writers. I would not be on this journey without them and wouldn't want to be.

I am grateful for my blog mates at Killer Characters (www.KillerCharacters.com) for letting my characters speak on the twentieth of each month.

The mystery community is wonderful. I belong to the Mystery Writers of America. I owe a special thank-you to Sisters in Crime, particularly the New England chapter. If I hadn't joined that organization, I don't think you'd be holding this book in your hand.